HOP-TU-NAA AND HOMICIDE

An Isle of Man Ghostly Cozy

DIANA XARISSA

Text Copyright © 2018 Diana Xarissa
Cover Copyright © 2018 Linda Boulanger – Tell Tale Book Covers

ISBN: 1719407681
ISBN - 13: 978-1719407687

All Rights Reserved

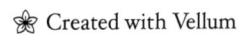

❦ Created with Vellum

For Jinny the witch, who was probably a perfectly nice person, really.

AUTHOR'S NOTE

One of my favorite parts of writing my books set on the Isle of Man is being able to share some of the many unique and interesting things about the island with readers around the world. Hop-tu-Naa is one of the those things and I'm delighted to share it with you in this, the eighth book in the Isle of Man Ghostly Cozy Series.

Hop-tu-Naa takes place on the 31st of October each year. It is actually a celebration of the Celtic new year, marking the beginning of winter. The day is celebrated across the island, and there are events at Cregneash as well, but they are not exactly as presented in this story. My children were taught the Douglas version of the Hop-tu-Naa song and they sang it as they went around our neighborhood each year, collecting treats. (I still make them sing it on Halloween night before Trick or Treat.)

As I said, this is the eighth book in the series. I always recommend reading my books in order (alphabetically). The characters do change and develop as the series progresses, but each book should be perfectly enjoyable on its own if you prefer not to read them all.

This book, unlike my Isle of Man Cozy Mysteries series, is mostly written in American English because Fenella grew up in the US. As she's now living on the Isle of Man, a UK crown dependency, her friends on the island tend to use British English (with a touch of Manx now and again). I work hard to keep this consistent throughout the story, and I do apologize for any errors that creep in.

This is a work of fiction. All of the characters are entirely fictional. Any resemblance they may bear to any real persons, living or dead, is entirely coincidental. The shops and restaurants in the book are also fictional creations. The historical sites and the island's history and traditions are all real. The events that happen at those historical sites within this story are fictional, however.

If you'd like to get in touch, my contact details are available at the back of the book. Thank you for spending time with Fenella and her friends.

1

"Did you say Harvey will be back tomorrow?" Shelly Quirk asked as Fenella Woods jogged up to join her on the promenade.

"Yes, and sooner would be better," Fenella told her, struggling to catch her breath as she slowed to a walk.

"Wooof," Winston said. He jumped up and down and then pulled on his leash.

"Calm down, big guy," Shelly said. "You've worn Fenella out."

Winston looked up at Fenella and then sighed and fell into step next to her.

"I am sorry," Fenella said once she could speak. "I've been racing up and down the promenade with you every day for the last week and I don't seem to have gotten any better at it, have I?"

"Oh, I don't know. I'm pretty sure you went a little further today than yesterday," Shelly told her.

"I think you're just saying that to make me feel better."

"I wouldn't do that," Shelly protested. "Fiona and I walked further while you were gone, anyway."

"Maybe Winston and I were just slower," Fenella suggested. She pushed her sweaty hair out of her eyes and then sighed. "Poor Winston deserves better."

"I'm sure you're giving him a better workout than Harvey does. Harvey is considerably older and he always has Fiona with him."

Fenella nodded. "I hope you're right. I was happy to keep the dogs for the week while Harvey is away, but I'd really forgotten how much work they are."

"I had as well," Shelly said, "but it's been fun having them again, especially since you know for sure that it's only temporary."

This was the second time Fenella had looked after the two dogs. Winston was a huge furry beast who seemed to have an endless supply of energy and a deep passion for the sea. Thus far he'd only managed to get away from Fenella and into the water twice while he'd been staying with her. Fiona was a much smaller animal who needed much less exercise. While she followed Winston into the water at every opportunity, Fenella suspected that was because she was devoted to her large friend, not because she actually enjoyed splashing in the sea herself.

The first time Fenella had kept the animals had been when both of their owners had disappeared under strange circumstances. When Fiona's owner passed away and Winston's owner, Harvey Garus, returned, Harvey had taken over responsibility for both animals. This time around, Fenella had actually volunteered to keep them both as Harvey had been invited to attend an awards ceremony in the US. She'd thoroughly enjoyed having them, but she was really looking forward to Harvey's return as well.

"Have they had enough for now?" Shelly asked.

"I hope so. I know I have," Fenella laughed. "Thank you for walking Fiona so that I could run with Winston."

"You're very welcome. You know I love spending time with the little beasts. It reminds me of why I have Smokey."

Shelly lived in the apartment next door to Fenella's. Some months earlier she'd adopted an older cat called Smokey, who kept the sixty-something widow company without placing too many demands on her time.

"Yes, well, it's been fun having them both, but Katie and I are really looking forward to the peace and quiet when they've gone."

Fenella had a cat of her own, a kitten really, that she'd named Katie. The kitten had wandered into Fenella's apartment one day, right after Fenella herself had moved in, and now Fenella couldn't imagine life without the tiny black and white ball of love and attitude. Katie had accepted the two dogs into the family, letting them have space in the king-sized bed in Fenella's bedroom with her and Fenella, and sharing the sunny spots in front of the windows for long naps, but Fenella was sure that the tiny animal was growing tired of having the two visitors in the apartment all the time.

"What time does Harvey get back?"

"He'll be back in the morning, but he's going to go home and have a nap before he picks up the dogs," Fenella replied. "He's promised to get them before five, though."

"Assuming his flights are all on time."

"Well, yes, that."

"And if he does manage to get them collected tomorrow, are we still on for Saturday?"

"Oh, yes, please," Fenella replied. "I'm excited to have the chance to learn more about Hop-tu-Naa."

"It's certainly a uniquely Manx holiday," Shelly told her, "and Cregneash is an interesting place to visit, Hop-tu-Naa or not."

"I can't believe I've been here for seven months and I've not been to visit it yet. What sort of historian am I? I haven't visited very many places, really. I just can't seem to get motivated to do much of anything."

Fenella had unexpectedly inherited her aunt Mona Kelly's estate. She'd used the inheritance as the excuse she'd needed to change her entire life. After quitting the university teaching position she'd held since she'd finished her doctorate degree, she'd sold her house and all of its furnishings, dumped the man she'd been with for over ten years, and moved to the island with no plans to return to Buffalo, New York even though it had been her home since she'd started college at eighteen. Life on the island was nothing like she'd expected it to be, but she was happier than she'd ever been, in spite of some of the more unpleasant things that had happened since she'd arrived.

"You've been rather busy," Shelly pointed out. "I should really be dragging you out more, too. I was a teacher for my entire career. I've no excuse for not making you visit every historical site on the island."

Fenella laughed. "I think you've had quite enough going on in your own life this past year."

Shelly had been widowed not much more than a year earlier. In the shock of her initial grief, she'd sold the house she'd shared with her husband, taken early retirement from her job, and bought the apartment in Douglas that was next door to Fenella's aunt's apartment. According to Shelly, Mona had saved her life, helping her deal with her grief and teaching her to embrace life again. Fenella wasn't sure what Shelly had been like before her husband's untimely death, but she had grown to love the woman's flamboyant dress sense and exuberant personality.

"Anyway, it should be an interesting day. They've all sorts of activities planned, including a chance to learn the traditional Hop-tu-Naa song and dance," Shelly said.

"There's a song? And a dance?"

"I thought I told you about the song. If we get anyone coming around on Hop-tu-Naa night, they should be singing the song, or rather the Douglas version of the song."

"There are different versions?"

Shelly laughed. "There are different versions that are sung in different parts of the island."

"The island is too small for there to be different versions," Fenella protested.

"Each town has its own version. Each town has its own distinct personality, too. Surely you've realized that by now."

Fenella hesitated and then nodded. "I suppose you're right. I don't get out of Douglas that often, but just a few miles away in Ramsey, things do feel different."

"And they sing a different version of the Hop-tu-Naa song."

"Saturday should be fascinating."

"I'm sure it will be."

The pair were just about back to their apartment building. The dogs were even starting to look a bit tired as they walked the last few yards and then crossed the road.

"What are your plans for the rest of the day?" Shelly asked as they all boarded the elevator together.

"You know I don't like to leave the dogs alone, at least not for long. I'm nearly out of food, but at least this time I was able to plan for their visit. I should have enough to keep us all fed through tomorrow."

"Maybe we should get a pizza delivered. Then you can save whatever you have left, just in case Harvey doesn't get back."

"Are you hungry for pizza?"

"Actually, I'm hungry for garlic bread. I was going to sneak that into the order if you agreed," Shelly said sheepishly.

Fenella laughed. "Let's get pizza, then," she said. "I feel as if we haven't seen each other in ages. The dogs have been keeping me confined to my apartment."

"And when we are together, we're both walking different dogs," Shelly added. "Should I bring a bottle of wine when I come over?"

"If you want wine, please do. I'm not really drinking much these days. The dogs are hard enough work when I'm cold sober."

"We can go the pub tomorrow night, after the dogs have gone home. That will be more fun. Anyway, fizzy drinks go best with pizza."

Fenella nodded. "I have lots of soda in, anyway. I stocked up because ShopFast was having a sale."

"And then, after dinner, we can take the dogs out for their last walk of the night," Shelly sighed. "I know I'll miss them, too, but right now I'm quite tired of all the walking they need."

"Maybe Fiona will be too tired to go far. I can take Winston and you and Fiona can sit on a bench and wait for us."

"We'll see. She hasn't been tired any other night."

"No, and I'm sure I haven't thanked you enough for helping with the dogs every day while Harvey's been away. I'm hugely grateful. I'm not sure I would have managed on my own."

"You would have, if I hadn't been around. Anyway, I was glad to help. I would have kept the animals myself if Smokey didn't hate dogs."

Shelly went back to her own apartment to give Smokey her dinner. Fenella opened her door and then stepped back and let the dogs go first, unfastening their leashes as she did so. They both bounced into the large living room and then on to the kitchen.

Fenella could hear Winston slurping up water and she knew from experience that Fiona would be doing the same, just much more quietly and daintily.

Katie looked over from the chair she was curled up on and then seemed to roll her eyes at Fenella. "He doesn't mean to be noisy," she told the animal.

"I think it's sweet," Mona said as she walked out of the kitchen. "I love having the dogs here."

Mona was either a ghost or something conjured up by Fenella's overactive imagination. Either way, Mona was completely unable to help with the extra work that the two dogs created. "Yes, well, I've enjoyed having them, but I'm looking forward to giving them back to Harvey tomorrow," Fenella said.

Mona sighed. "Do they have to go back tomorrow? We could just keep them through the weekend, couldn't we?"

"No, we can't. They need to go home, where they belong. I'm exhausted from all of the walks at all hours of the day and night. Besides, feeding them has completely blown my budget for the month."

Mona laughed. "As if that's truly a concern," she scoffed.

Fenella flushed. When she'd first arrived, she'd been thrilled to find that she'd inherited the gorgeous luxury apartment that she now called home. Her lawyer had been vague about what else was included in Mona's estate, so Fenella had settled in and begun to live frugally while she tried to work out whether she could afford to write the book she'd always wanted to write or whether she should think about looking for a job instead.

A more recent meeting with her lawyer had revealed that Mona's estate was a good deal more extensive than Fenella had dared even imagine. She'd discovered that she owned properties all over the island, had large bank balances in several banks, and owned a fortune in stocks and bonds. Although that meeting had taken place some months ago, Fenella was still finding it difficult to think of herself as wealthy. What she'd found easier was giving up the idea, at least for now, of writing her book.

"You'll miss them," Mona predicted.

"I'm sure I will, but I'm sure Harvey has missed them while he's been away. He'll be delighted to have them back again."

Shelly arrived a short time later and the pair ordered far more pizza and garlic bread than they could eat.

"We can both have leftovers tomorrow," Fenella said when she put the phone down after ordering.

"I won't complain about that. I never seem to want to bother with cooking anymore."

"I hope nothing is wrong?" Fenella made the statement a question.

Shelly laughed. "I think I just got spoiled when Gordon was taking me out all the time, that's all. Now he's away for work more than he's here and I'm having to fend for myself."

Gordon Davison was a widower who was a few years older than Shelly. He'd been a friend to both Shelly and her husband, and since Shelly had been widowed the pair had begun spending time together. Shelly always insisted that they were just friends, but Fenella knew that Shelly was beginning to hope for more from the relationship. In the last month or so, though, Gordon had been traveling for work a great deal, leaving Shelly on her own.

"Do you hear from him often?" Fenella asked.

"Not often, exactly, but occasionally. He texts me when he's back at his hotel room some evenings, when it isn't too late. We chat for a bit, but it's, well, it's difficult. He's very busy, anyway."

"Will he be away for much longer?"

"He's back on Tuesday for the day, then gone again until early November. I don't really expect to see much of him until closer to Christmas. He's going to take a few days off around the holidays and he's suggested that maybe we could have dinner together a few times while he's back on the island."

"Are you okay with that?"

"Not really, but it isn't as if I have a choice," Shelly sighed. "I miss him. I have a lot of friends, but I feel as if Gordon and I were getting close. I don't know. Maybe it's better that he's gone. Maybe we both needed some time to work out how we really feel."

"How do you feel?"

"Confused, mostly."

The doorbell kept Fenella from replying. She paid the pizza delivery guy and then carried the food into the kitchen.

"It all smells wonderful," Shelly said as she pulled down plates for them both.

When they were seated together at the table with full plates of food in front of them, Fenella picked the conversation back up where they'd left off. "So you're confused?"

"That's the best word for how I feel, but I'm coping. Being busy with the dogs has helped, too. Anyway, let's not talk about Gordon anymore. Let's talk about your love life."

Mona, who was sitting at the kitchen counter, laughed. "This will be a short conversation," she said.

Fenella frowned at her, but she couldn't disagree. When she'd first moved to the island she'd felt overwhelmed by attractive men who seemed interested in her. One by one they'd all seemed to disappear, leaving her as alone as Shelly.

"There isn't anything to talk about," she told Shelly, trying not to sound bitter.

"I thought you and Peter were cute together," Shelly said, referring to the man who lived right next door to Fenella.

"I like him a lot, but we're just friends. He's always busy with work, and he's out most evenings as well. I'm not sure if that's work-related or if he's seeing someone, but he certainly isn't pursuing me any longer."

"What about Donald? When will he be back?"

"Probably not until the new year. His daughter is improving slowly, but she has a long way to go."

Donald Donaldson was wealthy, worldly, and attractive. He'd been an ardent suitor, taking Fenella out as much as he could when he was on the island. His many business interests meant that he traveled a great deal, however. Just after he'd told Fenella that he was quite serious about her, his daughter had been in a car accident. Phoebe had been living and working in New York City and Donald had dropped everything to be with her. He was hoping to bring Phoebe back to the island for her rehabilitation, but arranging what the woman needed was proving difficult, even with all of Donald's money.

"I'm not sure I want to ask about Daniel," Shelly said, giving Fenella a sympathetic look.

"You can ask, but nothing has changed," Fenella replied.

Fenella found it difficult to talk about police inspector Daniel Robinson. The pair had first met over a dead body and their friendship had developed from there. They were starting to explore the idea of taking things beyond friendship when Daniel had been sent on a lengthy course in the UK. While he was gone they'd kept in touch infrequently, mostly whenever Fenella found herself caught up in the middle of yet another police investigation. The man had returned several weeks ago and he and Fenella had had an awkward reunion when they'd bumped into one another in ShopFast a few days after his return.

"Remind me of what he said when you saw him in ShopFast," Shelly said.

"I've told you this story a million times," Fenella sighed. "He said hi and then he introduced me to the very pretty and very young woman with him."

"Tiffany Perkins." Shelly made a face.

"That's the girl. They met on the policing course. According to Daniel, she's been looking to move out of London, where she'd been working, so she wanted to have a look at the island."

"And she's staying with Daniel while she's having this look?"

"Yes, because he has plenty of room in his house for guests."

Daniel lived in a four-bedroom house on the outskirts of Douglas. Tiffany could have been staying with him and sleeping in one of the spare bedrooms. Fenella was worried that she was sleeping in Daniel's bed, though.

"And you haven't seen him since?"

"Nope. He hasn't called me, or texted me, or anything. That was over a month ago, so I have to assume that he's not interested in me any longer."

"Nonsense," Mona said. "He's just behaving like an idiot. He'll come to his senses eventually."

Fenella only just stopped herself from replying to her aunt. Shelly couldn't see or hear the woman, so Fenella chomped down a slice of garlic bread before she blurted out something that might make Shelly think she'd lost her mind.

"Maybe he's just really busy at work. There have been a whole load of burglaries in Douglas in the past month."

"I'm sure he's busy with work and with Tiffany."

"Surely she isn't still here?"

Fenella shrugged. "I was at the rental house the other day, just making sure that it's ready for new tenants, and there were two cars in Daniel's driveway."

One of the other properties that Fenella had inherited from Mona just happened to be a house that was almost exactly across the street from Daniel's home. Her lawyer, Doncan Quayle, paid a company on her behalf to manage renting out all of her various properties, but Fenella had let her brother stay at the house on Poppy Drive. Once he'd gone home to Pennsylvania, Fenella had been oddly reluctant to let Doncan find new tenants for the home.

"You need to let someone else move in there," Mona said. "Then you won't be able to visit whenever you want to watch Daniel."

"I'm not watching Daniel," Fenella snapped.

"I didn't say you were," Shelly said in surprise.

"No, I'm sorry," Fenella replied, glaring at Mona, who was laughing. "I just feel guilty every time I visit that house. I feel as if I'm spying on the man, even though I'm not, not really."

"Perhaps you should ring him and ask him to tell you exactly what's going on," Shelly suggested.

"Or I could simply pretend that nothing is going on and carry on with my life," Fenella countered. "He doesn't have to explain anything to me. His actions tell me everything I need to know about where I stand with him, anyway."

"I really thought you two were good together," Shelly sighed.

"Yes, well, I liked him a lot, but it wasn't easy being involved with a police inspector. I'm probably better off without him."

"Maybe you should give your ex another chance."

Fenella laughed loudly. "I wouldn't get back with Jack if he were the last man on earth," she told her friend. "Being alone is much better than being with him ever was."

After ten years of trying to convince herself that she was in love with Jack Dawson, Fenella had been relieved to finally have an excuse to end their relationship when she'd moved to the Isle of Man. The pair had worked together as professors at the same university where Fenella had studied. Even in the earliest days of their romance, Fenella had never felt as if Jack were completely right for her, but the relationship had been comfortable and easy, even if she did find herself almost constantly looking after the man.

"So we need to find you a new man," Shelly suggested. "I'm going to give the matter some thought."

"I don't want a new man. Truly, I don't. I'm perfectly happy on my own. Anyway, I have Katie. Men are an unnecessary complication."

Mona sighed. "Are you quite certain that we're related?" she asked.

Fenella shook her head at her aunt. When she'd first moved to the island, Fenella had been surprised to learn that the woman she'd only met a few times as a child had something of a wild reputation on the island. Mona had never married and she seemed to have amassed her fortune thanks to the generosity of a number of men with whom she'd been involved. Maxwell Martin had been her primary source of support, letting her live in the hotel that he owned for many years. When the hotel was converted into luxury apartments, he'd given Mona the largest and most luxurious as her own. It was that apartment that was now Fenella's home.

"Maybe we're both better off on our own," Shelly said. "At least we have each other."

"Exactly, and we have a lot of fun together, you and I." Fenella washed down her last bite of pizza with a sip of soda and then sighed. "Except maybe not so much with the dogs," she said as Winston bounded into the room, barking excitedly.

"He can't need to go out again, can he?" Shelly asked.

"I'm sure he wants to, whether he actually needs to or not. I'm also sure I'm not taking any chances with all of my lovely furniture and carpets." Fenella got to her feet and headed for the living room. "Maybe you and Fiona can simply wait here for us," she suggested as she got Winston's leash back down.

But Fiona wasn't happy with that idea. As Fenella and Winston headed for the door, she raced over to it and began to bark loudly.

"Let me get my shoes back on," Shelly said. "Then we can split up again if necessary."

"We won't need to this time. I'm far too tired to go jogging again, even if Winston isn't."

Shelly and Fenella walked the dogs the length of the promenade again, letting them stop to sniff every flower and investigate every bush.

"See, if we had men in our lives, we couldn't do this," Shelly said as she and Fenella dropped onto a bench. The dogs happily continued to explore the area, at least as far as their leashes would allow.

"Yeah, yay being single," Fenella replied.

Shelly laughed. "That didn't sound sincere."

A moment later both dogs began to bark excitedly. Fenella looked up to see a pair of joggers running toward them. As they got closer, Fenella's heart sank.

"Sugar," she said under her breath.

"Sugar?" Shelly echoed.

"When I started teaching, I forced myself to substitute more appropriate language for the swear words that I had formerly used," Fenella explained. "Sugar is one of the those substitute words."

"Why did you, oh..." Shelly began and then trailed off as she recognized the new arrivals.

"Winston," Daniel Robinson said. "How nice to see you again." He stopped running and fussed over the large dog and his smaller companion for a minute before smiling brightly at Fenella and Shelly.

"Hi," Shelly said, "and welcome back."

Daniel grinned. "I've been back for about a month, but I've been too busy to socialize. Hopefully things will get quieter soon."

"Daniel?" the girl with him said.

"Oh, sorry, Tiffany Perkins, this is Shelly Quirk. She's another of my friends on the island. You already met Fenella, of course."

Tiffany gave Shelly a small smile. "I'm too sweaty to offer my hand, but it's nice to meet you," she said, "and of course I remember Findella. Where did we meet, again?"

"At ShopFast, just after you'd first arrived. I didn't realize you were still here, actually," Fenella replied, without bothering to correct the woman's pronunciation of her name. There was no doubt in her mind that the mistake had been deliberate.

"I'm simply having too much fun to leave," the girl replied with a shrug. "Daniel has been wonderful to me, letting me overstay my welcome."

"I'm just sorry we don't have any openings at the constabulary right now, but I'm sure something will open up for you somewhere soon," he replied.

"I won't complain if it takes a while longer. I'm really enjoying my holiday on the island," Tiffany said, "but that dog looks as if he needs a good run. Would you like me to run with him for a short while?" she offered.

"That's a great idea," Daniel said. "Winston loves running. Let us take him for a bit," he told Fenella.

She glanced at Shelly and then handed the leash over to Daniel, even though she didn't really want Tiffany anywhere near Winston. Daniel and Tiffany began to jog lightly together, picking up their pace as Winston tried to race ahead.

"I hate her," Shelly said in a conversational tone as they watched.

"That makes two of us, but you can see why Daniel is enamored. She's gorgeous and she's in great shape. I watched them running on the beach. She was running hard and she wasn't even short of breath when she got here."

"Never mind," Shelly said, patting Fenella's hand. "She's unemployed from the sound of it. Hopefully she'll find a job soon, far, far away from here."

Fenella sighed and then looked down the promenade. She watched as Daniel handed Winston's leash to Tiffany. Tiffany bounced away from the man, down the steps, and onto the beach.

"I don't want Winston on the beach," Fenella said angrily. She got to her feet and began to walk quickly toward Tiffany.

She wasn't quite close enough to shout at the woman when Winston noticed her. He clearly recognized that his time on the sand was limited, so he turned and ran toward the water, pulling Tiffany behind him.

"Stop," Tiffany shouted shrilly. Winston ignored her as he dashed into the waves.

Tiffany ran after him, struggling to hold onto the leash as she went. Winston glanced back over his shoulder and then dove into a huge wave. As he splashed up and down in the surf, Tiffany lost her grip on the leash. She lunged for it, losing her balance and falling face first into the sea.

Fenella couldn't stop herself from laughing as Tiffany tried to get up. Winston clearly thought she was playing some sort of game, so he rushed over and began to pounce through the waves next to her.

"That was wonderful," Shelly said as she joined Fenella on the promenade overlooking the scene below.

"Winston is having fun, anyway," Fenella said as the big dog tried to climb into Tiffany's lap.

"I should go and help," Daniel said.

Fenella jumped. She hadn't noticed the man's approach. "I should have told you not to take him on the beach," she said.

"I knew better from past experience," Daniel replied, "and I told Tiffany to stay on the promenade, but she wanted to run on the sand. It's more of a challenge."

"Then she should have left Winston with you," Fenella said.

"Which is what I told her," he agreed. "Now Winston needs a trip to the groomers."

"I hope they're still open." Fenella glanced at her watch. "I think Thursday is their late-night opening." She was still having trouble adjusting to life on a small island where late-night opening meant that some shops stayed open until nine one night a week. It was rather different from the shopping malls open until nine every night and the superstores that were open twenty-four hours a day, seven days a week, back in Buffalo.

"I'll take him, as it's my fault he's covered in sand and sea," Daniel said. "I'll bring him back to your apartment when they're done with him."

Fenella hesitated and then nodded. "You know where to find me," she said.

She glanced back down at the beach. Tiffany was squelching her way back across the sand, nearly dragging a dripping and penitent-looking Winston with her. Daniel met her as she walked back up the steps to the promenade and they had a short conversation. It ended when Daniel pulled out his wallet and handed something from it to Tiffany. As Shelly and Fenella watched, Tiffany stomped over to the nearby taxi rank and climbed into a taxi. Daniel and Winston headed off down the promenade toward the nearby dog groomers.

2

"I am sorry," Daniel said an hour later when he returned Winston to Fenella. "I shouldn't have let Tiffany take Winston."

"I should given you both instructions for walking him," she countered.

Daniel shrugged. "It all worked out in the end. Winston got to have some fun and then he got a nice bath. He's happy, anyway."

"I'm not sure that Tiffany is very happy."

"Yeah, well, I'll deal with that when I get home," Daniel said, sighing.

"Are you okay?"

"Me? I'm fine. Things are just, well, I don't know, complicated. I've been trying to find the time to come and see you. I'd really like to talk, but between work and having a guest at the house, I'm really busy."

"Do you have time for a quick chat now? I can make tea or coffee or something."

Daniel grinned. "I'd really like that." He'd only taken two steps into the apartment when his mobile rang. After glancing at the display, he frowned. "I need to take this," he said.

Fenella walked into the kitchen so that Daniel wouldn't think she was eavesdropping. Mona, on the other hand, went and stood right next to the man where she was sure to hear both sides of the conversation. It didn't take long.

"There's been another break-in at a house in Onchan," Daniel told her when he'd ended the call. "I have to go."

"You know where am I when you want to talk," Fenella told him as she walked back into the room.

"I do. Thank you," he said as he let himself out.

"Wooofff?" Winston said.

Fenella looked at the dog and then grinned. "I think you deserve a treat," she told him. "Tiffany might well win Daniel away from me, but at least I got to see her covered in sand, mud, and seaweed, dripping wet and furious, before she managed it."

Harvey was delighted to get the dogs back the next afternoon. Fenella was too tired out after a week of walking the pair every day to take herself off to the pub that night. Instead, she curled up with a good book and then watched mindless television until bedtime. She and Shelly had plans for Saturday and she needed to be well rested, anyway.

"I do love this car," she told Shelly as the pair made their way south in Mona's fancy red convertible.

"I do, too," Shelly replied. "I was afraid once you'd purchased your sensible car that you'd stop driving this one."

Fenella nodded. "I was afraid of that, too, but this one is perfect for outings like today's." It had taken Fenella many months of practice before she'd been ready to take the island's driving test, which was much more difficult than the one she'd taken at sixteen in the US. Passing it gave her access to Mona's sports car, though, so it had been worth all of the hard work. Once she'd discovered that she had considerable assets, Fenella had purchased a much more sensible car for her day-to-day needs. It was that car that she did her grocery shopping with and drove in the rain. Mona's car was for special occasions, like today, and driving it always made Fenella feel happy and carefree.

They drove further south than Fenella had ever been before, eventually arriving at Cregneash Village, a living museum that was dedicated to preserving the Manx way of life in the nineteenth century. Fenella had read about the village, but had never found the time to visit before. She parked in the small parking lot and then followed Shelly, who headed straight for the museum.

"Welcome to our annual Hop-tu-Naa celebrations," a man who looked around forty said to them as the entered the building.

"Thank you," Shelly replied. "It's my friend's first visit to Cregneash."

"In that case, take the time to look all around," the man urged her. "All of the cottages are open for visitors. There are different Hop-tu-Naa crafts and activities in most of them. I'm Oliver Wentworth from Manx National Heritage, and I'll be here all day if you have any questions about anything."

Shelly introduced herself and Fenella. "I promised Fenella that we'd carve some turnips," she told Oliver. "She's American, so she's only ever done pumpkins."

"Ah, pumpkins are for wimps," he laughed. "Carving a turnip is a real job." He told them where to find the turnip carving and then gave them a map of the site with all of the activities marked on it. "There will be lots of little ghosts and ghouls around, but there's plenty for adults to do as well," he assured them.

Fenella and Shelly walked a short distance and into one of the small thatched-roofed cottages. Inside, a couple were in a clinch that made Fenella blush.

"Oh, goodness," the woman gasped as she pulled away from the man. "We weren't expecting visitors just yet."

"Clearly," Fenella replied.

The woman giggled. "I am awfully sorry. I hope you won't tell on us and get me fired."

"You are a volunteer," the man pointed out.

The woman laughed again. She looked young, maybe twenty-five, and she was wearing in a simple dress that was no doubt historically accurate for the period when the cottage had been occupied. Her hair was a dark blonde that looked natural and her eyes were a lovely shade of blue.

The man with her appeared to be of a similar age. He was wearing modern jeans and a sweatshirt with the name of an American football team across it. His hair was short and dark and his eyes were brown.

"I still shouldn't be, um, well, anyway, good morning," she said to Fenella and Shelly. "I'm Karla, with a K, Pierce, and this is my very badly behaved husband, Phillip."

The man laughed. "I wasn't the only one behaving badly," he retorted.

"We're newlyweds, really," Karla continued, "so I hope you'll forgive us."

"When did you get married?" Shelly asked.

Karla blushed. "Just last week," she said softly. "It was something of an impulsive decision."

"Not for me," Phillip said stoutly. "I wanted to marry you the moment I first laid eyes on you."

Karla turned an even brighter shade of red. "Now stop," she said. "You mustn't say such things."

"Not even if they're true?" he questioned. "But I should get out of the way. I'm meant to be helping with the turnip carving, which sounds a difficult job."

"Yes, off you go. There will be dozens of small children here soon and they'll all need help," Karla said. She walked her husband to the door and then gave him a chaste kiss on the cheek.

"You'll have to do better than that later," he teased.

The girl blushed again and then pushed the man out the door. "But welcome," she said as she turned to Fenella and Shelly. "I'm meant to be talking about the different Hop-tu-Naa songs with our visitors today. Which part of the island did you grow up in?"

"I grew up in the US," Fenella told her.

"Oh, how exciting," Karla exclaimed. "I've always wanted to visit the US, but it's so expensive. Phillip and I are going to try to save up, though. We didn't take a honeymoon, not yet, anyway. I'd really like to go to New York and maybe Hollywood, but I'm afraid we'll have to save for years and years to be able to afford a trip like that."

Fenella was never sure exactly how to reply to people when they shared that sort of sentiment with her. Most of the people she'd met had a romanticized view of the US based on movies and television. She was always tempted to warn people that what they would probably find there wouldn't be what they were expecting.

"I grew up on the island," Shelly said after a moment.

"If you sing the Hop-tu-Naa song that you remember from your childhood, I can tell you which part of the island you're from," Karla replied.

Shelly shook her head. "I don't recall what version I sang as a child, really. I taught primary school in Douglas for a great many years so that version of the song is the one that is burned into my memory."

Karla laughed. "That's the one I learned when I was a child," she said. "For me, it will always be the right song to sing on Hop-tu-Naa, even though very few people agree with me."

"Do you know all of the songs, then?" Shelly asked.

"I've done my best to learn them for today," Karla replied. "My parents have been volunteering with Manx National Heritage for years and they always used to drag me along. Now that I'm older, I've started volunteering myself, but I don't have as much time to give as I'd like. Anyway, I did my best, and they've put me in here to teach the songs to visitors. Which one do you want to learn?"

Shelly looked at Fenella and raised an eyebrow.

Fenella laughed. "I'd rather have you explain them to me than teach me how to sing them," she said.

"I'll try, although you really need my mother for that," Karla told her. "Let me see what I have in the paperwork they gave me, though."

While Karla was flipping through a small binder filled with papers, the door to the cottage swung open. An older couple, probably in their late fifties, walked inside. They were both dressed in period costume and the woman was wearing a necklace and earrings made up of tiny plastic spiders.

"Perfect timing," Karla said, clapping her hands together. "Our guests were just asking about the story behind the Hop-tu-Naa songs."

"And you don't remember anything you were taught," the woman sighed.

"I remember a few things," Karla countered, "but you're the expert."

The woman laughed. "Hardly that, but I won't argue." She turned to Fenella and Shelly. "I'm Harriet Jones," she said, "and this is my husband, Henry. I've been a volunteer with Manx National Heritage since the early days of my marriage. Women weren't expected to work in those days, so I volunteered instead. Henry just gets dragged along and he's too nice to complain about it, at least in front of visitors."

Fenella and Shelly both laughed and then introduced themselves.

"How much do you already know about Hop-tu-Naa?" Harriet asked.

"I've read a bit, but I don't really remember much," Fenella said. "Which is shocking, as I was a history professor before I moved to the island."

"Did you read that Hop-tu-Naa is actually the observance of the Celtic New Year? It's a celebration of the successful harvest. Farmers waited until after harvest, when all of their preparations for winter were complete, and then they celebrated," Harriet told her.

"So Happy New Year," Fenella laughed.

"Yes, indeed," Harriet replied. "Karla can sing a few Hop-tu-Naa songs for you, if you'd like. Each part of the island has its own version of the song, but many of the modern versions are about Jinny the witch."

"Who was she?" Fenella asked.

"As with everything in Manx history, there are differences of opinion on that one, but many people believe that the song refers to a woman called Joney Lowney who was tried for witchcraft around 1715," Harriet told her.

"Oh, dear. Did she get burned at the stake or something else horrible like that?" Fenella wondered.

"Oh, goodness, no," Harriet laughed. "She was sent to prison for a fortnight and fined a few pounds. I believe she probably would have had to stand at the various market crosses for penance, as well."

"That doesn't sound too bad," Shelly said.

"Only one person was ever executed on the island for being a witch," Harriet told her, "and that was nearly a hundred years before Jinny's trial."

"I really should learn more about the island's history," Fenella said. "Everything I hear about it fascinates me, but I've been incredibly lazy since I've been here."

"You made a lot of changes in very short order," Shelly pointed out. "I think being lazy for a short while is understandable."

"There's a special dance for Hop-tun-Naa as well," Harriet said after a moment. "We can teach you the basics in just a few minutes and then you can join in the dancing later."

Fenella shook her head. "I'm hopeless at dancing, but you should teach it to Shelly."

Shelly laughed. "Maybe later. I really want to carve my turnip before it gets too busy."

"That's a good point, actually," Henry said, speaking for the first time since he'd been introduced. "Once the site fills up with small children, it gets difficult to do much of anything."

"Let's get off to the turnip carving, then," Shelly said. "That's the main reason I came, after all."

Fenella followed her friend out of the cottage and down a short walkway. A man in period dress coming the other way stopped and nodded at them.

"Good morning," Shelly said brightly.

"Aye, good morning," he said. "Let's hope it stays quiet, anyway."

"Quiet?" Shelly repeated. "Aren't you hoping for a crowd?"

He shrugged. "For those of us who live here, crowds aren't always good. They spook the animals, for one thing." He bowed slightly and then continued on his way.

"Goodness, I hope we don't spook any animals," Fenella said. "I can't imagine that would be good."

Shelly laughed. "I doubt we have to worry. I'm sure it's the large quantities of screaming children that have him so grumpy."

"He was rather grumpy, wasn't he?" Fenella agreed.

Phillip Pierce, on the other hand, seemed to be in a wonderful mood. He was laughing and talking with another man as Shelly and Fenella walked into the large barn where the turnip carving was supposed to be taking place.

"They look like rutabagas," Fenella said.

"Rutabagas?" Shelly repeated. "I don't know what those are, but these are what we call turnips here on the island."

"Well, they're bigger than what I was picturing. I couldn't imagine how anyone would carve what I think of as a turnip."

Shelly shrugged. "Divided by a common language," she suggested.

Fenella laughed. "Something like that."

"Ah, ladies, step right up," Phillip called to them. "Pick your turnip, but choose wisely. You want the best possible shape for your carving, after all."

Shelly seemed to study the long row of turnips available before she selected one. Fenella just grabbed the one that was closest to her. As she had no idea what she was doing, there seemed little point in being fussy.

"Excellent choices, both of them," Phillip said. "Now I'll just give them a little bit of drill action and then you can get started."

"Drill?" Fenella questioned.

"You can try hollowing it all out by hand if you prefer, but it will take you quite a while. We usually drill a few holes into the turnips to help you get started," he explained.

Fenella and Shelly watched as the man drilled several holes into each of their turnips. When that was done, the vegetables were returned to them and the hard work really began. Once they were roughly hollowed out, it was time to carve a design into the hard body of the turnips.

"I had high hopes of doing something incredibly creative," Shelly whispered to her friend in the barn that was slowly filling up with people. "But now I think I'll be happy with two eyes and a mouth."

Fenella rubbed her hand, which was aching from the effort she'd already put in. "Maybe mine will be a Cyclops," she said.

Shelly laughed and then went back to work. A short while later, as the barn began to get crowded and noisy, both women were happy to declare their work done.

"Mine looks as if a badly supervised five-year-old made it," Fenella sighed as she picked up her finished product.

"Mine isn't much better," Shelly assured her. "Maybe we should just leave them down here somewhere on a bench or something."

"Oh, no," Fenella said firmly. "After all of my hard work, this stupid thing is getting pride of place in my apartment until it gets too moldy to keep."

Shelly laughed. "You make a good point, really. I just hope mine doesn't scare Smokey too badly."

Fenella looked at the lopsided face she'd carved. "Katie is made of sterner stuff. She'll be fine," she said, mentally crossing her fingers that the kitten might be frightened enough to give Fenella the excuse she needed for trashing the ugly turnip.

"We should put these in the car before we do anything else," Shelly suggested. "So they don't get lost or damaged while we're doing other things."

And so no one sees how terrible they are, Fenella added in her head. The pair locked their turnips in the trunk of Mona's car.

"Let's go see what else we can find that's fun to do," Shelly said brightly.

Fenella laughed. "I'm not sure that particular activity was fun, but I'm sure there must be some fun to be had here."

As they walked back toward the museum, they were stopped by Oliver Wentworth. "Ladies, ladies, it's time for some dancing," he told them. "Follow me."

Fenella glanced at Shelly. She didn't really want to try dancing, but she knew that Shelly had enjoyed learning a few traditional Manx dance steps during Tynwald Day. She didn't want to get in the way of her friend's fun, even if she did feel as if she had two left feet herself.

"It truly isn't difficult," Oliver assured them both. "The Hop-tu-Naa dance is one of the easiest of the Manx dances."

"You would say that," Fenella replied.

He laughed. "Try it. If you don't have fun, you can quit after the first five minutes. We've been lucky enough to get a local band to provide the music. The Islanders play a great mix of traditional Manx music and more modern covers. Today they'll be focusing on the traditional songs, of course."

Fenella still wasn't sure, but she followed Shelly and Oliver into the large hall. A few musicians were warming up and Fenella recognized Henry Jones as one of them. After a minute he stopped playing and fell into a conversation with the man next to him.

"Come and meet the musicians," Oliver said. "I like to introduce them to everyone before they start playing. I find it encourages them to play at a reasonable pace, at least in the beginning."

"We've already met Mr. Jones," Fenella said when they'd reached the small group of men.

"You must call me Henry, though," he told her.

"This is Paul Baldwin," Oliver said, nodding at the younger man who had been speaking with Henry. "He's one of the best front men The Islanders have ever had. He's actually only just back from the UK for a short visit before he makes it big over there."

Paul was probably around thirty. He had long dark hair that was pulled back into a ponytail and dark eyes. Fenella thought he looked like he should have been in a boy band in his younger days.

"He'd do just fine back here," Henry said.

Paul shrugged. "It's a tough business. I had some fun and made some contacts. Now I'm home for a while, anyway. If I'm very lucky, I might hear back from one or two of the people I met while I was away. If not, I'll have to try again in the new year."

"It is the new year," Oliver laughed. "That's what Hop-tu-Naa is all about."

"Are you trying to get rid of me?" Paul demanded.

Oliver laughed. "Not at all. We need your talent. I'm not saying the band isn't great without you, but it's definitely a lot better with you."

"I think we were just insulted," Henry said with a laugh.

"You know I didn't mean it that way," Oliver replied.

"We need to warm up," Paul interjected. "It was a pleasure to meet you both," he told Shelly and Fenella.

Oliver introduced the women to the other three men in the band. Fenella forgot their names almost as soon as she'd heard them. The large room was starting to fill up as the men moved onto the stage.

"Where should we go?" Shelly asked Oliver.

"Why not stay here?" he replied. "I'm going to need volunteers to help me show everyone the steps. You two can be my volunteers."

Fenella opened her mouth to object, but she was drowned out by the band. For several minutes they played various Manx tunes, to the great delight of the crowd. It didn't take long for Fenella to notice that Oliver had been correct. Paul was very talented.

"Paul's talents are wasted with this lot, but they're all we have," Oliver said as a song ended.

"He's very good," Fenella agreed.

"Now it's time for some dancing," Oliver announced. He stepped out in front of the band and grabbed the microphone. "Happy Hop-tu-Naa," he called out to the small crowd.

"Happy Hop-tu-Naa," everyone repeated back.

Fenella noted that it was mostly families with young children in the space. She could see several men holding badly carved turnips. Most of the women were holding toddlers or younger children as they watched the band.

"How many of you have done the Hop-tu-Naa dance before?" Oliver asked.

A few people clapped and a few others headed for the door. Oliver laughed. "This is going to be fun," he said. "We'll try it once and anyone who isn't having fun can leave after that, okay?"

His words stopped at least a few people from leaving, Fenella noted.

Oliver waved at Shelly. "We have a volunteer," he said happily.

When Shelly joined him, he slowly took her through the steps for the dance. They practiced it several times before Oliver urged everyone in the room to try it.

Paul was standing near Fenella, so he offered his arm. "May I have the honor?" he asked.

Fenella blushed and then let the man lead her through the steps. Oliver hadn't lied. It was a fairly easy pattern and it wasn't long before she was starting to feel confident with it.

"I think we're ready for music," Oliver said.

"And there I must sadly leave you," Paul told Fenella. "Duty calls."

Fenella laughed. "Thank you for the dance."

Shelly rejoined Fenella as the musicians got into position. "Oliver has to call the steps," she told Fenella. "That leaves me free to dance with you."

Feeling as if she was probably going to regret it, Fenella fell into place with Shelly as her partner. The music started and the dance began. Several minutes later she and Shelly were both laughing and trying to catch their breath.

"You've all done incredibly well," Oliver said.

Fenella looked at Shelly and then giggled. She hadn't done incredibly well, but she had managed not to fall over. That had been harder than she'd expected, due to the number of small children who were simply ducking in and out between the dancers rather than trying to do the steps. Occasionally a harassed-looking mother would try to chase one of them, adding to the confusion.

"Let's try it again," Oliver suggested. "Maybe parents with smaller children could stand around the outside and keep their children out of the way. I'd hate for any little ones to get trampled."

The band started again and things did seem to go more smoothly this time, right up until a little boy who was probably two decided to have a tantrum. As he raced into the middle of dancers and threw himself on the ground, screaming, dancers began veering away in every direction. The boy's mother tried to grab him, but things were chaotic for a minute before the band suddenly stopped and the room went quiet.

"I'm so sorry," the woman said, her face bright red with embarrassment. "I'm not sure how he got away from me."

"He got away from you because you were on your phone," an older woman said.

The child's mother pressed her lips together and then scooped up the child and quickly walked out of the room with him.

"She was on her phone," the older woman said. "She wasn't paying him any attention."

"I think it's time to let our musicians have a break," Oliver said. "We'll start again in fifteen minutes."

As the room began to empty, Fenella looked at Shelly. "Do you want to stay and do some more dancing after the break?"

Shelly shrugged. "It was fun, but I feel as if we've done it now. Anyway, I'm getting hungry. I know there are meant to be food trucks down here somewhere. Maybe we should go and get some lunch."

"Lunch sounds perfect," Fenella agreed.

"I hope you'll be back for more dancing later," Oliver said as the pair headed for the door.

"We'll have to see how the days goes," Shelly told him. "We want to try everything that's on offer."

"My favorite type of visitors," he smiled. "You'll have to come back once we start doing our Old Manx Christmas weekends," he told them. "They're nearly as much fun as Hop-tu-Naa."

"Oh, yes, let's," Fenella told Shelly.

"There will be more dancing," Shelly warned her.

"I'm willing to try again. It was more fun than I thought it would be, and besides, Christmas is my favorite holiday," Fenella said.

They walked back outside and then followed their noses to the large parking area where the food trucks were set up. A dozen small tables with chairs around them were inside the tent on the grass next to the parking area.

Fenella and Shelly walked past every truck, reading each menu, before they decided what they wanted. Once they both had plates full of food, they found a table in the tent and settled in to enjoy their meal.

"I hope you're both having fun," Karla said brightly as she walked past their table a few minutes later.

"We are, thank you," Shelly replied. "Has it been terribly busy in your cottage?"

"Goodness, yes, but I love every minute of it, especially the small children. Phillip and I plan to start working on adding to our family in the new year, so it's all good practice," the girl replied. "I only get a short break, though. I'd better go and get some lunch."

The small tent was filling up and Fenella watched as Karla got her food and then looked around for somewhere to sit. She was about to wave to Karla when Paul walked in behind her. He said something to the girl that made her laugh. They talked for a few minutes and then left the tent together.

"Would you mind terribly if we joined you?" Harriet Jones asked a moment later.

"Of course not," Shelly replied. "We're just about finished, anyway."

"Don't rush off on our account," Henry said as he slid into a chair. "We can't stay long, anyway. We're on a very tight schedule."

"Oliver is a slave driver," Harriet said loudly, laughing when Oliver, who'd just walked into the tent, looked over. He waved and then joined them.

"I just want to give our visitors the best possible experience," he said. "If you only wanted to work half of the day, you shouldn't have volunteered for the whole day."

"The volunteer form didn't offer a half-day option," Harriet told him.

Oliver grinned. "That was smart planning on my part, then."

Harriet and Henry both laughed. "We love being here," Henry said. "I wasn't even expecting a lunch break. I brought sandwiches and everything."

"I'm not sure that Phillip will get a lunch break," Oliver told him, "but we're running low on turnips, so he should finish early. I'm going to walk over there now and see how he's doing. If he's nearly out, we'll have to start telling people as they arrive."

"Tell him that he's welcome to my sandwiches if he doesn't get away before the food trucks are done," Henry said. "I'll walk over myself shortly. Maybe I can help out so he can gobble down a sandwich or two."

After lunch Fenella and Shelly spent several additional hours enjoying the site. The man who'd warned them about spooking the animals was giving tours of the farm.

"I'm Josh Gentry," he said to the small group that had gathered for the first tour. "I live here at Cregneash as an employee of Manx National Heritage. I run the farm, using traditional methods. If you'd like to follow me, we'll visit a few of my animals and see some of the traditional equipment that I use."

Fenella found the tour interesting, but she couldn't quite imagine wanting to be a farmer. It seemed like incredibly hard work, especially using the traditional methods that Josh seemed to prefer.

"It is hard work," he said in reply to someone's question, "but it's totally worth the effort."

They all ended up back in front of the museum. A large sign over the door read "Sorry – we are out of turnips."

Fenella looked at Shelly. "I almost feel guilty that we did some," she said quietly.

"I don't. We were here nice and early. If people want to come to these events towards the end of the day, they have to expect to find that they've missed out on things."

"Hello, again," Karla said as she walked out of the museum building. "It's nearly time for the dance through the village. I hope you're both taking part?"

"Oh, I don't know about taking part," Shelly said. "We are looking forward to watching, anyway."

"I wish I knew where my darling husband was," Karla sighed. "We're supposed to dance together, but he hasn't turned up yet. I hope he doesn't think he needs to clear up the entire barn. We'll get to that later, after the visitors have gone."

"We can walk over and check for you, if you'd like," Shelly offered.

Karla frowned. "It probably doesn't matter. I'm sure I can find another partner." She turned and walked away, heading back toward the cottage she'd been working in earlier.

"Let's walk over to the barn anyway," Fenella suggested. "We're less likely to get asked to take part in the dancing if we're hiding in the barn."

Shelly laughed. "What if I want to take part in the dancing?"

"Then you stay here and dance. I can hide in the barn by myself."

Shelly shrugged. "Actually, I wouldn't mind taking part. Maybe I will stay here. Oliver did suggest that we might partner for it."

"You stay and dance with Oliver," Fenella said quickly. "I'll just walk over and see what Phillip is doing."

"You won't really hide in the barn, will you?"

"No, not really," Fenella said. But if I can get Phillip talking, I'm not going to rush out of it, either, she added to herself.

It seemed as if everyone at Cregneash was hurrying in the opposite direction as Fenella made her way toward the barn.

"It's time for the village dance," Harriet Jones said as she rushed past Fenella.

"Yes, I know," Fenella said to the woman's back.

The doors to the barn were shut and another sign about the lack of turnips was taped on one of them. Fenella knocked and then pushed the door open.

"Hello? Phillip? Are you still in here?" she called.

She could hear music starting, so she ducked inside the barn. "Phillip?" she said loudly, feeling foolish. No doubt he'd shut the doors and gone to find his wife. There were bales of hay in neat stacks around the room. Earlier in the day, they'd been covered in turnips. Now they were all empty.

Fenella sat down on one and wondered how long she could stay in the barn before anyone noticed. It wasn't that she hadn't enjoyed learning the Hop-tu-Naa dance, it was just that she didn't fancy trying it in the middle of the village. After a few minutes, she began to feel guilty. She probably wasn't supposed to be in the barn, not unsupervised. She got to her feet and headed for the door. As she glanced around one last time she noticed a shoe. It was sticking out from behind a few hay bales, lying on its side.

"How could someone lose a shoe?" she asked in a voice that sounded far too loud in the empty barn. Her stomach churned as she walked closer, her brain already expecting what she was going to find.

Phillip Pierce was lying on his side behind the bales of hay. One of the drills he'd been using earlier was next to him, its cord seemingly wrapped tightly around his neck.

3

Fenella backed away from the body, trying to remember to breathe as she went. There was no doubt in her mind that the man was dead. She shut her eyes tightly and almost immediately tripped over a hay bale. She jumped back up to her feet and then turned and ran to the door.

"Just breathe," she said softly to herself as she dug around in her handbag for her mobile phone. "Breathe in and out, and in and out," she told herself in a low voice. She could hear music and laughter in the distance as she punched 999 on her phone. It wasn't the first time she'd had to use the police emergency number, but she couldn't help but hope that it might be the last.

"What is your emergency?" a bored voice asked.

"I need the police," Fenella told him. "There's been an accident."

"I'll connect you," the voice replied.

"Castletown policing. How can I help you?" a cheery female voice said when the call was answered.

"Ah, yes, I'm at Cregneash Village and there's been an accident," Fenella said.

"What sort of accident? Do you need an ambulance?"

"I'm pretty sure he's past needing one," Fenella said, blinking back unexpected tears. "I believe the man was murdered."

"My goodness, really?" the woman gasped. "I'll have to find you someone quickly, then, won't I? Where are you exactly?"

"At the barn in Cregneash Village. There are tons of people here for the Hop-tu-Naa celebrations."

"Oh, I wanted to go to those, but I had to work today. Do you know if they're having them again tomorrow?"

"I'm sorry, but I don't."

"I'm going to need your name."

"It's Fenella, Fenella Woods."

"Ah, Mona's niece. Have you really found another dead body?"

Fenella sighed. "You've heard of me?"

"We had a briefing about you," the woman told her. "Inspector Robinson told all of the dispatchers to make sure to take you seriously if you ever rang. I'm also meant to ring him and let him know that you're in trouble."

"Oh, don't bother the man on a Saturday," Fenella said quickly. "Just get someone down here quickly."

"That's already being taken care of. I've put out an all-island text request. You're quite some way from our station, so I'm hoping there might be an off-duty constable nearby. He or she will be able to start the ball rolling until an inspector can get down there."

"The sooner someone gets here, the better."

"In the meantime, if you can just keep everyone away from the body, that would be great," the woman said brightly.

"I can try, but I don't even know if the barn has more than one door."

"Oh, that is a problem, isn't it? Never mind, just do your best. I'm sure someone will be on the way soon."

"What are you doing?" a loud voice asked.

Fenella was so startled that she nearly dropped her phone. She turned and tried her best to smile at Josh Gentry, who'd come up behind her.

"There's been an accident," she said. "I've just called the police."

"What sort of accident? What's happened?" he demanded.

"Oh, dear, it sounds as if you have company," the woman on the phone said.

"Yes, I do," Fenella replied. "We just need to wait for the police," she told Josh.

"The police? Surely you should have rung for an ambulance? We should see if there are any doctors in the crowd, though. There are enough people here that we should be able to find a doctor or a nurse, wouldn't you think?"

"I'm pretty sure he's dead," Fenella replied.

"Who's dead?" Josh shot back.

Fenella took a deep breath. "I shouldn't say anything more."

Josh took another step closer to her, clearly angry. "Who's dead in my barn?" he demanded.

"That's quite enough of that," someone said from behind Josh.

Fenella sighed with relief as she recognized the young man who'd just arrived. "The police are here," she said softly to the woman on the phone. "Thank you for your help." She dropped the phone into her bag.

Josh turned around. "Who are you?" he asked.

"Constable Howard Corlett, Douglas Constabulary," the man replied, shifting the baby he was holding from one hip to the other. "I was here for the celebration."

"Great, wonderful, you go back and celebrate. I can sort whatever is going on here," Josh said.

"I'm afraid it isn't that simple," the constable replied. "Ms. Woods, if I could speak to you, please?"

"You two know each other?" Josh asked.

The constable nodded and then stepped around Josh. He took Fenella's arm and led her a few steps away. "What did you find?" he asked in a low voice.

"A man called Phillip Pierce," she replied. "I'm sure he's dead and I'm pretty sure he was murdered."

Howard hadn't stopped watching Josh as Fenella had spoken. Josh seemed to be inching his way closer to the barn doors. "I'll just have a look in the barn, then," Howard said loudly.

"Whatever. I have better things to do, anyway," Josh said. He turned and walked away without looking back.

"I hope you know his name and where I can find him again," Howard said to Fenella. "I can't exactly chase after him with the baby in my arms."

"He's lovely," Fenella said, staring at the tiny boy.

"Thanks. Would you mind holding him for a minute? I don't want to take him into a crime scene. I'm sure he'd have no idea what he was seeing, but I'd still rather he didn't see anything, if you know what I mean."

"Sure, I can hold him," Fenella said, feeling odd about the entire situation. The constable handed her the baby, who almost immediately began to cry.

"He's at a clingy stage," the man said, "and my wife is off dancing somewhere. I've texted her twice, but she hasn't replied. I'm sorry to leave you with him, but I have to see what's going on here."

Fenella nodded. "You go. After what I saw in there, a crying baby doesn't seem so bad."

For what felt like hours but probably wasn't, Fenella rocked, bounced, and talked to the child. Every time she turned around, he'd twist his body, trying to see where his father had gone. By the time the constable walked back out of the barn, Fenella was exhausted.

"Sorry about that," the man said as he took the baby back again.

"It wasn't a problem," Fenella lied politely.

"I've rung for backup," he told her. "The local inspector is already on his way and I've mobilized the crime scene team. Every constable in the area is on his or her way here to start taking statements from the site's visitors. I recognized the man from when Odin was carving his turnip, but I don't know his name or anything about him."

"He's called Phillip Pierce and he was a volunteer here, along with his wife, Karla. Her parents are here, too. They're called Henry and Harriet Jones."

The man nodded. "I'd be taking notes if I didn't have my hands full," he said apologetically.

"I can try holding him again, if you want."

Howard shook his head. "What I want is for my wife to turn up," he muttered.

A few minutes later a pair of uniformed constables arrived. They spoke to Howard and then began unrolling crime scene tape. When Fenella's mobile buzzed, she looked at Howard.

"Can I see who that is?" she asked.

"Yes, but don't respond, please."

The message from Shelly was brief. *What's going on?*

"Do you need me to stay here?" Fenella asked Howard a moment later.

"Yes, please. You'll need to speak to the inspector," he replied.

"Howard? What's going on?" a voice called from the pathway to the barn. "There are constables everywhere and they didn't want to let me through."

One of the uniformed constables had stopped the very pretty young woman from getting any closer. Howard smiled at her. As he approached her, it was obvious from the baby's reaction exactly who the woman was. Odin's little face lit up and he held out his arms towards the woman, babbling excitedly at her.

"You'll have take Odin home," Howard said. "I'm going to be here for a while."

"This isn't even your jurisdiction," the woman argued. "Surely someone from the south of the island should be in charge."

"I was first on the scene. When the inspector gets here, he may simply take my statement and send me home, or he may ask me to stay and help. I don't know at this point."

"How will you get home?" she asked worriedly.

"I can get a taxi or a ride from someone. Don't you worry about me. You take good care of Odin and I'll see you later. I'll try to text when I have a better idea of what is happening."

The woman nodded, but she was clearly unhappy with the circumstances. Fenella watched as she walked away. Odin waved at his father over her shoulder and Howard kept waving back until the pair was out of sight. Then he spun on his heel and walked back into the barn.

Shelly texted two more times before a potbellied man with the shaggy grey hair and beard appeared. He spoke to each of the constables before he walked into the barn. When he emerged a few minutes later, he headed straight for Fenella.

"Ms. Woods? I was hoping to get to retirement without ever meeting you," he said. "I'm Inspector Kenneth Nichols. Everyone calls me Kenny. I need to take your statement. Let's see if we can find a bench or something. I hate taking notes standing up."

Fenella nodded and then followed the man as he stomped around the barn. There was a small bench under a large tree nearby.

"Have a seat," he told Fenella before he sat down next to her. He pulled out a battered notebook and a pen. "I've had this notebook for ten years," he told her. "Every serious crime that's happened in the south of the island is recorded in its pages. It's usually pretty quiet down here."

Swallowing hard kept Fenella from blurting out the apology she felt she owed the man. He couldn't possibly be blaming her for Phillip's untimely death, she told herself.

"Let's start at the beginning," the man said. "Start with what you had for breakfast."

Fenella did her best to remember everything that had happened that day. The man took extensive notes, occasionally making her stop and then repeat herself so that he was sure he hadn't missed anything. She felt tired and incredibly thirsty when she finished.

"Right, now start at the end, when you found the body, and work backwards, please," the man said.

"What do you mean?"

"I mean, start with finding the body and then slowly take me backwards through your day, from activity to activity. I'd appreciate it if you could repeat every conversation you had in full, too."

"I just did all of that," Fenella said.

"Yes, I know, but you did it forward. Now I want you to do it backwards. Sometimes remembering things differently helps people recall additional details."

Fenella was too tired to argue with the man. Instead, she did her best to repeat everything in reverse order. When she got back to breakfast, she leaned back on the bench and sighed.

"Right, what did you touch inside the barn?" the man asked.

"Nothing on my second visit," she replied. "When my friend and I were carving our turnips, we used several of the tools, but that was early this morning. I'm sure dozens or maybe even hundreds of people have used them all since."

Kenny nodded. "Constable Jones is taking a statement from your friend, Shelly, right now. Once I've had a chance to compare the two, I'll let you and Shelly go. I'd like you to wait here until that's completed, and I'd appreciate it if you didn't discuss the case with anyone on your way out."

"I won't," Fenella promised.

"We won't be releasing the victim's name until we've had a chance to notify the next of kin. We still need a formal identification, as well. It's very important that you don't tell anyone who you found."

"I won't tell anyone anything."

The man got to his feet. "If the press start bothering you, let me know. I can put a stop to that."

He walked away, leaving Fenella alone on the bench. When her phone buzzed, she glanced at the display.

I will be at your flat at seven to discuss Phillip Pierce. Text me back if that's a problem. Daniel.

"You've been back on the island for nearly a month and you haven't had time to visit. I find one measly dead body and all of the sudden you're free?" she said to the display. "I've half a mind to tell you I'm busy."

Except as she sat there, watching the crime scene team members coming and going, all she could think about was how much she wanted to talk to Daniel. Even if they were never going to be anything more than friends, she trusted him and she knew he was a good investigator. The case would be solved more quickly if it were given to him rather than to Inspector Nichols, or at least that was what Fenella thought. She was still sitting on the bench when the body was removed from the barn. Once she'd realized what was happening, she'd looked away, feeling incredibly sad for Phillip and his young bride.

"Okay," Kenny said a few minutes later. "You're free to go. Constable Corlett will walk you through the village to your car. Your friend is waiting there for you."

Fenella nodded and then got to her feet. "Thank you," she said, although she wasn't sure why.

The man nodded. "I'm sure I'll be in touch," he told her.

"Are you okay?" Howard asked as he fell into step next to Fenella.

"Not really. I just want to get home," she told him.

He nodded. "Are you going to be okay to drive?"

"Yeah, I'm fine. Driving will give me something else on which to focus, too."

"If you find you're having trouble, stop and take a taxi or let your friend drive," he told her.

"Yes, sir," she muttered. They'd reached the museum now and Fenella realized that they hadn't seen anyone else anywhere in the village. "Where is everyone?" she asked.

"We're trying to question people as quickly as we can and then send them on their way," Howard replied. "The victim's friends and family members are being looked after in the museum building."

"I feel so sorry for his wife. They were newlyweds, you know."

"I didn't know. I haven't been involved in any of the questioning. That's very sad, assuming she didn't have anything to do with the man's death."

"They were newlyweds," Fenella repeated, feeling shocked.

"And I'm just a bit jaded from everything that I've seen in policing," the man told her. "Don't mind me, and please don't tell the inspector that I was discussing the case with you."

"Inspector Nichols did say that I wasn't to talk about the case at all," Fenella sighed.

"He's trying to keep as much as he can out of the local papers."

"Well, they won't hear anything from me. With the number of people who were here today, though, they've probably already heard something."

"They had a reporter here, covering the festivities," Howard sighed. "She got the scoop of her life, but now she's desperate for more information. We aren't releasing the victim's name yet, for example."

They'd reached the small parking area, and Fenella was surprised to see that it was nearly empty. Shelly was standing next to Mona's car, chatting with a uniformed constable.

"We should have lunch one day," the constable told Shelly as Fenellla and Howard joined them.

"Yes, let's," Shelly agreed. "Ring me. You have my number."

The woman shrugged. "I can't take it from your official statement, but I'm sure I'll be able to find you anyway."

Shelly nodded. "I'm easy enough to track down. It was really good to see you again."

The young woman gave Shelly a hug and then flushed as she looked at Howard. "Mrs. Quirk was my teacher when I was six," she explained. "She taught me how to read and write and that boys were nothing but trouble."

Howard grinned. "All very useful lessons," he said.

"I may have changed my mind about boys since then," the woman laughed, "but I've not stopped loving to read."

"Are you ready to get out of here?" Shelly asked Fenella.

"More than," Fenella said with alacrity.

The two constables stepped away from the car and watched as the women climbed inside. Fenella took several deep breaths before she turned the key and put the car into gear. It stalled immediately, as she'd completely forgotten about the clutch.

"Are you okay to drive?" Shelly asked.

"I will be in a minute," Fenella replied. "I just have to focus."

This time, as she put the car into gear, she pressed down on the clutch. With her mind firmly focused on her driving, she carefully exited the parking lot and turned onto the road. They were halfway home before Shelly spoke.

"The constable I was questioned by wouldn't tell me anything," she said. "I don't even know who's dead."

"I've been told I can't tell anyone anything."

"I see."

"Let's wait until we get home," Fenella said. "I can't talk and drive, at least not on this particular subject."

Shelly made a few innocuous comments about the weather for the next several minutes. Fenella gave appropriate responses; at least she hoped her responses were appropriate. She wasn't really paying attention.

Once she'd parked the car in the garage under their building, she closed her eyes and took several deep breaths.

"Are you okay?" Shelly sounded concerned.

"I will be. It was all a bit, well, difficult," Fenella told her. "I'm badly shaken."

"Let's get upstairs. I'm sure Katie will make you feel better."

That thought was just what Fenella needed to get her moving. She climbed out of the car and began to follow Shelly toward the elevators.

"We almost forgot our turnips," Shelly exclaimed, stopping and turning back toward the car.

"I'm not sure I want mine," Fenella said sadly.

Shelly glanced at her. "Let's take them upstairs, anyway. You don't want them rolling around in your boot for the next month."

Fenella opened the trunk and Shelly grabbed both turnips. "I can keep yours for you, if you'd like," she offered.

"Maybe just for now."

"I'll just put these down somewhere and then I'll be over," Shelly said when they reached the sixth floor.

Fenella nodded and then let herself into her apartment. The incredible sea views nearly always made her smile, but today she felt as if nothing would cheer her up.

"My goodness, what happened?" Mona demanded. "You look as if you've lost your best friend. Shelly is okay, isn't she?"

Shelly's knock on the door answered that question, anyway. Fenella let her in and then sat down on the first couch she encountered. Katie jumped into her lap, and began to purr and Fenella stroked her back.

"Katie knows something is wrong," Shelly said.

"Yes, and she's trying to help," Mona added. "You'll feel better if you tell me all about it, though."

Shelly sat down on the couch next to Fenella. "Shall I tell you what happened after you left?" she asked as she patted Fenella's arm.

"Yes, please," Fenella replied.

"Oliver found me where you'd left me and insisted that I dance with him," Shelly said. "If I were twenty years younger, I think I'd be smitten."

Fenella smiled. "Maybe he likes older women," she suggested.

"I think he might like younger men, actually," Shelly told her, "but he was great fun to dance with, anyway."

"So you danced?"

"We did. All the way from the entrance to the site, down the road past the cottages, and then back again. I thought we'd turn and go past the barn, but we didn't."

"I wonder why?"

"It was probably because we were running out of time," Shelly said. "The musicians started late, and then Paul rushed up to join them after half of the first song, so they had to start again. It was all a bit chaotic, but it worked out in the end."

"Why was Paul late?"

"I've no idea."

Fenella frowned. She'd liked the talented young man. Was it possible that he'd been late to the dancing because he'd been busy murdering Phillip Pierce?

"Anyway, after we finished our dancing, we all went back to the museum for some treats. The small children in costume were given them first, but everyone got something in the end. Then the first uniformed constable showed up and everyone got very serious and sad."

"Did you see Constable Corlett anywhere?"

"Actually, I did. He was holding a baby, which I assume was his, and watching the dancing. When we walked back up to the museum, he was gone, though."

Fenella nodded. "What happened after that?"

"More police came and they moved us all into the museum. It was quite cramped at first, but they began to interview people right away and they seemed to get through them very quickly."

"I hope they weren't too quick," Fenella sighed.

"Eventually it was my turn and I talked to a lovely constable called Mike. He had me walk him through my entire day, starting with breakfast, which seemed to take ages. I would suggest that he was more thorough with me than they were being with other people."

"Probably because you're my friend and I found the body."

"Yes, well, whatever the reason, we talked for ages, and then when we were done, I was escorted back to the main part of the museum and told to wait there. That's when I had a little chat with Karla."

"With Karla?"

"Yes, she came over and sat down next to me. She wanted to know what was going on, and I told her, in completely honesty, that I had no idea."

"The police wouldn't tell you anything?"

"Not one thing. From past experience, I guessed that a body had been found somewhere, possibly under suspicious circumstances, but I didn't mention that to Karla, of course."

"No, of course not."

"Anyway, she asked me what was going on, and while we were talking one of the police constables came and stood right behind me. Obviously, with him standing there, I wasn't going to tell Karla what I was thinking."

"What else did Karla say?"

"She'd obviously been crying. She asked me if I'd seen Phillip and then asked where you'd gone."

"What did you tell her?"

"I said that you didn't want to dance so you'd gone for another walk around the site. It seemed likely that the body you'd found was Phillip's, as he was the only person obviously missing, so I didn't want to tell her that you'd gone to the barn."

"That was smart," Fenella said with a sigh.

"It was Phillip, wasn't it?" Shelly asked in a low voice.

Fenella knew she wasn't supposed to tell Shelly anything, but she couldn't lie under the circumstances. "Yeah, it was Phillip," she said.

"And judging from the size of the police presence, he was murdered, wasn't he?"

Fenella hesitated and then nodded. "That would be my guess, anyway," she added.

"You should know," Mona said.

Fenella frowned at her. It was hardly her fault that she kept stumbling over dead bodies. It wasn't as if she was actively looking for them.

"I'm sorry," Shelly said. "You found him, then?"

"Yes, and then I called 999. They found Constable Corlett and sent him to find me."

"The last time I saw him he was carrying his baby around."

"He still had the baby when he got to the barn. I actually held the baby while Howard took a look at the body."

Shelly shivered. "It was good of him to keep the baby from seeing something so awful."

"I wish someone would have kept me from seeing it."

Shelly rubbed Fenella's back. "I can't imagine how dreadful it must have been for you."

"It was pretty bad, especially when we'd just met the man and he'd seemed so happy and so nice."

"He did seem to be a very nice young man."

"So who could have wanted him dead?" Mona asked.

Fenella stared at the woman. It was a very good question. Who could have wanted the personable young newlywed dead?

"Once Shelly is gone, you'll have to tell me about all of the possible suspects," Mona said. "I especially want to hear about his wife."

Karla couldn't possibly have killed the man, Fenella thought to herself. The couple were clearly devoted to one another.

"Is Inspector Nichols still in charge down there?" Shelly asked.

"Yes, he is."

"I met him once about twenty years ago," Shelly said. "He seemed good at his job, but I don't know that he's ever had to investigate a homicide before."

"He said something about having one notebook for every major crime that had happened in the past ten years. He seemed to think that the murder was going to take up far too many pages in it."

Shelly laughed. "That sounds like him. I was helping out at a school that was desperately short of teachers for a few weeks and someone was stealing things from the common room. As I said, he was good at his job. He found the culprit by the end of the day, in fact, but I would have a lot more confidence in Daniel's ability to find the killer."

A knock on the door made Fenella wince. "Speak of the devil," she said as she stood up and walked to the door.

4

Her mostly forced smile faded immediately when she opened the door and found not just Daniel but also Tiffany on her doorstep.

"Hello," she said, immediately feeling stupid.

"Hello," Daniel replied, smiling at her. "I hope you don't mind that Tiffany came along. Since this is just an informal chat, I thought it might be helpful for her to hear what happened. She may be able to offer a different perspective."

Fenella's mind was racing as she let the pair into the apartment.

"What an amazing view," Tiffany gasped, "and what a beautiful flat. But where are the dogs?"

"They aren't my dogs," Fenella explained. "I was just dog-sitting for a friend."

"Oh, that's a shame. I was looking forward to seeing them again."

"You can find them on the promenade every day," Fenella told her. "Just walk up and down a few times and you're sure to see them."

"I may just have to do that," Tiffany giggled.

Shelly and Fenella exchanged glances.

"Are you okay?" Daniel asked as he and Tiffany took seats.

"I'm fine. Would you like a drink or something?" Fenella replied.

"I don't want anything, but thank you," Tiffany said. She wriggled her nose and then sneezed.

"I'll have a cold drink if it isn't too much bother," Daniel said.

"I'll get it," Shelly offered, "and one for myself. Do you want anything?" she asked Fenella.

"No, I'm good," Fenella replied. What she wanted was for Tiffany to leave, but she couldn't very well say that out loud.

"I'd like the annoying blonde woman to leave," Mona said. "Why doesn't anyone ask me what I want?"

Fenella caught her eye and winked at her. Mona grinned. "Why did Daniel bring this woman with him?" she demanded.

As Shelly walked back into the room, Tiffany sneezed again.

"Goodness, pardon me," she said. Shelly handed around the drinks and then picked up a box of tissues and gave them to Tiffany. The girl blew her nose, which was turning quite red.

"So what happened today?" Daniel asked Fenella.

She sighed. "Inspector Nichols told me not to talk about it," she said.

Before Daniel could reply, Katie walked into the room. She looked around for a moment and then ran over to Tiffany and jumped up into her lap.

Tiffany shrieked and leapt to her feet, dumping Katie onto the floor. "A cat?" she shouted. "You didn't tell me she had a cat," she said to Daniel.

"I didn't think it mattered," he replied.

Katie hissed at the woman and then climbed into Fenella's lap. Fenella gave her a cuddle, brushing down her fur that was standing on end. "It's okay," she whispered.

"I'm sorry," Tiffany said, clearly struggling to compose herself. "I'm allergic to cats, you see."

"How unfortunate," Shelly said.

"I'm going to have to go," Tiffany announced. "Come on, Daniel."

He blinked and then sighed. "I'm sorry," he said to Fenella. "I'm going to have to take Tiffany home. I'll come back later."

"It's getting quite late," Tiffany said. "Perhaps you can have your little chat another day." She sneezed three times in rapid succession before grabbing a tissue.

Daniel stood up. "Are you sure you're okay?" he asked Fenella.

"I'm sure," she lied. "You go and look after Tiffany. Clearly she needs you more than I do."

"Yes, that's probably true," he muttered, glancing around the room.

"What does that mean?" Mona demanded.

Fenella shrugged as she followed Daniel and Tiffany to the door. "I'll ring you," Daniel said in the doorway.

"Great," she replied unenthusiastically.

He raised an eyebrow and then followed a sneezing Tiffany down the corridor. Fenella watched as they boarded the elevator and then she shut the door.

"Why did he bring her?" Shelly asked.

"I've no idea," Fenella replied, "but I'm very glad Katie was here. You get treats for that," she told the kitten. In the kitchen she gave Katie a handful of treats and then refilled her food and water bowls.

"We never had any dinner," Shelly said, sounding surprised.

"We didn't, did we? I'm not actually hungry, though."

"You've had a shock. You should eat something."

Fenella shrugged. "Nothing sounds good."

"I'll make us both something. How about spaghetti? That's quick and easy."

"If you want, but don't make much for me," Fenella said. "I don't know if I have any of the ingredients in, though," she added.

"I have everything in my flat. Do you want to move over there?"

"Don't you dare," Mona said.

"Do you mind staying here?" Fenella asked.

"No, not at all. I can go and get everything I need in two seconds."

"Bring Smokey back with you."

Shelly laughed. "I'll have to make two trips, then."

Fenella opened the door for her and then stood and waited for her friend to come back. Mona paced behind her. "This is stupid. Shut the door and tell me what happened," she demanded.

Shelly walked back in, juggling a large shopping bag and a sleepy-looking cat. When she put Smokey down, Katie raced over and began to talk to her in a series of meows and yowls.

"She's complaining about Tiffany," Shelly said.

"I don't blame her," Fenella laughed.

They settled in the kitchen. Fenella set the table while Shelly cooked dinner. Mona sat at the counter on one of the stools. That kept her out of the way and meant that Shelly was unlikely to accidentally sit on her, anyway, Fenella thought.

"What are you going to tell Daniel when he rings?" Shelly asked as she worked.

"I don't know that I'm going to tell him anything. I was told not to discuss the case with anyone. Daniel himself said it was an informal meeting. If he's not talking to me as a police inspector, surely he falls into the same category as everyone else on the island?"

"I don't know about Daniel, but I'd definitely put Tiffany in that category," Shelly said.

"Oh, no," Mona said. "She belongs in a category all her own."

Fenella took a sip of her drink to keep from laughing. "I just hope Inspector Nichols wraps the whole thing up in a day or two."

"Do you think he will? Was there anything obvious at the scene to suggest who the killer was?" Shelly asked.

"I didn't look very closely, but he hadn't written anyone's name in blood or anything like that," Fenella told her. "Maybe the police found something when they searched that I couldn't see from my single, very quick glance, though."

"Was there a lot of blood?" Shelly asked. As soon as the words were out of her mouth, she spun around and looked at Fenella. "You don't have to answer that. Let's talk about something more pleasant. What are you giving out for Hop-tu-Naa?"

"There wasn't any blood," Fenella replied, "and I haven't any idea what to give out on Hop-tu-Naa. Will we actually get kids coming to the door? Does security let them in?"

"Security tends to look the other way on Hop-tu-Naa, at least as far as small children in costume are concerned. And everyone on the island thinks that Promenade View Apartments are full of rich people, so the building has become something of a popular destination for Hop-tu-Naa."

"Really? Oh, dear," Fenella said. "I shall have to go shopping, then."

"Mona always gave out candy bars, not the little miniature ones, but regular ones that cost like fifty or sixty pence a bar."

"And how many kids should I expect?"

"A hundred or so."

Fenella nodded. "And I can't let the kids down," she muttered.

"Of course not," Mona said. "You can afford a bit of chocolate. Just don't buy too much. You'll get tired of it if you have to eat it for weeks on end."

It was impossible for Fenella to imagine getting tired of chocolate, but she couldn't argue with Mona in front of Shelly, so she bit her tongue. A moment later Shelly put steaming plates of spaghetti on the table.

"Should we open a bottle of wine?" she asked.

"As much as I'd love a drink, I don't really think it would be wise," Fenella replied. "Especially if Daniel is going to ring later."

"He won't," Mona said. "That little trollop won't let him."

"He'll probably decide it's too late to ring tonight," Shelly said, "and a glass of wine might help you sleep."

Fenella thought about it for a minute, and then shook her head. "I won't sleep anyway and wine sometimes give me nightmares. I'll just eat my dinner and then go to bed and hope for the best."

Shelly sat down and then took Fenella's hand. "I'm sorry," she said, giving her hand a squeeze. Fenella squeezed back and then they both focused on eating for a short while.

"This is delicious," Fenella said after she'd taken several bites. "I'm sure I saw you using a jar of sauce, but it tastes really fresh."

"It was a jar, but I added some fresh basil and some Parmesan cheese," Shelly told her. "I've yet to find a jar of sauce that can't be improved upon."

"I need to make a note of the brand and details. It's much better than the stuff I've been buying."

The pair talked about local politics and the weather as they finished their meal. Mona sat and stared out the windows at the sea below them, not speaking.

"I brought some microwave chocolate puddings for pudding," Shelly said as she cleared their plates.

"You shouldn't have done that," Fenella protested.

"Of course I should have. I wanted one and I don't mind sharing."

Fenella laughed and then devoured her dessert. "That was also delicious," she said as she scraped up the last bits of chocolate sauce.

"I hope you're feeling better," Shelly replied.

"I'm sure I'll be fine. It was just such a shock, that's all."

Shelly insisted on loading the dishwasher and started it running. Then she wiped down the kitchen. "It's getting late," she said when she looked at the clock on the wall. "Are you going to be okay on your own?"

"I won't be on my own. I have Katie."

"And me," Mona added.

"I can stay for a while longer," Shelly offered.

"No, you and Smokey need to get home and get some rest. I'll be fine."

"Let's go for brunch tomorrow. We can go to a place in Laxey that does the huge brunch buffet, my treat."

"You don't have to treat, but brunch sounds great. I didn't know it was a UK thing."

"It isn't. I think one of the owners of the restaurant is American. They started doing it about a year ago and it's proven very popular. I can't believe we haven't done it before, actually."

Fenella let Shelly and Smokey out and then shut and locked the door. She sank into the nearest chair and stared at the sea. Katie climbed into her lap and began to purr loudly.

"Go on then," Mona said. "Tell me everything."

Fenella thought about arguing, but Mona was the only person with whom she truly felt as if she could safely discuss the case.

"We got to Cregneash around ten," Fenella began. She told her aunt everything that had happened, including every conversation that she'd had with everyone at the village. Mona only yawned a couple of times and she stopped yawning and sat up a bit straighter when Fenella reached the part about walking into the barn.

"And then I called 999," Fenella concluded, "and Constable Corlett appeared."

"So who killed the poor man?" Mona asked.

"I've absolutely no idea," Fenella snapped.

"The wife has to be the number-one suspect."

"They were newlyweds."

"That doesn't prove anything. Maybe they were already miserably unhappy."

"They didn't seem unhappy. They seemed madly in love."

"Maybe Karla is a very good actress."

"Maybe, but I don't think she killed her husband."

"So who do you think killed him?"

"Probably someone that he works with or something. There were hundreds of people there. Maybe someone got mad because he ran out of turnips or maybe he didn't drill someone's the way he or she wanted it drilled. It could be anything."

"I hardly think the man was killed over a turnip, even on Hop-tu-Naa," Mona said. "What did he do for a living?"

"I've no idea."

"That's disappointing. We'll have to find out."

"No, we won't. Inspector Nichols will have to find out. The case is his problem. I'm not getting involved."

"Tell me about Karla's parents again. Did they like Phillip?"

"How should I know? I only met them very briefly."

"What did they say about him?"

"Nothing at all that I remember."

"That could be significant," Mona said.

"I can't imagine why."

"What about the other men in the band with Karla's father? Did any of them say anything about Phillip?"

"Not to me. I barely spoke to them. The one I talked to the most was Paul, but we talked about dancing and music, not Phillip."

"You saw Paul talking to Karla," Mona mused.

"Yes, and I also saw about five dozen other people talking to Karla.

She was a volunteer at the site. She was always talking to someone, every time I saw her."

"What about Oliver? Did he like Phillip?"

"Again, I've no idea. He never mentioned the man to me, and I never thought to ask him. I suspect he was grateful to all of the volunteers, though."

"You said Karla has been working there for years?"

"Yeah, because her mother has. Phillip said something that made me think that it was his first year helping out, but if it was, he caught on very quickly. He was doing a great job with the turnips when I saw him, anyway."

"Tell me about the man you met outside the barn right after you found the body."

"Josh Gentry? I don't know anything about him."

"Except he seemed to resent the visitors, didn't he? Maybe he killed Phillip to discourage people from coming to Hop-tu-Naa next year."

"That seems a bit extreme, really, doesn't it?"

"I suppose that depends on how upset he truly was about the visitors."

"He took several of us on a tour around the farm," Fenella reminded her. "While he wasn't exactly warm and welcoming, he was pleasant enough."

"Maybe he was just in a good mood because he was planning to murder Phillip."

Fenella laughed. "I think that's a stretch, I really do."

"So who do you think killed the man?"

Fenella sat and stared at her aunt for a full minute before she replied. "I've absolutely no idea. He seemed like a perfectly pleasant young man who was completely in love with his wife and happy to volunteer his time to help at an event that was important to her."

"She said it was an impulsive marriage, didn't she?" Mona asked.

"Something like that," Fenella said, trying to remember the girl's exact words.

"That could be important."

"Maybe the murder was completely random," Fenella suggested. "Maybe someone went into the barn to carve a turnip and found

Phillip there alone without any turnips. Or maybe it has something to do with Phillip's work. Maybe he was a drug smuggler or maybe he embezzled millions from someone and they tracked him down and killed him."

"I don't trust Karla," Mona said, "but I'd trust her before I'd trust Tiffany."

Fenella frowned. "Yeah, there is that," she said bitterly.

The pair talked for a while longer, but Fenella simply couldn't answer any of her aunt's questions. Eventually Mona gave up. "I'm going to have to go and see what I can find out from other sources," she said.

"What other sources?" Fenella asked, sure that her aunt would probably make up some wildly improbable source just to annoy Fenella.

"I thought I'd go and see if the local paper for tomorrow is ready yet. It's all computerized now and ever so easy to hack."

Fenella opened her mouth to question her aunt, but Mona had already faded away. She sighed and then looked at Katie, who was fast asleep on her lap. "It's bedtime," she told the kitten.

Katie opened one eye and then yawned. Fenella laughed as the animal reluctantly climbed down to the floor.

"Sorry I had to wake you up to tell you to go to bed," Fenella told her.

Katie didn't reply, and when Fenella walked into her bedroom a minute later the animal was already in her place in the center of Fenella's bed.

"I'm here to arrest you," Tiffany Perkins said in a bright tone. "You need to come with me."

"You can't arrest me," Fenella told her. "I have to look after Katie."

"Oh, I'll look after Katie," the girl replied. "I have a special place in mind for Katie."

"I won't let you have her. She can stay with Shelly while we talk."

"We aren't just going to talk, though. You're going to prison."

"To prison, but why?"

"I have to do everything I can to keep you away from Daniel, you see. He's far too fond of you, but he'll forget about you eventually. Once he's done that, I can let you out."

"I don't want Daniel to forget about me."

"I don't care what you want. You can come with me nicely or I can get out my handcuffs and drag you out kicking and screaming."

"I haven't done anything wrong."

"I think you have, and what I think is all that matters."

"I have rights. You can't just arrest a person because you don't like them."

"I'm young and thin and beautiful. I can do whatever I want," Tiffany laughed. "You're old and you've gained ten pounds since you've been on the island. I can't imagine what Daniel ever saw in you, really."

Fenella felt tears in her eyes. "I'm a nice person," she said desperately.

"Even if you do keep getting caught up in murder investigations? I did suggest to Daniel that maybe you killed Phillip Pierce, just to have an excuse to see him. He's giving the idea some thought."

"I didn't kill anyone," Fenella said. She said it again louder and then began shouting it as Tiffany moved closer and tried to grab her wrists. Fenella took a giant step backwards and then hit the floor. Katie yowled as Fenella sat up on the floor and blinked several times.

"I fell out of bed," she said slowly.

"Merrow," Katie replied.

It was three o'clock and far too early for anyone to be awake. Fenella got herself a drink from the kitchen and then crawled back into bed. As soon as she was settled, Katie moved up and snuggled against Fenella's arm. The kitten's presence was soothing and after a while Fenella managed to fall back to sleep.

When Katie began tapping on her nose the next morning, Fenella was momentarily cross. "I just got back to sleep," she said, trying to focus on the clock. It was eight, a full hour after the time when Katie normally woke her.

"I suppose I should thank you," she muttered to the animal as she climbed out of bed.

"Mmmeooowww," Katie agreed.

"Okay, thank you," Fenella replied, "and thank you for cuddling with me after my nightmare. Tiffany was trying to arrest me, you see. It was horrible."

"Yoooowwwllll."

"Yes, I know you don't like her, either, but she can't actually arrest me. She doesn't even work for the police."

"That doesn't mean you don't have to take her seriously," Mona said.

Fenella jumped, spilling the water she was using to fill up her coffee maker all over the counter. "I didn't know you were here," she gasped as she reached for paper towels.

"I'm here because I'm worried about Tiffany. Daniel is too nice to get tangled up with a woman like her."

"He's old enough to know what he's doing."

"You're only saying that because you're upset with him. I think Tiffany is taking advantage of him."

"What if she is? What can I do about it?"

"You need to talk to him, but you need to get him alone first. He's never going to be able to explain what's going on with Tiffany around."

"He said he'd call me to talk about the case."

"But he may well do that when he's with Tiffany. You need to get him to visit you here and then you need to kiss him."

"Kiss him? I can't do that."

"You've done it before."

"Yeah, before Tiffany. I can't kiss him now. He's obviously not interested in me now."

"He couldn't take his eyes off of you yesterday."

Fenella shrugged. "He's living with Tiffany. That tells me everything I need to know."

"Maybe it isn't what it appears."

"Or maybe it's exactly the way it appears."

"It's a shame Donald is away. He would keep you busy so you could stop worrying about Daniel, and he'd make Daniel nicely jealous, too."

Fenella sighed. "I've never had good luck with men. I should have known that nothing would change on the island."

"You just need to meet someone new. There are plenty of men out there, but sometimes they take a bit of effort to locate. You need to start going out more. Get Shelly to go with you. She needs to shake Gordon up before he decides that they should just stay friends forever."

"Where would we go?" Fenella asked, in spite of her misgivings. Taking advice from Mona seemed ill advised on a number of different levels, really.

"Everywhere, of course. The local pub is fine once in a while, but you should be going out every night. Pubs, clubs, restaurants, casinos, you should visit them all."

"I'm too old."

Mona laughed. "I was still going out every night after my ninetieth birthday. You are only as old as you feel."

"Then I feel too old."

"Darling, I know that you're upset about Daniel's behavior. I will give you exactly twenty-four hours to get over it and then we'll start working on a plan. I'll see you tomorrow." Mona faded away, leaving Fenella alone.

"Twenty-four hours isn't very long," Fenella complained to no one.

"Meeroow," Katie said.

"Yes, I know Daniel and I agreed we would see other people, but I didn't expect him to take up with a twenty-five-year-old woman with cat allergies."

Katie shrugged and then jumped down. She raced into the kitchen and began to shout.

"It isn't time for lunch yet," Fenella told her. "We only just had breakfast."

She switched on the television and watched a few hours of daytime programming. "That was good," she told Katie when she finally pushed the off button. "I've learned all about the latest makeup trends, saw a trailer for a film I don't want to see, and caught up on the love lives of a bunch of celebrities I'd never heard of before."

Katie ignored her in favor of shouting over her empty food bowl.

Fenella filled it and the animal's water bowl and then opened her refrigerator. There was very little in it besides milk and soda.

"I need groceries," she sighed, "and I really need them before I can eat lunch."

Katie glanced up from her bowl and then went back to it.

"Sure, you don't care either way. I always have cat food." She looked in the freezer, hoping for a forgotten pizza or something, but aside from a few tubs of ice cream, it was empty. It took her a minute to convince herself not to simply eat her way through all of the ice cream instead of having a proper lunch.

"Look at me, being all grown up," she muttered as she shut the freezer door. She found her shoes and headed down to the parking garage. On the way down she tried to decide which car to take, but even before she started thinking about it, she knew she'd take her boring and sensible car. It was simply a matter of practicality for things like grocery shopping.

She walked up to the car as she dug around in her bag for the keys. It wasn't until she'd emptied the entire bag onto the garage floor that she remembered that she'd left the keys for the sensible car in the drawer in her kitchen before she and Shelly had headed down to Cregneash. As she put everything back into her bag, she thought about going back for the keys, but her stomach rumbled loudly and interrupted her thought process.

Taking Mona's car felt like a huge indulgence and Fenella knew that she wouldn't be able to buy everything on the long list that she had tucked in her handbag, but as long as she got enough for lunch today, she'd be better off than she had been.

The trip around the grocery store didn't take long. Fenella tried to be careful as she selected items, constantly reminding herself of the tiny trunk in Mona's car, but she was starving, so chocolate cookies and cakes seemed to throw themselves into her shopping cart at every turn. She was studying the vegetables, trying to plan an evening meal, as the chocolate bars called her name.

"Hello," a tall man with dark hair and thick glasses who was wearing the store's unattractive uniform said. "What are you thinking of buying?"

"My body weight in chocolate," Fenella replied.

The man laughed. "As the fruit and veg manager, I recommend you try eating your body weight in lettuce instead. It 's much better for you and it will fill you up faster."

Fenella shrugged. "But it won't be anywhere near as satisfying."

"Maybe you could have a nice salad and then have a few squares of chocolate for pudding."

"Maybe."

"I make a wonderful salad with mixed greens and fruits and then put spicy chicken on the top. It isn't quite a good as chocolate, but it's very tasty."

"That does sound good," Fenella replied. *But then, I'm starving, so just about everything sounds good,* she added to herself.

"Maybe I could make it for you one night," he suggested.

Fenella flushed. She'd not realized that the man was flirting with her. She'd assumed he was simply trying to sell her fruit and vegetables. "Oh, my goodness," she said. "I don't think, I mean, I didn't, sorry, but I don't think so."

"It's the uniform, isn't it?" the man asked. "I promise I have regular clothes. Some of them are even attractive."

Fenella laughed. "It isn't the uniform. I'm just, well, not really looking for a man right now."

"I have a sister who's single," he said, raising an eyebrow.

"No, I'm not, that is, I'm sort of seeing someone," Fenella replied, not entirely truthfully.

The man shrugged. "If it doesn't work out, you know where to find me. I'm usually lurking in between the broccoli and the cauliflower. It's almost always quiet over there."

Fenella laughed again. "It was nice meeting you," she said. She grabbed a few random vegetables, feeling very much as if the man were watching her every move, and then fled to the safety of the checkout lines.

As she loaded far more bags into the trunk of Mona's car than she felt should fit, she shook her head at her behavior. *He seemed a lovely man, really,* she thought. *He wasn't unattractive and he was funny. Maybe I should have given him a chance,* she thought.

She drove home still thinking about the man. Was she being a snob, refusing to consider dating a man who worked in a grocery store? Or was she truly so emotionally invested in Daniel that she couldn't get past him? Donald was another matter, of course. Before he'd left he'd urged her to give him a proper chance and she'd thought she'd been prepared to do that.

It took her three trips back and forth to get all of her shopping from the car into the apartment. "How did all of this fit in that tiny trunk?" she asked Katie.

"Meow," Katie said.

"Yeah, I know. Everything about Mona is magic," Fenella sighed.

She made herself a sandwich, eating it while standing at the counter. Once that was gone, she grabbed an extra-large chocolate bar and curled up with that and a murder mystery. An hour later, she'd eaten the entire bar, which hadn't been the plan.

"I need a long walk," she told Katie, who ignored her. "It was better when the dogs were here and I had to walk every day for hours," she added.

Katie yowled at her and then disappeared into the bedroom.

"Sure, take a nap," Fenella called after her. "You never want to go for a walk."

When Katie didn't reply, Fenella found her shoes and stomped out to the elevators. The promenade was reasonably quiet as Fenella made her way from one end to the other. She'd hoped she might run into Harvey and the dogs, but they were nowhere to be seen. In no great hurry to get back to her apartment, she stopped at the small convenience store that was only a short walk from home.

They were having a big sale on ice cream now that autumn had arrived, and Fenella found herself grabbing multiple tubs of discounted deliciousness.

"Are you having a party?" the twenty-something girl behind the counter asked as she rang up the ice cream.

"Yeah, I am," Fenella replied. *A party for me, although I may even invite Shelly to join me,* she added to herself.

"Have fun," the girl said as she handed Fenella her bags.

Feeling as if she probably shouldn't have bought so much ice cream after just having purchased so many cakes and cookies, Fenella made the short journey back to her apartment. The bags were heavy and seemed to cut into her hands, and as Fenella walked she wondered if Tiffany Perkins ever ate ice cream.

The elevator in her building seemed to take ages to arrive, and when it finally did there were nearly a dozen people waiting for it. That meant that they stopped on every single floor before finally getting to the top. Fenella took a few steps off the elevator and then stopped. Daniel was standing in the corridor, staring at her. He was alone and he looked angry.

5

"Hello," Fenella said as brightly as she could.

"Hello," he replied. "Where have you been?"

"I went for a walk on the promenade," she replied. "I didn't realize that I needed to inform the police when I went out. Should I call 999 next time I fancy a stroll, or would the non-emergency number work as well?"

Daniel frowned. "I rang earlier and you didn't answer. Then I texted you and you didn't answer. I was worried."

Fenella swallowed a dozen different replies. While she tried to think of something suitably neutral to say, she shifted all of the bags to one hand and then dug around in her bag for her keycard. It was, as always, at the very bottom.

Daniel stood watching her, not speaking as she pulled it out and opened her door. She walked into her apartment and then looked back at him. "Did you want to come in?"

"Yes, please," he said.

He shut the door behind himself and then followed Fenella into the kitchen. He didn't say a word as she struggled to fit too much ice cream into her freezer. When she finally managed to stack things just right and get the freezer door shut, she turned around and sighed.

"I was out grocery shopping earlier," she said. "My phone died while I was there. I plugged it in to charge when I got back and left it here when I went out for my walk."

She crossed into the living room and picked up her phone. She had three text messages from Daniel, all simply requesting a chat. "Sorry about that. What do you want to talk about?"

"May I sit down?" he asked.

"Sorry, sure," she said.

He sat on one of the couches and then looked around the room. "Your furniture is lovely," he said. "All of the pieces are antiques, aren't they?"

"I believe so, although Mona may have purchased them new and then simply kept them for a very long time."

Daniel nodded. "She was very wealthy, wasn't she?"

"Yes." There was no other way for Fenella to answer that question, really.

Daniel sighed. "But I didn't come to talk about Mona. This visit is strictly professional."

"Is it?"

"I've been asked to assist with the investigation into Phillip Pierce's murder."

"Isn't that unusual?"

"I can't really comment on how the island is policed."

Fenella flushed. This Daniel wasn't nearly as nice and friendly as the man she'd come to care about previously. If this was the effect Tiffany was going to have on him, she had even more reason to dislike the young woman.

"Right, so you have questions for me?" Fenella asked.

"I'd like you to take me back through the day," he told her.

"Again? Oh, come on. I gave Inspector Nichols a full accounting of everything that happened and then he made me go through it all backwards. You must have his notes."

"What I have or don't have isn't relevant," Daniel countered. "I'd like to hear the whole thing from you directly."

Fenella really wanted to argue, but Daniel was acting very much like a policeman rather than a friend. She didn't want to find herself answering questions at the police station rather than in her own apartment.

"Can I get myself a cold drink, then? This will take a while."

"Sure."

"Would you like one? Or tea or coffee?"

Daniel hesitated and then nodded. "A cold drink would be good."

She got cans of soda for both of them and then did her best to walk the man through her day, from breakfast to finding the body.

"Who did you see as you walked to the barn?" was Daniel's first question when she was done.

"Everyone, really. It was time for the dancing, so everyone, visitors, staff, and volunteers alike, were all heading for the museum."

"Did you see anyone else walking the other way?"

"I was the only person pushing against the crowd. A few people even commented on it."

"And when you reached the barn, was there anyone around?"

"No, it was creepy and quiet, like I said. I wasn't sure if the barn was locked or not, but there wasn't anyone around to ask."

"Where did Josh Gentry come from, then?"

"What do you mean?"

"When you came out of the barn, Josh appeared. Where did he come from?"

"The village center, I suppose."

"Did you see him when you were on the way to the barn?"

Fenella closed her eyes and tried to think. She hadn't really been paying much attention to the people that she'd passed, aside from smiling at a few that she'd recognized. "I don't specifically remember seeing him, but that doesn't mean that he wasn't in the crowd somewhere," she said eventually.

"Could he have come out from behind the barn?"

Fenella tried to remember where the man had been when he'd first spoken to her. "He came up behind me," she said. "I was watching the barn doors. It's hard for me to picture it exactly, though."

"I may need you to accompany me to the site. I'll be visiting later today to get my first look. I hope you'll be available later in the week if I visit again."

"I can make myself available," Fenella said.

Daniel nodded. "Tell me what you thought of Karla."

"What I thought of her? I thought she seemed incredibly young and very much in love."

"And Phillip?"

"He seemed crazy in love with his wife and eager to make her happy."

"By volunteering at the village?"

"Exactly that. He said something that made me think it was his first time there."

"What about Josh Gentry?"

"I barely spoke to the man. He didn't seem very happy about all of the visitors to the site, but he gave us an excellent tour. He was clearly devoted to the animals under his care and he was passionate about the farming practices that they are using down there."

Daniel raised an eyebrow and then made a few notes. "Are you considering making a donation to Cregneash, then?"

"A donation? What do you mean?"

"I just thought, with all your money, that you might be looking at helping fund the village and its projects, that's all."

"All my money?" Fenella repeated, feeling confused. To whom had the man been speaking, and what had they told him?

"Tell me about Harriet Jones. Did she seem to like her son-in-law?"

"He'd gone before Harriet and her husband arrived at the cottage. I never saw the pair together, but she certainly didn't say or do anything that made me think she didn't like the man. He never came up in the conversation, though."

"Do you remember anything odd in her interaction with her daughter?"

"Odd? Not at all. She teased Karla about not remembering anything she'd been taught over the years, and then she told Shelly and me all about Hop-tu-Naa. That was the extent of our conversation."

"You had lunch with them."

"They sat at our table with us after Shelly and I had nearly finished. We exchanged pleasantries and then Shelly and I left them there."

"What about Henry Jones?"

"What about him? He seemed very nice. He was quiet when we were with his wife and daughter in the cottage, but he talked more when he was with his bandmates. I don't remember him saying much of anything over lunch, but I've already told you about every conversation that I had with everyone."

Daniel nodded. "Tell me about the men in the band with Henry."

"I really only remember Paul Baldwin. I was introduced to the others, but I forgot their names almost immediately."

"Why do you remember Paul, then?"

"We spoke to him for a few minutes, for a start, and he was kind enough to dance with me for a short while. Also, Henry told us that Paul was very talented, so I was looking forward to hearing him perform."

"And was Henry correct?"

"Absolutely. The man is very talented."

"What did you think of Oliver Wentworth?"

"He was great fun. He was very enthusiastic about the site and Manx National Heritage, and he was determined to make sure that everyone visiting had a wonderful time."

"And did you have a wonderful time?"

"I was having fun, right up until I found Phillip's body."

"If you were having fun, why were you hiding in a barn rather than dancing?"

Fenella shrugged. "I'm not a very good dancer. I felt uncomfortable with the idea of trying to perform in front of that many other people."

"What made you decide to go back to the barn?"

"Karla had mentioned not being able to find Phillip, so I thought I would look for him. I thought, if he was stuck cleaning up, that I might give him a hand so that he could get away and join in the dancing."

"You weren't a volunteer, though. Why would you feel as if you needed to help with the cleaning?"

"I didn't feel that I needed to help, but I was willing to help. Maybe I'm just bored, sitting around my apartment all day with nothing to do, but I felt as if it would be nice to feel useful for a few minutes. I was sure that Phillip would be eager to join his wife for the dancing, so I thought I would volunteer to help him get finished." Fenella frowned. She hadn't expected to have to justify her actions to the man.

"Did the barn still need cleaning?"

"I don't know. I don't know how clean it's normally kept. The turnips were all gone and the tables that everyone had been working on had been put away somewhere. I didn't see any of the drills or carving instruments lying around anywhere, either. Someone must have cleaned away all of that, anyway."

"Tell me about the carving instruments you just mentioned."

"They were mostly plastic knives and scoops. Phillip had a few proper metal knives that he let some of the adults use, but they were pretty dull. Carving my turnip was really hard work."

"Yes, you mentioned that you'd carved a turnip. I'd like to see it, please."

"I don't have it. I was too upset after what happened to want to have it in my apartment."

"You threw it away?"

"No, Shelly kept it with hers."

Daniel nodded. "So I can ask Shelly to let me see both of them."

"I suppose so."

"Excellent. I'll do that next."

Fenella wanted to ask the man why he cared about the turnips, but his detached behavior didn't seem to invite questions. Instead, she took a sip of her drink and waited for the next question.

"You're quite certain the knives were dull?" was what Daniel asked after a moment.

"I'm quite certain that the knife I was given was dull. The one Shelly had wasn't any better. I know that because we were each convinced that ours was worse, so we traded. They were both terrible. Phillip may have had an entire box full of incredibly sharp knives tucked away somewhere, but if he did, he didn't share them with Shelly and me."

"Why would he have kept them tucked away if he had them?"

"I not suggesting that he actually had any tucked anywhere," Fenella replied, starting to get impatient. "I'm just saying that I don't know what else he might have had. I can only tell you about the knives that Shelly and I were given."

"How many knives did the man have?"

"I've no idea. He had a large box full of various tools. He drilled holes in our turnips and then handed us each a plastic spoon and a plastic knife. After we'd worked for a while, he offered us metal knives to try. As I said, they weren't much better."

"I've never carved a turnip. Take me through the process."

Fenella took a long drink from her soda. Daniel was clearly being difficult; the question was why he was trying to make her so miserable. If he wanted to hear about turnip carving, he was going to get an earful, she decided.

Half an hour later she was done giving him the very detailed account of exactly what went into carving a turnip. She sat back feeling slightly smug. When she started out, she'd hoped to drag the telling out for fifteen minutes. Having achieved double that, she could only hope that Daniel would stop asking her such stupid questions.

"Can you show me the Hop-tu-Naa dance?" dashed her hopes.

"No, I can't," she replied steadily. "I only did it a few times and I've done my best since then to put it out of my mind. I'm sure Shelly could show you. She actually seemed to enjoy it, and you're going to see her anyway about the turnips."

Daniel nodded. "What about the Hop-tu-Naa songs?"

"What about them?"

"Can you sing any of them for me?"

"Again, you're better off with Shelly. I wasn't truly paying attention and they all seemed quite complicated, really."

Daniel made another note. His phone buzzed and he frowned. A glance at the display had him frowning even more. Before he could slip the phone back into his pocket, it rang. He sighed and answered the call.

"I'm working," was the first thing he said after hello.

"Homicide investigations aren't nine to five. You, of all people, should understand that."

"You don't work for the police here. I can't bring civilians with me when I interview people."

"I still have at least two more witnesses to speak with before I'll be done for the night. You have dinner if you're hungry. I'll grab something before I come home."

"Sometime between now and midnight. It would be sooner if I could stop talking and texting with you and do my job."

He shook his head as he ended the call and dropped his phone back into his pocket.

"I hope everything is okay," Fenella said, trying not to smile.

"It's fine. Tiffany is just bored and wants to help. She's an excellent investigator. I'm sure she'd be an asset to the team, but she can't just volunteer to help with a murder investigation."

"I assume she's applied for a job with the constabulary over here."

"She would, if we were currently taking applications. Unfortunately for her, we aren't."

So why is she still hanging around, Fenella wondered.

"Do you think Shelly is home?"

"I don't know. I'm not sure what her plans were for today."

"Can you ring her and ask her to join us? See if she can bring the turnips with her."

Fenella wanted to ask him why he wanted to see the turnips, but she felt awkward doing so. Instead, she picked up the phone and called Shelly.

"Hello?"

"It's Fenella. Inspector Robinson is here, taking my statement, as he's been asked to assist on the investigation into Phillip Pierce's death. He was wondering if you could come over and answer a few questions for him."

"Since when do you call him Inspector Robinson?"

"Since circumstances warrant it."

"Oh, dear. Is he being difficult?"

"That would one way of putting it."

"And he's sitting there listening to your end of the conversation, isn't he?"

"Yes."

"Which do you like better, Chinese or Indian food?"

"Chinese," Fenella said, feeling confused.

"Who was taller, your mother or your father?"

"My mother."

"What is six times eight?"

"Forty-eight."

"Who kisses better, Donald or Jack?"

Fenella laughed. "Donald, by a long way."

Shelly chuckled. "Do you think Daniel is desperately trying to work out what we're talking about now?"

Fenella glanced over at the man, who was studying her with a confused look on his face.

"Yes, absolutely."

"I'll be right over."

"Oh, and bring the turnips. The inspector wants to have a look at them."

"Why?"

"Wrong person."

"Wrong person? Oh, you mean I'm asking the wrong person. He won't tell you, or you didn't ask because he's being difficult."

"The second one."

"Oh, this is going to be fun," Shelly said before she hung up.

"Not likely," Fenella muttered at the receiver before she put it back.

"What isn't likely?" Daniel asked.

Fenella stared at him for a minute and then found herself blinking back tears. There were so many things she wanted to say, but none of them seemed exactly right. Before she could work out an appropriate reply, Shelly knocked.

When Fenella opened the door she couldn't help but laugh. Shelly was standing there, holding a turnip in each hand. She'd put tiny candles inside them and they were almost, but not quite, spooky.

Daniel had walked up behind her, and when he started to laugh, Fenella felt a bit better. She stepped back to let Shelly in, taking care not to get too close to Daniel, who was still laughing. Shelly walked into the kitchen and set the turnips on the counter.

"Fenella told me that you only had plastic spoons and dull knives to work with, but I was still expecting something better," he said after he'd had time to inspect the turnips more closely.

"I can assure you that we did the very best we could under the circumstances," Shelly told him. "If you think you can do better, you're welcome to join us next year."

"I may have to take you up on that," he replied, picking up one on the turnips and then putting it back down again. "No offense, but I can't imagine doing any worse."

"Well, I'm offended," Shelly said. "It was hard work, carving that stupid thing. I don't think you can criticize, not when you haven't done it yourself."

"Maybe next year," he replied. "Please show me exactly how the carving went."

Shelly frowned. "I'm not sure what you mean."

"Fenella, can you give Shelly a spoon and a knife? Shelly, pretend you're starting over and show me how you carved the turnip."

Fenella handed her friend the items. Shelly put them down on the counter and then picked up her turnip. "It all starts with the drill, of course," she told Daniel.

"Why?"

"Because turnips are too difficult to empty out without power tools," Shelly replied. "We always used drills to start them off when I used to do them with the kids at school, too."

"And that was Phillip's job?" Daniel checked.

"Yes, mostly. He put a bunch of neat holes into the top of each turnip and then gave us each a few tools and left us to carve on our own."

"Show me what you did," Daniel said.

Shelly did her best to recreate the way that she'd dug out the insides of the turnip and then carved the face into its flesh. Daniel watched closely.

"Why am I doing this, exactly?" Shelly asked as she worked.

"I'll explain in a minute," he replied, "when you're finished."

After Shelly had walked the man through the entire process, he turned to Fenella. "Did you do yours the same way?"

"Yes, more or less. I didn't do as well as Shelly, but that's obvious when you look at our results."

Daniel looked at the two turnips and then chuckled. "I'm not going to comment on the finished products," he said. "Shelly, can I see your hands, please?"

Shelly shrugged and then held out her hands, palms down. "Turn them over, please," Daniel said. When Shelly complied, he spent some time studying them.

"Fenella, can I see your hands, please?" he asked.

She held out her hands, palms up, wondering what Daniel was doing. He took her right hand and rubbed his finger across her palm. "You have a blister here."

Fenella shivered at his touch, and when their eyes met, she felt her face flood with color. "From digging out the turnip," she said, pulling her hands away.

"Did either of you see Phillip doing any digging or carving?" Daniel asked.

"He only drilled ours and left us to our own devices, but there were a few small children there and I did see him helping one of them with the digging out on his turnip. The little boy's parents were both on their phones and weren't paying any attention to the child," Shelly said.

"So he may have helped with dozens of turnips throughout the course of the day," Daniel suggested.

"I expect he did," Shelly agreed.

Daniel sighed. "That answers that, then."

"That answers what?" Shelly demanded.

"Phillip had some blisters and sore patches on his hands. Inspector Nichols assured me that they were the result of turnip carving, but I wanted to see for myself exactly what damage he could have done during the process."

Shelly nodded. "If you want, I can go and buy a few turnips and you can have a go at carving one yourself."

"It's a tempting thought, but I think I'll leave it for now. I'm satisfied that the marks are consistent with what I've seen today. I really appreciate your cooperation."

"You know I'm always happy to help," Shelly replied.

"I know and I appreciate it. Not everyone is as cooperative."

Fenella thought he couldn't possibly be talking about her. She'd answered all of his questions, and she hadn't said a single word about Tiffany Perkins, either.

"Do you have more questions for me?" Shelly asked.

"I'd like to take a complete statement from you, actually," he replied. "It would be better if we did it where Fenella can't hear us, though."

"We can go over to my flat," Shelly said.

"Or you can use the living room and I'll stay here in the kitchen," Fenella said, feeling annoyed with the man. There was no reason why he couldn't take Shelly's statement in front of her. He would have done so three months ago, before he went away. Before he met Tiffany, a little voice added, making Fenella frown.

"Let's stay here but move into the living room," Daniel said. "We might want Fenella's input at some point and that will be easier if we're here."

Shelly shrugged and then followed Daniel into the living room. Fenella didn't move until they were out of sight. Then she sighed. "What the heck am I meant to do in here?" she said in a whisper.

"Meroooww," Katie suggested.

"It isn't time for your dinner yet," Fenella countered, "but you may have a treat because you're behaving well."

Katie ate her treat and then disappeared into the living room. Fenella felt oddly left out on her own in the kitchen as Katie vanished.

"When in doubt, bake," she said softly. She had plenty of ingredients in the apartment after her trip to the grocery store earlier. What she needed now was some chocolate chip cookies. The first batch was just coming out of the oven when Shelly stuck her head into the kitchen.

"What are you making?" she demanded. "Daniel and I can't concentrate because something smells delicious."

Fenella laughed. "Just chocolate chip cookies. Do you want a few?"

"Yes, please."

Fenella pulled down three plates and piled four cookies onto each plate. She handed two of the plates to Shelly, along with a handful of paper napkins.

"Thank you so much," Shelly said.

"I always recommend milk with cookies," Fenella grinned. "Would you like a glass of milk?"

"Not for me, but Daniel might like one. I may be back."

Fenella poured herself a glass of milk and tried her first cookie. She'd only just swallowed when Shelly returned.

"Daniel would like some milk, if it isn't too much bother," she said.

Fenella poured a second glass of milk and handed it to her friend. "What is the man playing at?" she asked Shelly in a whisper."

"I've no idea, but I'm hoping I can ask him a few questions once he's full of cookies and milk," Shelly replied in a low voice.

A few minutes later both Shelly and Daniel walked into the room.

"Thank you for the cookies and milk," Daniel said, putting his empty glass and plate on the table. "They were delicious."

"I hope they haven't spoiled your dinner," Fenella told him.

"Dinner? Oh, yes, I suppose I should start thinking about dinner," he replied.

"I can make my famous shepherd's pie, if you want," Shelly offered. "It only takes about an hour to throw together and bake, assuming I have all of the ingredients to hand."

Daniel looked at his watch and then frowned. "I really should go back to the office and do my reports."

"Do you want shepherd's pie?" Shelly asked Fenella.

"Oh, yes, please," Fenella laughed. "I like anything I don't have to cook myself. I'll save some cookie dough to bake right after dinner. Then we'll have fresh cookies to enjoy."

"You've sold me," Daniel sighed. "A lovely meal prepared by someone else and hot cookies for pudding. I can't resist that combination."

Shelly and Fenella exchanged glances. Daniel was staying for dinner? What did that mean, Fenella wondered.

He went with Shelly to her apartment to get the ingredients she needed for their meal. While Shelly prepared everything, he told the women about the course in Milton Keynes.

"It was excellent, really," he concluded after talking about the different subjects that had been covered and never once mentioning Tiffany's name. "And it's already resulted in my being asked to help Inspector Nichols with the case at Cregneash, so it's already proving worthwhile."

"And where does the beautiful young Tiffany Perkins fit into all of this?" Shelly asked.

Daniel shrugged. "She paid her own way on the course, as her previous employer didn't have the necessary funds. It's all a bit of a mess, really, as she offered to pay her own way because she really wanted to take the course, but her employer didn't fully understand the time commitment. When he found out that she was going to be away from her position for such a long period of time, he told her he couldn't keep her job open for her."

"Oh, dear," Shelly said.

"Yes, it was unfortunate, but she wasn't worried because she was sure that the course would help her find a new constabulary that would be happy to have her. Sadly, it hasn't worked out that way yet, but it's early days," Daniel added.

"The constabulary on the island isn't hiring?" Shelly asked.

"Not at the moment," Daniel replied, "and if they were, they probably wouldn't want to hire Tiffany anyway. The course has given her impressive qualifications, but she doesn't really have the experience to go along with them. She also has rather high expectations for salary. I really hope she finds something soon, but she may have to temper her expectations."

"And she's staying with you while she's looking?" Shelly asked.

Fenella tried to look uninterested as she waited for Daniel's reply, but she felt as if she were sitting on the edge of her seat.

"She wanted to see the island, so I invited her to come for a short stay. I never thought she'd stay this long," Daniel said. He flushed and then glanced at Fenella. "It's fine, though."

Shelly raised an eyebrow. "It doesn't sound fine."

"What did you get up to while I was away?" Daniel asked Shelly. "Are you still seeing Gordon?"

Shelly flushed. "We're just friends," she said too quickly. "He's traveling a lot for work at the moment. I don't get to see much of him."

The oven timer buzzed just as the silence began to feel awkward. "And that's our shepherd's pie, all ready," Shelly said, jumping to her feet.

Fenella got down plates and Shelly spooned out generous portions of the delicious-smelling meal. Just before everyone sat down to eat, Fenella slid the last tray of cookies into the oven.

"They should be ready to eat when we've finished our meal," she said as she sat down between Shelly and Daniel.

"This is delicious," Daniel said after a few bites. "Thank you so much."

"You're very welcome. I love to cook and I don't do it nearly enough," Shelly said.

"It's wonderful," Fenella agreed. "Thank you."

Daniel's phone buzzed as Fenella was pulling the cookies out of the oven. He glanced at the display and then sighed. "I need to take this," he said as he got to his feet.

Fenella and Shelly both listened as his voice carried back into the room as he spoke.

"I told you I'm interviewing witnesses."

"At least another hour, maybe more."

"I'll get something to eat. You worry about you."

"That isn't any of your concern."

"I need to go. I'm working, remember?"

"If not, you can take a taxi, surely?"

"I've no idea, but I'll give you some money to cover it."

"I don't have time for this. I have to go."

When Daniel walked back into the kitchen he looked upset.

"Cookies?" Shelly asked.

Daniel looked at the plate in the center of the table that was stacked with cookies that Fenella had just taken out of the oven. "Yes, please," he said.

Several minutes later, when the plate was empty, he got to his feet. "I need to go to the office and get my reports done," he said. "If I find that I have any more questions for either of you, I'll be in touch."

"The next time you aren't working, you should come to the pub with us," Shelly said as she and Fenella followed the man to the door. "The Tale and Tail is the nicest pub in the world. I'm sure there wasn't anything like it in Milton Keynes."

"No, there wasn't," he agreed. "I missed it." He opened the door and stepped through it before looking back over his shoulder. "I missed both of you, too," he added before he shut the door behind himself.

6

"And on that note, we're off to the pub," Shelly said before Fenella could speak. "I'll just help you tidy the kitchen and then we'll go."

Fenella thought about arguing, but she was too confused about everything to do anything other than follow Shelly back into the kitchen.

Shelly loaded the dishwasher while Fenella cleaned up the mess that making cookies had made.

"Go and change," Shelly told her when they were done. "Put on something gorgeous from Mona's wardrobe and do your hair and makeup. Tonight you need to be fabulous."

"I don't want to be fabulous," Fenella said, blinking back unexpected tears. "I want to stay home and eat chocolate and cry."

"That's exactly why we're going out," Shelly said. "Maybe we'll have some luck and you'll meet a thoroughly unsuitable man with whom you can flirt outrageously. Tonight is not a night for sitting at home and feeling sorry for yourself."

"Why not?" Fenella demanded.

"Because life is too short and the Tale and Tail is too wonderful. We'll go and have a glass of wine or maybe even two. You'll have plenty of time to feel sorry for yourself when you get home, if you still want to, but hopefully you'll be too tired to do anything other than fall asleep."

"I don't know about that, but I'll try," Fenella said. Shelly went back to her own apartment to get ready while Fenella headed for her bedroom. Along with the fortune that she'd inherited from Mona, Fenella had also inherited the woman's incredible wardrobe of custom-made clothing. Everything had been made by a very talented local designer, and for some reason every item that Fenella had tried on from the seemingly unlimited supply had fit her perfectly.

Tonight will be the night that all goes wrong, Fenella thought as she pulled open the wardrobe. The first dress she saw was exactly what she needed for a quick trip to the pub. It was black and it had a casual simplicity that meant it wouldn't look as if she were trying too hard. "It's not going to fit," she told Katie as she slid the dress over her head.

"Meerooowwww," Katie said from her spot on the bed.

"Yes, okay, it fits perfectly," Fenella admitted. She turned slowly in front of the mirror. It was a wonderful dress and it made her look better than she felt. She dug out a pair of Mona's shoes and then twisted her hair into a knot at the back of her neck. A bit of eyeshadow and a coat of lipstick completed her look. A tiny drop of Mona's perfume from its elegant cut crystal decanter made her feel extra special.

"Will I do?" she asked Katie.

The kitten looked at her and then shrugged, clearly not interested in Fenella's appearance.

"I won't be late," she promised the animal. "You be good."

As soon as the words were out of her mouth, Fenella rushed off to shut the bathroom door. If it was left open when Katie was alone in the apartment, the kitten had a bad habit of unrolling the toilet paper and shredding it. Fenella checked that the box of tissues next to her bed was tucked into a drawer and then she headed for the door.

"You look wonderful," Shelly said when she opened her door a moment later. "Mona had such beautiful clothes."

"She did, didn't she? I can't quite believe that they all fit me."

"It is strange, but maybe it's something to do with how they were made. You've given me three dresses from that wardrobe and they all fit me perfectly, even though I'm not shaped anything like you or like Mona."

Fenella shrugged. "Maybe it's just magic," she said, only half joking.

Shelly looked at her for a minute and then laughed. "Mona was nothing if not magic," she sighed. "I do miss her, you know."

If you only knew, Fenella thought.

The Tale and Tail was only a short walk away. Even on a cool October night, the pair didn't mind walking. As they entered the warm and inviting room, Fenella was reminded again of why the pub was one of her favorite places in the world. It had formerly been the library in a large seaside mansion. The new owners had opted not to change much in the space. They'd turned the mansion into a luxury hotel and added a large bar to the middle of the library. What they hadn't done was remove the books, which was what made the pub such a special place. Besides books, the pub was famous for its cats. There were at least half a dozen who called the pub's scattered cat beds home, and Fenella often thought that if she took the time to count them she might find ten or fifteen of the animals spread around the space.

"Why aren't there ever any kittens?" she asked the bartender as he poured them their glasses of wine.

"All of our cats are spayed or neutered before they're allowed inside the pub," he replied. "They're all rescue cats that were left at a shelter or abandoned in the street. As long as they can get along with other cats and our customers, we take them from the shelters when the shelters can't keep them."

"How wonderful," Fenella said.

"I'm surprised you aren't overrun with abandoned animals," Shelly said.

"You'd be amazed how many of our cats get adopted by our customers," the man told her.

"I didn't realize they were adoptable," Shelly said. "I got my cat from the local shelter."

"We don't actively seek homes for our cats. As far as we're concerned, they are home here, but if a customer becomes exceptionally attached to an individual animal and we believe the feeling is mutual, we're prepared to consider letting that customer adopt," he explained.

Feeling as if she loved the pub even more than ever, Fenella followed Shelly up the narrow winding staircase to the upper floor. It was practically deserted, so they easily found a table with a few comfortable chairs around it, with easy access to a section of bookshelves. They sipped their wine and perused the shelves for a few minutes before Shelly spoke.

"Are you okay?" she asked.

"I'm fine," Fenella replied with a sigh.

"For what it's worth, I didn't get the feeling that Daniel was very happy with Tiffany."

"But she's living with him."

"She's staying with him. That's a very different thing."

"I don't know about that. Regardless, he's acting weird toward me. He's acting as if he isn't interested in me at all."

"No, he's acting as if he's very interested in you but feels as if he shouldn't be," Shelly countered.

"What does that mean?"

"I mean when I was alone with him, he asked me a dozen questions about you. He was very concerned that you'd been upset about finding the body, for one thing."

"He never said anything of the kind to me."

"He can't take his eyes off you when you're together."

"I don't believe that."

"Because the thought scares you."

"Maybe, and maybe we should just talk about something else."

Fenella sipped her wine and read the titles off the spines of a dozen books. She was startled when she heard music.

"What's that?" she asked Shelly.

"I've no idea," Shelly replied. "Let's go find out."

The pair took the elevator down to the lower level where they were surprised to see a small band had set up in the corner of the room.

"The owners thought it was time to try something different," the bartender said when the women approached the bar. "We're going to start having live music one or two nights a week. If you don't like the idea, do let me know. The owners want to keep our regulars happy."

Fenella looked over at the band, who were playing a song she recognized from Cregneash. "It's the band from the Hop-tu-Naa day," she said to Shelly.

Shelly turned and stared at the band. "It is, isn't it?" she replied. "It's The Islanders. They're very good, really, but I'm not sure I want them here, exactly."

"At least they aren't too loud. We can always go upstairs if we want to talk," Fenella pointed out.

"Yes, that's true. In the meantime, we appear to be their only audience, so maybe we should stay for a while."

Fenella grinned. Other than the bartender, she and Shelly were the only people on the ground floor aside from the band. "Perhaps the two couples who are still upstairs will come down once the band gets going properly."

"Let's hope so," the bartender said. "Otherwise they'll be playing to an empty room."

A small makeshift stage had been set up on one side of the room and a few rows of chairs and couches had been arranged facing the stage. Fenella and Shelly sat together on one of the couches as the band finished their song. They both clapped politely at the end.

"Thank you, ladies," Paul Baldwin said, "but we've met, haven't we?"

"Yes, at Cregneash yesterday," Shelly said.

Paul frowned. "Oh, dear. I'm trying hard to forget that yesterday happened."

The band began to play another song and after a moment Paul started to sing. They played three songs in succession before they were ready for a break. One of the men that Fenella dimly remembered meeting previously headed for the bar while the other men put their instruments down and stepped off the stage.

"That was rather rude of me," Paul said apologetically as he walked over to sit next to Shelly. "The event at Cregneash was really good, right up until, well, until poor Phillip's untimely death. I can't quite get my head around it, really."

"I thought you could use a drink," a voice said. Fenella looked at the man who was holding a beer mug out toward Paul. He appeared to be around sixty, with grey hair and blue eyes. There was something attractive about the man, and while Fenella was sure he'd been on stage with the band tonight, she was also sure she hadn't met the man yesterday.

"Ah, thanks, Todd. You keep this up and you might get a permanent place in the band," Paul laughed.

The man grinned. "I told you I don't want a permanent place. I'm happy just filling in now and again when you're stuck. But now you must introduce me to your friends."

"I'm terribly sorry, but I don't remember your names," Paul said to Shelly and Fenella with an apologetic smile. "I meet a lot of people at shows, you understand."

"Of course," Shelly said. "I'm Shelly Quirk and this is Fenella Woods."

"It's a pleasure to meet you, Shelly," the man said. He shook Shelly's hand and then smiled brightly at Fenella. "And you," he said, taking her hand and giving it a squeeze. "I'm Todd Hughes. I'm just filling in for Henry Jones, who is much more talented than I am."

Of course, Henry isn't here, Fenella thought. She should have noticed that.

"I hope Henry is okay," Shelly said as Todd sat down next to Fenella.

"He and Harriet are staying with Karla. She's devastated," Paul explained.

"The poor girl. She told us that she and Phillip were newlyweds," Fenella said. "Had they known each other for long?"

"Oh, yes, we all grew up on the island," Paul said. "Although Phillip's family moved across when he was about twelve. He just moved back recently when he took a job with one of the banks."

"So they were childhood sweethearts?" Shelly asked.

"Not really. As I recall, they were just friends in those days. If anything, Karla and I were childhood sweethearts, although I'm a few years older than she is, of course. But we were a couple during her teen years, off and on, anyway. Of course, those were the years when Phillip was across," Paul explained.

"And then you moved across and Phillip came back?" was Shelly's next question.

"Something like that. I wanted to give music a proper go, you know? And I haven't given up on my dream, either. I'm back for a short while, but it's only a temporary return, if things go to plan," Paul said.

"You deserve success," Todd said. "You're incredibly talented. I'm just afraid you're too nice to succeed in the music business."

Paul laughed. "Don't let the façade fool you. I can be nice here, because I'm playing to a crowd of two just for fun. I'm nowhere near as nice when I'm working across."

Todd shrugged. "You know I'll do what I can to help."

"Yes, and I appreciate that," Paul said. "Todd may not look like it, but he was a very successful musician in his day."

"Really?" Shelly said. "The name isn't familiar." As soon as the words were out of her mouth, she blushed. "I mean, I'm terrible at recognizing famous people. Don't mind me."

Todd laughed. "You're fine. No one has ever heard of me," he assured her. "I was a session musician. I played in the background of any number of big hit songs, but unless you enjoy reading the fine print on album covers, you'll not have heard of me."

"Don't be modest," Paul said. "He was one of the best in the business and in huge demand in his prime. And he made a fortune doing it."

"A small fortune," Todd said with a shrug. "But I was happy to be in the background, just getting paid to do what I love."

"And getting to work with some of the biggest names in the business," Paul added.

"That was a huge bonus," Todd agreed. "If I had children or grandchildren, I'd have lots of great stories to share with them."

"Oh, share with us," Shelly invited.

Todd laughed. "Well, I suppose I could tell you one quick story, before we have to get back to work."

Shelly and Fenella were both fascinated as the man told them a story about a few of the antics of a very famous singer that had happened while they'd been on tour together in Australia. "I played keyboards for that tour and then told his manager that I didn't want to travel with him again," Todd concluded. "I came home and slept twenty-two hours a day for a week, just to get caught up."

"And now we should get back up there," Paul suggested. While they'd been talking, a handful of additional customers had wandered in. The new, larger audience seemed excited by the idea of a live band. Paul and the others performed a dozen songs, including several that Fenella remembered from Cregneash but also some that she was sure she'd heard on the radio recently. When they were ready for another break, they received a large round of applause from the dozen or so people watching.

There were three girls who looked to be in their mid-twenties sitting together on one of the sofas. As the band members came off the stage, one of them got up and crossed to Paul. She whispered something in his ear that made him blush. He shook his head and then crossed to the bar.

"He's going to have to get used to that," Todd said as he sat back down next to Fenella. "I hope you don't mind if I join you," he added.

"Of course not," Fenella said. "Who needs to get used to what, then?"

Todd shook his head. "Sorry. I was talking about young Paul and the girl. When you're in a band, you attract a lot of attention from women. Even us session musicians used to get, um, offers during or after shows. A lot of times, the women were hoping I would introduce them to the lead singer, but usually they'd settle for, well, spending the night with me, if that was the closest they could get to the star."

"My goodness," Shelly said. "What a horrible thought."

"It is, rather," Todd agreed. "I should add that I never actually accepted any of the offers that were thrown at me over the years. I'm no angel, but I got married very young and I was brought up to believe that being faithful mattered."

"Good for you," Shelly told him. "Did your wife use to go to your shows?"

"Sometimes. As I said, we never had children, but in the early days she was working more steadily than I was, so she usually stayed home and paid the mortgage while I traveled around and tried to make a name for myself."

"That sounds like hard work," Fenella said.

"It was. And then, just when I started to succeed, she fell ill." He frowned. "I should have simply come home and looked after her, but she insisted that I keep going. You're only as good as your last show in this business. If I'd taken time off to look after her, I would have had to start over again."

Fenella could see pain in the man's eyes. "I'm sure she understood," she said softly.

"Oh, she did. As I said, she encouraged me to keep going, but I'll never stop feeling as if I let her down anyway," he sighed. "I was in Los Angeles, performing with, well, it doesn't matter who, but someone huge, when they rang to tell me that she wasn't going to make it. I flew home that night and got to her bedside just in time to say goodbye." He stopped and cleared his throat. "And then I flew back to LA and got back out on the stage the next night."

"My goodness, that was brave," Shelly said.

"It was cowardly," he corrected her. "I buried my feelings in my work, and each success just seemed to remind me of how much of a failure I truly was." He stopped and shook his head. "I don't know why I'm telling you both all of this. I never talk about myself."

"We're good listeners," Shelly told him, "but don't tell us more than feels comfortable for you."

"There isn't much more to tell. I spent another twenty years on the road, still staying faithful to the only woman I'd ever loved, and then I met someone else. I settled in London to be close to her and then, about a year ago, I lost her, too. That's when I decided to move back to the Isle of Man. The wife and I lived here when we were first married, and we used to holiday here after we moved to the UK. Anyway, I have a friend here. I came to visit him recently and realized that the island feels more like home than anywhere else in the world, so here I am."

"And the island is better for it," Shelly said firmly.

Todd laughed. "I don't know about that, but I haven't regretted my choice. Harvey was right. Once you get here, the island gets you under its spell."

"Harvey? That wouldn't be Harvey Garus, would it?" Shelly asked.

"Yes, it would. Do you know Harvey?"

"Very well. I knew he was involved in the music business before he retired to the island," Shelly explained.

"Yes, he was one of the best managers out there. He managed my career for me, and at least ninety percent of my success was down to him."

"Don't listen to him," Paul interjected. "He would have been a success anyway. He's that good." He dropped into the chair next to Shelly and sighed. "I've just told those women that you're my father-in-law," he told Paul in a low voice. "It was the only thing I could think of to get them to leave me alone."

Todd nodded. "What's my daughter called?" he asked.

Paul shrugged. "I didn't bother to give her a name. Do you think we need one?"

"Just to be safe, let's make sure we're telling the same lie," Todd said. "Call her Elizabeth. If we would have had children, we would have called a daughter Elizabeth."

"Can I call her Liz or something?" Paul asked.

"You'd have to ask her that," Todd teased.

Shelly shook her head. "Surely it would be easier to just tell the girls that you aren't interested?"

"I don't want them to feel insulted or anything," Paul said. "Sometimes it's easier to lie."

Fenella wondered if the man had used the same logic when talking to the police about Phillip Pierce's murder. A dozen questions sprang to her lips, but before she could ask any of them Todd stood up and reminded Paul that they had another set to do.

"Should we stay for the last set?" Shelly asked.

Fenella looked at the clock on the wall. It was later than she'd realized, but she was really enjoying the music and the evening out. "I'm happy to stay, but if you're tired, we can go home."

"No, I think I'd like to stay. It's been ages since I've had a late night, but I can lie in tomorrow as late as I like."

"Katie will wake me at seven for her breakfast," Fenella sighed.

"Get everything ready before you go to bed tonight, then you just have to dump her food into a bowl and you can go back to bed," Shelly suggested.

"I may have to do that," Fenella laughed.

By the time the band finished, the crowd had thinned back down. Besides Shelly and Fenella, only one couple who looked to be in their mid-forties were left when Paul took his final bow.

"Thank you for sticking with the whole show," he told them as the band began to pack up their things. "I hope you didn't stay because you felt as if you had to."

"Not at all," Shelly said quickly. "We truly enjoyed ourselves."

The other couple got up and headed for the door. They stopped at the bar and said a few words to the bartender before they left. As the door swung shut behind them, the bartender gave Paul a quick thumbs up.

"We're here again next Sunday," Paul told Shelly. "That's as far ahead as they've booked us for now, but I'm hoping we might get a few more weeks in. I need the practice. There's nothing like performing for a live audience, even a very small one, to keep one's skills up."

"Maybe we can find some friends to bring with us next week," Shelly said. "You deserve a larger crowd."

"Do you think Henry will be back next week?" Fenella asked.

"She wants to get rid of me," Todd laughed. "I didn't think I was that bad."

"Not at all," Fenella said quickly. "I'm just concerned about Henry."

"We all are," Paul replied, "but I'm more worried about Karla than about anyone else. What happened just doesn't make any sense."

"Murders don't often happen on the island," Todd said. "I can't help but wonder if maybe Phillip brought some sort of trouble back to the island with him from across."

"He'd been back for six months or more, though," Paul said.

Todd shrugged. "I suppose I just like that idea better than thinking that someone from the island killed him."

"It must have been an accident," one of the men in the band said.

"The police haven't said exactly what happened. Maybe he slipped and fell and hit his head and the police just think it was murder."

"I think the island police are smarter than that," Shelly said. "If they think it was murder, it was murder."

"But who could have wanted to kill the man?" Paul asked.

"Maybe it was something with his work," one of the band members said. "He worked for one of the banks, right? Maybe he found out that someone was embezzling from the bank."

"I suppose that's a possibility," Paul said, "but it seems farfetched."

"What other possibilities are there? Aren't most people killed by the person closest to them?" Todd asked.

"That would be Karla," Paul said, shaking his head. "They were only married just last week. She couldn't possibly have had anything to do with it."

"What about Henry?" someone asked. "He didn't seem too happy about the marriage."

"You can't possibly be accusing Henry of anything," another band member snapped. "He wouldn't hurt a fly and you know it. Now that wife of his is a different matter."

Everyone laughed. "I can see Harriet killing someone if she felt justified, but as far as I know, she liked Phillip and was happy about the marriage," Paul said.

"Maybe it was that man from Manx National Heritage that did it. You know, the one who kept telling us to pick up our rubbish every time we put a cup down anywhere," someone said.

"Except Josh wouldn't hurt a fly, either, quite literally. He won't permit the use of pesticides at Cregneash. I can't see him actually raising a hand to anyone," Paul said. "No one had any reason to kill Phillip."

"Maybe someone else was upset about Phillip and Karla's marriage," Shelly suggested. "She said something about them getting married impulsively. Was she involved with someone else recently?"

"Not that I'm aware of," Paul said, "and I think I would know."

Fenella wondered what he meant by that, but before she could ask the bartender interrupted.

"We're ready to close for the night," he told them. "I'm sorry you didn't get a larger crowd, but everyone who was here had good things to say about you. We'll try to advertise next week's show more. If you aren't busy, the owners have suggested you try again on Tuesday evening, though."

"This Tuesday?" Paul asked. He looked around at the others, most of whom nodded. "Yeah, okay, we'll do Tuesday."

"Great. I hope we can get a bigger crowd for you," the bartender said.

"A bigger crowd would be nice, but as long as you're happy, we'll play to just you and the cats," Paul told him.

The bartender laughed. "They seemed to enjoy the show, anyway," he said. "They all came downstairs and watched."

Fenella looked around. It seemed as if every cat bed was occupied and most of the animals seemed to be watching as the band finished packing up their things.

"We should get home, then," Shelly said, getting to her feet.

Fenella stood up and then stretched. "I shouldn't have just sat there in between sets," she said. "I feel as if I need a long walk to work out the kinks in my back."

"I'd be delighted to escort you along the promenade for a short while," Todd offered. "Assuming it isn't raining, that is."

Fenella flushed. "It's awfully late," she said quickly.

"Then I'll simply walk you both home," he offered.

"We're only a few steps away," Fenella told him. "We're fine on our own."

"I'm sure you are, but I'll feel better seeing you safely home," the man said. "It's old-fashioned, but it's the way I was raised."

Shelly laughed. "Come on, then, let's go," she said, taking the man's arm.

He offered his other arm to Fenella, and after a moment's hesitation, she took it. They walked together as far as the pub's door and then had to separate to get through it. The night was clear and fresh and Fenella found herself wanting that walk again as she breathed in the sea air.

"Let's walk for a bit," Shelly said. "It's too nice out here to head straight inside."

The trio strolled down the promenade for several minutes. "Everything looks different at night," Fenella said after a minute. "All the lights makes it seem like a fairy tale or something."

"It's beautiful," Todd agreed. "I never get tired of the scenery here."

After a short while, Shelly sighed. "I'm getting tired," she said. "I'm going to turn back. You two can keep going, though. I'll be fine on my own."

"I'm not letting you walk back alone," Todd said. They all turned back toward home.

As the entered the lobby of Promenade View Apartments, Shelly stopped. "Okay, I'm home now. You two can go and finish your walk."

Fenella hesitated. She wanted to keep walking, but she wasn't sure about being alone with Todd, who was, after all, a stranger.

"Ring me when you get home, though, so that I know that Todd isn't really a serial killer or anything," Shelly added.

"I'll ring you soon," Fenella promised as she and Todd turned back around.

Todd was laughing as they walked back outside. "No one has ever suggested that I might be a serial killer before," he said as he took Fenella's arm and guided her back across the road.

"After yesterday, it makes sense to be extra careful," Fenella said.

"Except I was working in London all day yesterday," Todd told her. "There's no way I killed Phillip Pierce."

"I thought you said you were retired?"

"I am, but an old friend needed someone to play keyboards at his wedding and I couldn't say no."

Fenella had read about a very famous musican who'd married for the fifth time the previous day. Surely that wasn't who Todd was talking about?

They walked in silence to the very end of the promenade. Todd stopped and stared out at the sea for a long while. "You're far too young and attractive for a man like me," he said conversationally. "But that doesn't mean that I'm not interested in you."

"I'm not that young or that attractive," Fenella replied.

He turned and then held out his hand. Fenella took it and he pulled her close to him. "May I kiss you?" he asked.

Fenella hesitated for a minute and then whispered her reply. When he finally lifted his head, Todd grinned at her. "I was starting to think that I was too old for this sort of thing."

He walked her back to her apartment and then kissed her again, just quickly, at her door. "I'll ring you," he promised after she'd given him her phone number.

She nodded and then let herself into her apartment. It was only after she was ready for bed that she remembered to call Shelly.

"I'm home, safe and sound," she said.

"Alone?"

"Yes, alone."

"I got the impression that he'd be a wonderful kisser."

"He is," Fenella replied.

7

Katie woke Fenella at seven the next morning, exactly as Fenella had predicted. Having followed Shelly's advice, Fenella stumbled into the kitchen and dumped Katie's food into her bowl before heading straight back to bed. When she woke up ninety minutes later, she felt almost human.

"Thank you for not disturbing me," she told Katie as she headed for the shower.

The look Katie gave her seemed to say "Who are you again?" but Fenella decided not to take it personally. After a quick breakfast of toast and a banana, Fenella wondered what she should do with her day.

"You need to go to the museum and meet Marjorie Stevens," she reminded herself. If she wasn't going to write her book about Anne Boleyn, maybe she should try doing a bit of research into the island's history. It would keep her mind active and help the island at the same time. Of course, Marjorie was probably very busy. Simply turning up on her doorstep unannounced wouldn't be right. No, she needed to call and make an appointment.

The sun was shining outside Fenella's window. What she really wanted to do was take Mona's car for a spin.

"Do you want to go for a ride in Mona's car?" she asked Shelly when her friend answered her phone a minute later.

"Yes, please," Shelly replied. "Now?"

"Give me five minutes."

Ten minutes later they were cruising across the island with the top down. Fenella had to turn the car's heating up as high as it would go to keep her teeth from chattering, but it was wonderful to feel the wind in her hair and to breathe fresh air.

"This is exactly what I needed today," Shelly said. "I'm stuck."

"Stuck? On what?"

Shelly laughed, but it sounded forced. "Do you remember when we talked about books once?"

"We've talked about books a lot."

"Yes, but the time when we talked about romances, and I admitted that I read them a lot."

"Oh, yes. I do remember that. You were going to try your hand at writing one, weren't you?"

"Yes, well, the thing is, I've been doing just that, trying, I mean, but I'm well and truly stuck."

"Congratulations," Fenella exclaimed. "I know from experience that writing a book is hard work."

"I don't deserve congratulations yet. I'm stuck on chapter two," Shelly said with a sigh.

"That's one more chapter than I wrote of my book."

"Maybe between us we've written a short story," Shelly said. "The thing is, I have my main character and I really like her, but I'm struggling with her love interest."

"Tell me the story," Fenella suggested.

"I thought it would be good to write something about an older woman. Older women need love, too. My main character was a teacher, but she retired early when her husband died unexpectedly."

"Really? She sounds familiar."

Shelly chuckled. "Yes, okay, I'm really writing about myself, although I've made my character a good deal more interesting than I truly am."

"Is the book set on the island?"

"It wasn't going to be, but I've never lived anywhere else, so I decided that it was probably easiest to simply set it here."

"It's a great location. I'm sure you can use the island's history and its amazing scenery to help bring the story to life."

"Sure, if I ever get past the first chapter. I need a man now, though, and I'm having trouble dreaming one up."

"If your main character is based on you, why not base your hero on John?"

"The character's first husband is based on John. I want the man who romances her in my book to be nothing like him."

"What about Gordon?"

"Romances need conflict. Gordon is far too nice to be a romance novel hero."

Fenella glanced at her friend. Was it possible that Shelly was getting a little bit tired of Gordon? "Is everything okay between you and Gordon?" she asked.

"I suppose so. I don't know that I miss him as much as I thought I would, though. He's incredibly nice, but, well, maybe we're missing some sort of spark."

"Or maybe you've been reading too many romance novels. Couples don't have to have conflict, you know."

"I know," Shelly sighed, "but they do have to have chemistry."

Fenella nodded. "And you don't have any chemistry with Gordon?"

"Maybe if he'd try kissing me just once, I would be able to answer that question," Shelly said sharply. "I don't mean to take it out on you, but it's all a bit frustrating, really."

"Okay, so Gordon won't do. What sort of conflict do you want between the couple?"

"I'm not sure I know. I was thinking that the hero would be sort of a jerk who never stays in a relationship for more than few weeks until he meets the heroine, but if they're both in the early sixties, that seems, well, odd."

"What about Donald? He'd make a good romance novel hero. He's rich and he has a terrible reputation with women. He's been married three times, too. Use him as your inspiration."

"Donald might be good," Shelly mused, "but aside from his reputation with women, what could bring him and heroine into conflict?"

"Maybe her house is on a plot of land he wants to buy," Fenella suggested. "He can be really obnoxious about trying to get her to sell and then fall in love with her."

"That's a good idea. It can be the house that she and her husband bought when they were first married so she can be stupidly stubborn about not selling, even though Donald is offering her more than the actual value of the property."

"Don't call the man Donald," Fenella suggested. "Just in case he finds out about the book."

Shelly laughed. "Maybe I'll call him Maxwell, in honor of Mona and her great romance."

"You could always base the hero on Todd," Fenella said after a few minutes. "He'd be a good romance novel hero, I think."

"He has a fascinating past and he's gorgeous and sexy," Shelly said. "If I were a few years younger, I think I'd be trying to catch his eye."

"He seems awfully nice, though. I can't imagine what sort of conflict you could create with him."

"I'm not even going to think about that. I'm going to focus on Donald and his determination to buy the house that my husband and I spent our entire married life making into a home."

"That sounds like a plan."

"Now I'm almost eager to get home and get back to work on my story."

"Do you want me to turn around?"

"Would you mind terribly?"

"Not at all. I just wanted to get out and get some fresh air and some sunshine. We've had both. Anyway, it's nearly time for lunch." Fenella had been planning on suggesting that they stop for lunch somewhere, but she had an apartment full of food, so going home wasn't a hardship.

Shelly nearly leaped out of the car as Fenella parked it. "I hope you don't mind if I dash away," she said. "I've just written the most wonderful scene in my head and I need to get it written down."

"Go, write," Fenella laughed. She watched as Shelly crossed the parking garage. When the elevator door didn't open immediately, Shelly headed for the stairs. By the time Fenella reached the elevator, it had arrived.

She was just finding her keycard when Shelly pushed open the door at the top of the stairs.

"Okay, so I should have just waited for the lift," Shelly gasped as she walked down the corridor. "But I was too excited. Remind me next time that we live on the sixth floor, though, okay?"

Fenella laughed. "If you get stuck again, come and visit me," she said. "I don't have any plans for today."

"I hope I'm going to be writing all day," Shelly said. "At the moment I feel as if the whole story is unfolding in my head."

After getting Katie her lunch, Fenella heated up some soup and made a sandwich to go with it. Once they were gone, she was back to trying to work out what to do with her day. "I should go and do something exciting," she said to Katie.

"Meerroow," the kitten replied before disappearing into Fenella's bedroom.

"You're going to take a nap, aren't you?" she called after the animal.

Katie didn't bother to reply.

"Maybe a puzzle book," Fenella muttered as she stared out at the sea. "Or a good mystery. Maybe you should borrow a few romances from Shelly."

"Maybe you should stop talking to yourself," Mona suggested as she sat down next to Fenella.

"I probably should," Fenella agreed. "What about talking to you, though? I mean, if anyone saw me now, they'd think I was still just talking to myself."

Mona yawned. "So, what did I miss while I was away? Have you solved that poor man's murder yet?"

"No, and as far as I know, neither have the police."

"That's a shame. Still, at least that means you should get to see Daniel once in a while, right? He won't be able stay away from you, not if you're wrapped up in a murder investigation."

"He was here last night," Fenella told her.

"I knew I should have visited last night," Mona frowned. "Max and

I had dinner and then he insisted on taking me dancing. I should have told him no, but I was never very good at resisting the man. Tell me all about Daniel's visit, then."

Fenella told her aunt what she could remember, stopping to eat a few cookies in the middle of the story. "Sorry," she said as she poured herself a glass of milk, "but I'd nearly forgotten I have cookies," she explained. When she was done with her snack, she sighed. "And then Shelly and I went to the pub," she concluded.

Mona studied her for a minute. "There's a story there, too, isn't there? But before we talk about what happened at the pub, we must discuss Daniel. The man is clearly still enamored of you."

"I'm not sure why you think that. That wasn't the impression I got from him at all."

"He spent hours here, having you tell him and then having Shelly show him how to carve a turnip. That was all just an excuse to spend time with you, obviously. And from what you've said about his conversations with Tiffany, it sounds very much like she's making him miserable. She'll be gone by the end of the month."

"I hope you're right about that, because I don't like her, but I'm not convinced that Daniel still has feelings for me."

"I won't bother to argue. It will all work out in the end. I'm sure of that now. I wonder who told the man about my money."

"What do you mean?"

"You said he made a few comments about money. Someone must have told him that you're incredibly wealthy. No doubt that's part of the problem."

"It shouldn't be a problem. It wasn't a problem before he went away."

"Maybe he'd never really thought about it before he went away. Someone must have said something. I wonder who it was, and I wonder what was said."

"Perhaps I'll ask Daniel the next time I see him," Fenella said.

Mona shook her head. "You won't. I know you better than that. But what happened at the pub, then?"

Fenella told her aunt about the band and the various conversations they'd had about Phillip's murder. She barely mentioned Todd as she went along, trying to keep the focus on the murder investigation.

"No one in the band could suggest any possible motives for the man's murder? That's unfortunate, but perhaps the men didn't know Phillip well. You said he and Paul had known each other as children?"

"Yes, that's what Paul said. He and Karla and Phillip were all childhood friends."

"And then Phillip left and Paul and Karla became a couple," Mona mused.

"It didn't sound as if it was anything too serious, from what Paul said. Anyway, they split up so that Paul could chase his dreams in the UK."

"But now he's back, and right after Karla and Phillip got married. The timing is interesting."

"Is it? Why?"

"It's almost as if Paul came back to reclaim Karla," Mona suggested.

"Even if he did come back when he heard the news, surely it was up to Karla to decide whether she wanted him back or not?"

"What if she said no, so he decided to get rid of his competition?"

"If I didn't know any of the people involved, I might believe that, but Paul's far too nice a man to do something like that. He may have been hurt when he found out that Karla had married someone else, but I can't even see him getting angry, let alone angry enough to kill someone."

"What if Karla's parents weren't happy about the marriage? What if they'd always liked Paul? Once he was back on the island, they simply had to get rid of Phillip, or so they thought."

"You think Harriet and Henry Jones killed Phillip in an effort to get Karla and Paul back together?" Fenella knew she sounded incredulous.

"The man's recent marriage to Karla is the only thing that I can think of as a possible motive for murder," Mona said. "Do you have other ideas?"

"Maybe it was something to do with his work. He worked for one of the banks. Maybe someone was stealing from them and he found out."

"Possible, but boring," Mona replied, "and that will be harder for us to find out more about, too. Do you know which bank?"

"No, but it will probably be in the local paper."

"Yes, I'm sure it is. Perhaps you should visit the appropriate bank and see what you can find out."

"You want me to go to the bank and start asking questions about Phillip Pierce?" Fenella said, shaking her head. "As if Daniel wasn't already annoyed with me enough."

"If you won't try to find out more about his work, then I'm going to continue to assume that Phillip was murdered because of Karla," Mona told her.

"Hey, whatever makes you happy. You can assume that he was killed because of aliens, if you want. I am not doing any investigating, no matter what you think."

"But you are going to see Todd again, aren't you?" Mona asked.

"What makes you think that?"

"There was just something about the way you said his name, whenever he came up in the conversation," Mona replied. "Your eyes lit up, as well. I will admit that he's a handsome man, but he's a musician, so you must be extra cautious about falling for him."

"You knew Todd?"

"Of course I knew Todd. He wasn't on the island often, but when he was here we moved in some of the same circles. He's an incredibly talented musician, as well. Max used to hire him to play at parties, although not nearly as often as Max would have liked. Todd never needed the work and he would have been invited as a guest to most events if he wasn't performing, you see."

"He seemed very nice," Fenella said.

"I always thought he was lovely. If I'd been twenty years younger and slightly less devoted to Max, I might have tried to get to know him better."

"I don't know that I'll be seeing him again, though. That's going to be up to him, I suppose."

"You really should listen to your answering machine once in a while," Mona suggested.

Fenella glanced over at the machine that was near the door. She hadn't noticed the blinking light when she'd come in.

"Hi, Fenella, it's Todd. I really enjoyed meeting you last night. I know this is short notice and whatever, but would you like to have dinner with me tonight? Ring me back if you have a chance. I'll book somewhere special, just in case it's a yes, but don't feel bad if you're busy. As I said, it's short notice." He recited his phone number before he disconnected.

"It is short notice," Mona said as Fenella wrote the number down. "He won't properly appreciate you if you make yourself available immediately."

"I'm not playing stupid games. He asked me to have dinner with him and I happen to be free, so why shouldn't I say yes?"

"Men like games," Mona told her. "Especially men like Todd. He's traveled all over the world as a musician. He's probably used to women throwing themselves at his feet. Be distant and a little mysterious. It will make him crazy."

"I don't want to date a crazy person," Fenella said dryly. "It's bad enough I have to live with one."

Mona laughed loudly. "My goodness, I didn't deserve that, but it was funny. Anyway, you must do what you think is best, of course."

"Thank you. I think I'll have dinner with Todd, then."

Fenella dialed the number he'd left and listened to the phone ring several times. She was about to give up when the man answered.

"Hello?"

"It's Fenella," she said, suddenly feeling shy.

"I'm glad I ran to answer, then," he replied. "I was practicing a complicated guitar riff and I wasn't going to bother, but I would have been furious with myself if I'd missed you."

"I didn't mean to interrupt your practice."

"I'm always practicing. Most of the time just for my own satisfaction, but today I was actually working on some of the songs for tomorrow night. Henry probably isn't going to make it again and I felt as if I let the band down on a few numbers last night."

"Speaking on behalf of the audience, you didn't," Fenella told him.

"I'm glad you feel that way, anyway, but that doesn't mean I won't be practicing all afternoon."

"I should let you go, then."

"But you haven't answered my question. Are you free for dinner tonight?"

"Yes, if you're sure you have time."

"I'll make time, no worries there."

"Okay, then," Fenella said, feeling her cheeks flush.

"I'll collect you at half six, if that works for you. A friend of mine just opened a restaurant in Ramsey that is getting good reviews. I thought we could go there."

"That sounds good," Fenella agreed. She'd heard about a new restaurant in Ramsey. A very well-known celebrity chef had opened it after a fight with a London food critic. From what Fenella had heard, wealthy Londoners were flying across just to have dinner there and then flying right back home again. If Donald had been on the island, he probably would have insisted on taking Fenella to try it as soon as it had opened.

She put the phone down and smiled at Mona. "Now I just have to find something to wear," she said.

"Wear the red dress that's three from the end on the left side of the wardrobe," Mona told her. "It's perfect for tonight."

Fenella didn't question Mona when it came to her wardrobe. The woman had excellent taste and gorgeous clothes and Fenella was just happy that Mona was willing to share them with her. She frowned now, though, when she pulled the dress in question out of the wardrobe.

"It's very low-cut at the front," she said hesitantly.

"It will look good on you," Mona said. "Try it on if you don't believe me."

"It isn't that I don't believe you," Fenella said. "It's my own eyes I don't believe."

A few minutes later she was standing in front of the large mirror in her bedroom. "It's very low-cut," she said.

"Yes, but it suits your figure," Mona countered.

"It certainly shows off my figure," Fenella said, "but this is our first date. I don't want the man to get the wrong idea about me."

"What were you wearing last night?"

Fenella told her about the black dress.

"No wonder you made such a good first impression," Mona said. "I loved that dress. But it does mean you must work harder tonight to make a good second impression. This is the perfect dress for that."

Fenella looked at herself again. It was a beautiful dress and it made her feel gorgeous and sexy, but she found herself blushing whenever she looked at the plunging neckline.

"Take two stiches in it, if you must," Mona said. "Timothy will roll over in his grave, but it won't ruin the lines of the dress."

Mona was, as always, exactly right. A few stitches made all of the difference. Fenella still felt just as wonderful, but without the embarrassment.

"It's perfect," she said happily.

"I think I shall go and change, too," Mona said. "I haven't seen Todd in years. I should make a bit of extra effort for him."

"He won't be able to see you," Fenella reminded her.

"Yes, I know, but I will know that I made the effort. That's what matters." Mona faded away while Fenella shook her head. Sometimes the woman made no sense at all. She changed back into her comfortable clothes and then curled up with a magazine. Perhaps she'd take a long, hot bubble bath before she got ready for dinner, she thought as she flipped through the glossy pages. The phone rang a few minutes later.

"Maggie, darling, how are you?" a familiar voice said.

"Jack, what do you want?" Fenella snapped. She wasn't feeling even the slightest bit of warmth toward the man, even after all of their years together.

"It's our anniversary," he replied. "I know you thought I'd forgotten, but I didn't."

"Our anniversary?" she repeated, feeling confused.

"Eleven years ago today we went out to dinner together for the first time," Jack told her.

"Really? Why do you remember that?" The man had never remembered Fenella's birthday, so it was odd that he suddenly was recalling their first date.

"I have every date that was significant to us burned into my memory," he replied.

"When's my birthday?" she countered.

"Oh, er, um, it's in December," he said, "but that date isn't significant to us as a couple. It's only significant to you."

"What about the date of our first meeting?"

"It was in August, or maybe July."

"It was in January, and I'm done with this conversation."

"You can't just hang up on me on our anniversary," Jack protested.

"It isn't really our anniversary. You probably have the date wrong."

"I don't. I'm positive."

"How can you be so sure?"

"I was just clearing out a drawer and I found the credit card receipt from our meal," he told her. "I'd saved it for all these years."

"Let me guess, it was in your big pile of receipts from everything you've charged since you graduated high school."

"I don't have receipts from that long ago. Anyway, I cleared everything out last week and I found the receipt from our first dinner together. We went to that little Italian place that quickly became one of our favorites."

Fenella laughed. "That wasn't our first date. On our first date, you took me to dinner at that little diner near campus, remember? I had the chicken and it was practically inedible, and you got food poisoning from your sandwich."

"My goodness. That was our first date? I'm surprised you agreed to go out with me again after that."

"I didn't always make the smartest decisions in those days."

"Hey, what's that supposed to mean?"

"Jack, we broke up over six months ago. Why are you still calling me?"

"Because I still love you and I miss you," he replied plaintively. "I want you to come back and fix my life for me. Everything was so good when you were here and now it's all a mess."

"What's wrong?"

"Everything. My laundry keeps shrinking and turning odd colors. I never have any food in my house and I keep forgetting to pay my bills.

Credit card companies get very grumpy when you miss a payment or two, did you know that?"

"I didn't. I never miss my payments."

"Yes, well, you used to help me keep track of mine, too. Now I have to do it all on my own and it simply isn't working."

"You don't need a girlfriend, you need a mother," Fenella snapped.

"I have a mother. She never liked you."

"I'm well aware of that."

"Anyway, she's busy with her own things, although she is coming to stay for a week at Thanksgiving. At least I'll have food and clean clothes that week."

"Jack, you're nearly sixty years old. Surely it's time for you to learn to look after yourself."

"I try, I truly do, but then I start thinking about the paper I'm working on and I forget all about real life. Real life isn't nearly as interesting as history, you know."

"I'm sorry, but you're going to have to start devoting a few minutes every day to real life. I'm sure once you get into some sort of routine, you'll be able to manage."

"That's exactly what I need. A routine. You can make one for me, right? You know what I need to do and when I need to do it better than anyone."

"Jack, I have my own life to live."

"Surely you can spare a few minutes to help out an old friend," Jack pleaded. "Just jot down a few notes for me about when I need to do things. I'll call you back in a few days and you can read me my list. Then, once it's all written down, I won't have to call you anymore."

Fenella frowned as she tried to think. If making a list for Jack would truly get him to stop calling, it was worth a few minutes of her time, she decided. "Okay, I'll make you a list, but once I've given it to you, you really must stop calling me all the time."

"Yes, of course, whatever you want," Jack replied. "I wish I would have thought of this before you left. You could have walked me through everything I'm supposed to know while you were still here."

"Yes, well, I'll do what I can, but it will only be a beginning. You'll have to add other things to the list, as I'm sure I'll forget something."

"Oh, I hope not. I'm really counting on you to fix everything."

I've been gone since March and nothing has changed, then, Fenella thought. "Have you been seeing anyone?" she asked.

"There is someone, but I don't want to talk about it. I don't want you to be jealous."

"I won't be jealous. I'll be happy for you. I want you to be happy." And maybe you'll be able to find someone to look after you so you can quit bothering me, she added silently.

"Yes, well, it's very early yet, but the department has just hired a new assistant professor and she's, well, she's very special."

"That's nice. What's her name?"

"Annabelle Simmons. She's quite a bit younger than I am, that's the only thing that worries me. She's only just earned her PhD."

"How old is she?"

"Probably around forty. She went back to school when her husband left her."

Fenella made a note of the name. She'd do a bit of online research on the woman the next time she had her laptop out. "I'm afraid I'm going to have to go," she told Jack.

"Let me guess. You have a date, don't you?"

"Yes, I do, actually."

"Who is it this time?"

"What's that supposed to mean?" Fenella asked.

"Every time I call you, you're just on your way out on a date and it never seems to be with the same man twice. I know you've mentioned someone called Peter as well as a Donald and a Daniel. Is tonight with one of them or someone else?"

"Someone else, actually. His name is Todd Hughes."

"Todd Hughes? Not the keyboard player? No, it can't be."

"He told me that he was a retired session musician. Apparently he played with a lot of different bands over the years."

"If I'm thinking of the right man, then that's right. He's played with just about every band that had any success in the seventies, eighties, and nineties. He plays keyboards mostly, but he plays about a dozen other instruments reasonably well. You know music is my guilty pleasure. Are you really having dinner with the Todd Hughes?"

"I don't know if he's the Todd Hughes, but I'm having dinner with a musician by that name. There could be ten men with the same name, all of whom play in bands, for all I know."

"I'm looking online right now. According to this, Todd is now retired and living in the Isle of Man. Life isn't fair," Jack complained. "I'd just about sell my soul to meet Todd Hughes, and you're going to have dinner with him. This wouldn't be happening if you'd let me move to the island with you."

"No, it wouldn't, because the man wouldn't be interested in buying me dinner if I had a boyfriend."

"But maybe we would have met him together and then he and I could become friends. I'll bet he still gets invited to amazing music industry parties."

"I didn't know you were interested in going to music industry parties."

"There are a lot of things you don't know about me," Jack said with a sniff. "And now I must go."

He put the phone down before Fenella could reply. She stared at her receiver for a second and then put it back in the cradle. It was time for her to get ready for her date with Todd, which made her feel nervous for many reasons.

8

Fenella studied herself in the mirror. Maybe she needed to take one more stitch in the neckline of the dress. As she reached for her sewing supplies, Mona made a noise behind her.

"Don't you dare do anything else to that dress. It's absolutely perfect the way it is right now. You'll ruin the fit if you fuss any further."

"I thought maybe one more stitch," Fenella said.

"No more stitches. I don't know why I share my wonderful clothes with you, I really don't."

"Maybe because you don't have a choice, being that you're dead and all."

"Now, that isn't nice," Mona said, looking sad. "I don't like being dead, you know. Well, okay, I like some parts of being dead, like not having to worry about dying any longer, but I'd rather be alive. Or maybe I wouldn't. Actually, being dead is quite freeing, in its own way. If I could simply be left alone to live my afterlife as I choose, death would be quite perfect, I suppose."

"Who isn't leaving you alone?"

Mona shrugged. "The administration would prefer if I would move on to the next part of the afterlife. Having me here is complicated for them, but as the choice is mine to make, they simply have to live with it. They do like to complain about it, though. Then there are the other ghosts and spirits. Some of them are incredibly difficult to get along with. And then there's Max."

"I thought you loved Max."

"I do love Max, but I don't think he quite understands that he's dead. He keeps talking about all of the things that he'd like to do one day, things that are quite impossible. And, of course, he misses Bryan terribly. He can't seem to understand why Bryan never comes to visit."

"Bryan was his business partner?"

"His partner, yes," Mona agreed.

"Where is he now?"

"I imagine he's moved on. He was always the more practical of the two. If he'd been told that he was expected to move on in a timely fashion, no doubt he did so. I expect he's watching over Max and wishing the dear man would do the same."

"Can't you suggest that to Max?"

"I can, but I'm not sure that I want to," Mona replied. "I'd miss him terribly if he went, you know. It's very selfish of me, but I love having him here with me, and I'm definitely not ready to go. I won't be leaving until you're properly settled on the island."

"How long to you think that will take?" Fenella asked, wondering if she really wanted to hear her aunt's answer.

"I thought you were well on your way when you and Daniel were together, but now that he's been momentarily sidetracked, well, perhaps you and Todd will have fun together for a while until Daniel comes back."

"What makes you think he's coming back?"

"I saw the look on his face when he was here the other day. He's still crazy about you, he's just stuck with Tiffany for the foreseeable future. It will all come right in the end for you and Daniel, unless you decide to fall in love with Todd."

"I only just met Todd. It's far too soon to talk about falling in love with the man."

"He'd be good for you, though. He probably has more money than you, and he's led a very exciting life. I'm sure he could introduce you to an amazing array of very famous people."

"I'm not really interested in meeting famous people," Fenella said thoughtfully. "I'm sure I'd just be awkward and tongue-tied around them. That wouldn't be any fun for anyone."

"How do I look, then?" Mona changed the subject. "I thought I should dress up for Todd."

Fenella looked over at her aunt. She was wearing a tiny little black dress that was perfect on her thirty-year-old figure. "I feel quite frumpy next to you," Fenella sighed.

"Take the extra stitches out of the dress," Mona suggested with a wink.

The idea made Fenella blush, which made Mona laugh. "Honestly, sometimes I do wonder if we're truly related," she said.

"It's a good thing Todd won't be able to see you," Fenella replied. "Otherwise he'd be disappointed that he's taking me out and not you."

"At the moment, I'm far too young for him," Mona countered. "You're much closer to his age."

A knock on the door stopped Fenella from reminding her aunt that she had been over ninety when she'd died. That was probably just as well, as Mona could be touchy about her age.

"You look stunning," Todd said. "These are for you." He handed her a bouquet of red roses. He was wearing a dark suit that was perfectly fitted to him. Fenella knew, from years of helping Jack buy suits, that it must have been expensive.

"That's a great suit," she said. "Come inside. I'll just put these in some water and then I'll be ready to go."

"Merrooowww," Katie objected.

Fenella laughed. "I'll just put these in some water and then feed Katie and then I'll be ready to go," she amended herself.

"What a gorgeous animal," Todd said. He bent down and stroked Katie's back. She snuggled up to him and then rolled over so he could scratch her tummy.

Fenella headed for the kitchen with Mona on her heels. "He likes Katie, anyway," Mona whispered. "I know you'll give him bonus points for that. Otherwise, he looks good. Age has made him more distinguished, but there's still something sexy about him as well."

Fenella very nearly replied. She only caught herself as Katie dashed into the room. Todd wasn't far behind.

"She said to tell you she wants her favorite tonight, with extra treats, as you are going out and she isn't," he announced.

"I suppose she can have her favorite, but she won't get her treats until I get home," Fenella laughed. She opened the cupboard and pulled down a can of Katie's food. "But the flowers get their water first," she added as she turned to find a vase.

"I can manage opening a can of cat food," Todd said. "If you'd like the help, that is."

"Just be careful you don't get anything on your suit," Fenella told him as she handed him the can opener.

"I'd rather something spilled on me than on you. That's a wonderful dress. It must have been made for you."

"It wasn't," Fenella told him as she filled up a vase with water. "It was made for my aunt, Mona Kelly. I inherited it, along with her estate."

Todd stared at her for a minute and then shook his head. "I'd heard that Mona's niece had moved to the island and I knew this was Mona's flat, but I still didn't put it all together, which was stupid of me. You're Mona's niece?"

"Yes, I am."

Todd sighed. "Remember what I said last night about never cheating on my wife? It was all true, but I'll tell you, if Mona would have ever given me a chance, I'd have taken it. She was amazing. Beautiful, but in an unconventional way. Smart, but adept at hiding it until she needed to put someone in his or her place. Funny, silly, gorgeous, amazing. I was crazy about her, and I was devastated when I heard that she'd passed away."

"You'll get over me eventually," Mona said, beaming at the tribute.

"She used to visit our family in the US when I was a child, but I never really knew her once I reached adulthood. I regret that now, of course," Fenella said.

"She had me here once or twice, to play for Max," Todd told her. "You know about Max?"

"Everyone tells me that he was the only man Mona ever loved."

"I tell you that," Mona interjected. "No one else could possibly understand."

"They had a very special relationship. When he fell ill, she did everything she could to keep his spirits up. She had the best food and wine flown in from all over the world. In the last few months of his illness, when he wasn't well enough to go out anywhere, she had people come here to entertain him. I came a few times to play, bringing odd friends with me, whoever was around."

Mona rattled off a list of some of the most famous singers in the world, from pop stars to country music icons and beyond. "They all came," Mona said softly. "They all came and played for Max." A single tear slid down Mona's cheek.

"Harvey arranged a lot of it for her, and he dealt with payments. Money was no object to Mona or Max, but most of us, well, we didn't want paying. Max and Mona were special and we were happy just to spend some time with them," Todd said.

"If these walls could talk," Mona sighed, looking around the spacious kitchen.

"It sounds as if Mona had a lot more fun here than I'm having," Fenella said. "After everything I've heard about her, that doesn't surprise me."

"I can make a few phone calls," Todd said. "Who would you like to have come and play for you?"

Fenella shook her head. "Right now I just want dinner," she replied.

Todd laughed. "I was so lost down memory lane that I nearly forgot about dinner. I'm starving, too. Let's go."

He gave Katie a quick pat and then he offered Fenella his arm. She stopped to get her handbag and slide on her shoes, and then she followed him out of the apartment. As they rode down to the lobby, she wondered if he'd have a limousine waiting for them outside. Instead, she found herself being helped into the passenger seat of an old American classic sports car. The steering wheel was even on the left side, suggesting that Todd had had the car imported from the US.

"I wasn't expecting this car," Fenella said after Todd had taken his place behind the steering wheel.

"I bought it in LA when it was brand new and I've moved it with me everywhere I've gone ever since. I have other cars, some of which are even practical, but this one is my favorite. I always use it for special occasions."

Fenella blushed. "You must take very good care of it."

"I do. I even fly a mechanic over from the US twice a year to change the oil and check everything over. That's less expensive than taking the car back and forth, anyway."

The drive to Ramsey didn't take long. Todd drove smoothly, with practiced ease, seemingly uninterested in speeding or showing off for Fenella. They chatted about the weather as they went.

"Do you worry about it when you park it?" Fenella asked as they climbed out of the car.

Todd shrugged. "Life's too short to worry about such things. I'm very fortunately in the position where I could repair or replace the car if anything happened to it, of course. That helps to mitigate any worries I may have."

The restaurant was small and there was a short queue of people at the door waiting to get inside. Todd and Fenella joined the back of the queue, and then Todd pulled out his mobile.

"Sorry about this, but I may be able to get us inside a bit faster," he told Fenella. He sent a quick text and then slipped his phone back into his pocket. A moment later the door opened and the famous chef who owned the restaurant stepped outside. Several people in the small crowd gasped before everyone seemed to begin speaking at once. From what Fenella could make out from the noise, they were all begging for a table, and sooner rather than later.

The man ignored everyone as his eyes searched the crowd. "Todd," he shouted after a minute. "There you are. I wasn't sure I believed you when you told me you were on the island."

"I live here now," Todd replied. "It's the perfect place for retirement."

"Tax advantages, eh," the chef winked. "Too bad I'm many years away from retirement myself. But come inside. I'll do you a special meal, something off the menu."

Todd stepped back and guided Fenella in front of him. They followed the chef into the building while several people muttered unhappily behind them.

"I don't think the people waiting are very happy," Fenella said in a low voice.

"We have a limited amount of space and limited opening hours. If people insist on simply turning up without a booking, we often can't accommodate them," the chef said. "We've only been open for a few weeks, so it's far too early to be thinking about expanding. Once the novelty wears off, we'll see if we're still turning people away."

"You will be," Todd said. "You could double your size and still be turning people away. The island needs more fine dining establishments like this one."

The man led them to a small table in the very back of the dimly lit dining room. "You're right next to the kitchen," the chef laughed. "This way I can keep an eye on you."

Todd held Fenella's chair for her and then took his own seat.

"Wine?" the chef asked.

"I'm driving," Todd replied.

"Do you still have that old American car? What did I offer you for it last time? I still want it, you know."

Todd shook his head. "Yes, I'm still driving it, and it isn't for sale. If you really impress me tonight, I might let you take it for a spin one day, though."

"I'd better get back to the kitchen, then," the man replied. "Tell me everything you don't like," he said to Fenella.

"Everything I don't like?" she repeated.

"Yes, exactly. I'm going to do you a special meal, but I don't want to give you things you don't like."

"I'm not terribly fond of seafood," Fenella said in an apologetic tone.

"Neither am I," Todd said.

"Yes, I remembered that about you," the chef said. "So no seafood for either of you. Anything else?"

Fenella thought for a minute and then shook her head. "I'm prepared to try just about anything else."

"Excellent. The first course will be out shortly. I'll send someone over to get your drinks order, as well."

The man disappeared into the kitchen. Fenella looked at Todd. "Our own special menu?"

"He's just showing off," Todd replied dismissively. "I just realized that I didn't introduce you to the man. Remind me when he comes back to correct that omission."

Fenella looked around the room. "It's lovey in here. The chandelier is gorgeous."

Todd looked up and then grinned at her. "I believe that is one of the chandeliers that used to hang in what was the grand ballroom of the Promenade View Hotel. When they decided to turn the building into flats, they sold off the gorgeous fixtures from the public areas. It's nice to see someone using some of them again."

"I'm surprised Mona didn't put one of them in her apartment," Fenella said. "It seems like something she would do."

Todd laughed. "It's probably too large, even for the grand sitting room in the flat. It might have taken away from the splendour of the view, too. It wouldn't surprise me to learn that she kept some of the serving trays and things from the old restaurant, though."

"There are some beautiful silver trays in my kitchen cupboards. Perhaps they are from the restaurant."

"Or maybe Max bought her them for Christmas or her birthday or just because," Todd smiled. "He loved showering her with gifts in between their frequent quarrels."

"I don't suppose you have any idea what they fought about?"

"Anything and nothing. They both had such huge personalities that their clashes seemed inevitable. They never stopped loving one another deeply, though, even in the midst of their most epic battles."

"I wish I'd visited the island when Mona and Max were still alive."

A nervous-looking waiter cleared his throat next to Fenella. "I don't mean to interrupt, but Chef asked me to take your drinks order?"

As Todd was driving and didn't want to drink, Fenella ordered a soda, too.

"I had a few glasses of wine last night, watching this amazing band perform. I don't need to drink tonight," she told Todd when he objected.

"I hope you really did enjoy last night," he replied. "I'm rather hoping you might come again tomorrow night."

"I won't promise, but I'd like to come if I can."

"I might just be in the audience myself tomorrow. Henry wants to play, but he isn't sure if he'll be up to it or not."

"I hope that means that Karla is doing better."

"I'm sure Karla will be fine. She's very young."

"Have you known her since she was a baby, then?"

"Off and on. I used to come to the island for breaks when I needed them. I'd arrive swearing that I wasn't going to play a single note for an entire fortnight or for however long I was planning on staying. Usually within twenty-four hours I'd be ringing around, trying to find somewhere to play. Henry used to let me join whatever band he was playing with at the time. Harriet always appreciated it when I took Henry's spot, because it meant Henry would get home earlier to help with the baby."

"Karla being the baby?"

"Yes. She probably wasn't any more work than any other baby, but Harriet seemed to struggle during Karla's early years. Maybe that was just because Karla was her first baby. They never did have any more, though."

"How often were you on the island over the years, then?"

"As I said, we lived here for several years, and then we used to visit two or three times a year. My wife loved it here and I enjoyed the music scene. It was completely unlike the cutthroat world I was used to living in. Here I could just play for fun and for the love of the music."

"So you've known Paul since he was young?"

"I probably met him fifteen years or so ago, when he was in his teens. The first time I saw him perform, it was already clear that he had real talent. Henry added him to his band and before long it was really Paul's band."

"He said something about being involved with Karla in their

teenaged years?" Fenella made the statement a question. The waiter dropped off their drinks and their first course before Todd replied.

"I remember young Karla hanging around a lot in those days. She seemed quite taken with Paul, but I don't think he paid her much attention, not until later. He's a few years older, maybe three or four, so she probably wasn't even in her teens yet when Paul first started working with the band."

"I'm not sure what this is, but it's delicious," Fenella said after a few bites. "Do you remember when Karla started seeing Phillip, then?"

Todd stared at her for a minute. "You seem very curious about Karla and Paul," he said eventually.

Fenella shook her head. "I'm sorry. Having found Phillip's body, I'm probably a little obsessed with the whole case. We can talk about something else, though. Whatever you like."

Todd put his knife and fork down and took Fenella's hand. "I didn't realize you found the body," he said softly. "In that case, your interest is understandable. Let me tell you everything I know about Karla and Paul and Phillip so you don't have to keep asking questions."

"We can talk about other things."

"And we will," he told her. He gave her hand a squeeze, and then released it and resumed eating. A moment later the waiter removed their empty plates and left them the next course.

"As I said, Karla used to hang out and watch the band practice and perform whenever she could. I could tell she had her sights set on Paul, even if her father didn't approve."

"Henry didn't approve?"

"At the time, I mentioned something about keeping an eye on Karla now that she was getting older and the band had a young and attractive lead singer, but he just laughed. I think he still thought of Karla as a baby, even though she was nearly into her teens. Anyway, nothing much came of it, not for a few years. I was traveling a lot, and then my wife passed away and I stopped coming to the island as much. The next time I saw them all, Karla was probably sixteen and she and Paul were very much a couple."

"Sixteen seems so young," Fenella sighed.

"My wife was fifteen when we met, and we were married on her eighteenth birthday," Todd told her. "I'd do it the exact same way again, given the chance."

Fenella smiled. "Things were different then, though, weren't they? People married younger and they stayed married through thick and thin."

"I suppose so. Anyway, Henry and Harriet didn't object, and Karla was clearly happy. I'm just telling you what I saw."

"Karla was happy? What about Paul?"

"I don't think he was unhappy, but from what I could tell, he was always more devoted to his music than to Karla. She didn't have any plans for what she wanted to do after school. When I asked her, she told me that she wanted to marry Paul and live happily ever after."

Fenella frowned. "Surely her parents encouraged her to do more than that with her life."

"I asked Henry about it, but he just laughed it off. Again, he and Harriet weren't worried, and it wasn't my place to interfere."

"So what happened next?" Fenella asked as Todd stopped to eat.

"Your next course," the waiter said as he exchanged empty plates for full ones.

"Next course? How many courses are there going to be?" Fenella asked.

"I believe Chef is planning for ten courses," the man replied.

"Ten? I can't eat ten courses," Fenella exclaimed.

"The portions will all be small," the waiter promised before he walked away.

"I can't eat ten courses," Fenella told Todd.

"Eat what you like and skip anything you don't like," he told her.

'What if I like it all?" Fenella sighed as she tasted the food on the plate in front of her. Whatever it was, it was truly incredible.

"Life got busy again; it was a few years before I came back to the island. Of course, I got in touch with Henry right away and he invited me to come and play with them again. Paul was even better than I'd remembered and he was starting to talk about going across to try to make it big. Every time he mentioned it, Karla would get upset, though. She didn't want to leave the island. After my fortnight's holiday, I told Paul that I'd do what I could to help him if he wanted to have a go in London."

"But he wasn't interested then?"

"Actually, he met me in London and I took him around to meet a few people. Then his mother fell ill unexpectedly and he returned to the island. He stayed here to help look after her for the next five years, which brings us up to about a year ago."

"And he was with Karla while his mother was ill?"

"I believe they broke up when he first went to London, actually. I think she was still angry with him for going, at least for the first year or two. I kept in touch with Paul, because I still wanted to help him if I could, but all I can tell you for certain is that he never mentioned Karla to me. I have to assume that means they were not longer seeing each other."

"So what happened a year ago?"

"Paul's mother finally passed away, and Paul rang me up. He was ready to have another go in London. I was already thinking about moving back here, but I met him in London and took him around again. He made some good contacts and I think he might actually find some success. I'm doing everything I can for him, anyway."

"That's very nice of you."

"He's very talented."

Another set of plates were exchanged. Fenella was pleased to find that the portions stayed small, but she was starting to get full anyway.

"And Karla married Phillip," she said.

"Yes, that was a bit of a surprise," Todd replied. "They'd grown up together, of course, but they hadn't seen each other in years. Henry told me he was shocked when Karla told him that they were getting married."

"Was Harriet surprised, too, or does Karla tell her mother more than she tells her father?"

"I think Harriet was as surprised as Henry was, but I've not actually discussed it with her, so I could be wrong. I don't think she and Karla are terribly close, though."

"They seemed to get along well when I met them."

"Did they? Maybe they've grown closer now that Karla is older. As

I said, Harriet seemed to find her difficult when she was very young."

"What about Phillip? Did you know him?"

"Not really. When Karla was younger, sometimes she'd have friends at the house when the band was practicing. I'm sure I met Phillip once or twice in that way, but he didn't make much of an impression on me. I got to know him a little bit in the past few months, since he'd been back on the island and I've been playing on and off with The Islanders."

"What did you think of him?"

"He seemed like a nice young man. A little, well, staid, maybe, but I thought that would probably be good for Karla."

"Do you have any idea who might have killed him?"

Todd sighed and then patted Fenella's hand. "I wish I did. Henry and I have been friends for a great many years. It's painful for me to see him so upset about something. Obviously, I worry about Karla, too. She's a sweet girl and she was so very happy with Phillip."

"Were you at the wedding?"

Todd shook his head. "They ran away to Scotland to get married," he told her. "Karla said afterwards that it was something of an impulsive decision."

"So her parents weren't there, either?"

"No, they didn't find out about it until it was all over."

Fenella frowned. "Did she know before she married Phillip that Paul was coming back to the island for a few months?"

"I don't know what she knew. I knew Paul was coming back and I'd discussed it with Henry. Whether he shared that information with his daughter or not, I can't say. I'm not sure why it matters, though. Paul and Karla split up years ago, remember."

"I just find the timing of the wedding to be odd," Fenella said. "It's probably just me, though. Why is Paul back on the island?"

"He needed a break from the pressure cooker that is London," Todd explained. "One of my contacts suggested that he try to put his own band together and maybe even try writing some of his own music. It's something he's always wanted to do, so he's given himself a few months out to work on those two things. He'll be back in London in early January, working on finding the right opportunity."

"And now he's caught up in a murder investigation," Fenella sighed. "I hope the police will solve the case quickly."

"I have a lot of faith in the island's constabulary. I'm sure they're doing everything in their power to work out what happened to Phillip. I can't help but hope that the whole thing may still turn out to have been just an unfortunate accident."

Fenella thought back to what she'd seen on the floor of the barn. There was no way the man's death had been an accident. Something in her expression obviously worried Todd.

"Time to talk about something else," he said quickly. He gave her hand a squeeze, and then sat back as the waiter delivered their next course. Once the waiter was gone, he began a lively story about a famous actor's birthday party where everything that could have gone wrong did.

Fenella was practically in tears from laughing when he finally finished the story. "You have led a fascinating life," she said.

"But I want to hear about you now," he countered. "Tell me your story."

She gave him a very abbreviated account of her life. "I'm afraid that wasn't very interesting," she said when she was done.

"I'm very interested," he replied softly.

Fenella felt herself blushing as yet another course arrived. Todd filled the rest of the evening with incredible stories from his life. In between each story, he insisted that she tell him something else about herself. The evening flew past, and after an incredible dessert, as they made their way back toward Douglas, Fenella found herself thinking that it had been a long time since she'd enjoyed herself that much.

"Thank you for a lovely evening," she told the man at her door.

"No, thank you," he said. He leaned forward and gave her a gentle kiss. "I hope you'll come and see us tomorrow night," he added, before kissing her again. The second kiss left Fenella breathless.

"If I don't see you tomorrow night, I'll ring you soon," he promised when he lifted his head. "Sleep well."

Fenella let herself into her apartment, still feeling slightly lightheaded.

9

"Did you have a nice evening?" Mona asked as Fenella made coffee the next morning.

"It was lovely," Fenella replied.

"Lovely? Tell me more."

"The food was incredible. Todd and the chef are friends, so he made us our own ten-course meal. I've no idea what I ate, but everything was delicious. Dessert was a chocolate soufflé, and there was very nearly a riot in the dining room when we were served because it isn't on the menu, apparently."

"And Todd was an interesting companion?"

"He was fascinating. His stories are amazing. I'd almost think he was making them up, but Jack was quite jealous that I'd even met the man. Apparently he's very famous in some circles."

"In musical circles, certainly," Mona agreed. "I was surprised that he remembered when I had him come to play for Max. Those little concerts were very special to me, but I didn't expect anyone else to remember them."

"He seems like an almost perfect man," Fenella sighed. "There must be something horribly wrong with him."

Mona chuckled. "Maybe he's the man you've been waiting for your whole life," she suggested.

"I don't know. It's far too early to say."

"And Daniel is still a problem."

"Daniel isn't a problem, exactly."

"Yes, he is. You'd started to fall in love with him before he went away, and now you're feeling disloyal when you think about Todd, even though Daniel is the one who's living with someone else."

"Maybe I should stop dating."

"Maybe you should just embrace everything that life offers you and stop worrying so much."

"Maybe," Fenella muttered. The knock on the door startled both of them.

"I'm a mess," Fenella said as she looked down at her pajamas.

"Yes, you are. I hope it isn't anyone important."

Fenella sighed. It was bound to be Daniel or Todd. It was always someone important when she looked her worst.

"Flowers," the man at the door said, handing Fenella a huge bouquet of roses. He turned and disappeared back down the corridor before Fenella could reply.

"Flowers," she said to Mona as she shut the door behind him.

"Let me guess, Todd had a wonderful time," Mona said. "Although it has been a few days since you've heard from Donald. Maybe he misses you."

Fenella carried the flowers into the kitchen and found another vase. Once the flowers were in water, she carried the vase into her bedroom. The flowers from last night were already filling the kitchen with fragrance. She pulled the card out of the middle of the bouquet before she walked back to the kitchen.

"Thank you for a wonderful evening, Todd," she read to Mona.

"Donald is slipping. He's not going to be happy when he hears about Todd."

"If he hears about Todd."

"Oh, he'll hear. If you don't tell him, someone else will. Todd gets talked about nearly as much as Donald, you know."

Fenella shook her head. "Why do people care? Todd should be able to have dinner with someone without the whole island talking about him."

"People are always interested in what the wealthy and the famous are doing. Make no mistake, people are talking about you, too."

"Which is probably why Daniel is avoiding me," Fenella sighed.

The phone cut across Mona's reply.

"Good morning," Donald's voice came down the line. "How are you?"

"I'm fine, thanks. How are you?"

"I've been better," he sighed. "No, that isn't fair. I'm just a bit fed up, really. Phoebe is improving, but slowly, and I'm ready to come home. I've had enough of living out of a suitcase and eating at fast-food restaurants. But none of that is your fault, and I didn't ring you to complain about my problems. Tell me what's going on in your life."

Fenella glanced at Mona. "Someone has already told him about you and Todd, so you may as well mention it," she said.

"Shelly and I went to Cregneash on Saturday and I found another body," Fenella said, leading with the story she hoped might distract the man.

"Oh, dear, you poor thing," Donald replied. "I hope it wasn't anyone you knew?"

"It was a man called Phillip Pierce," she said. "I'd met him earlier in the day, but we'd barely spoken. I met his wife, too. They'd only been married for a week."

"How sad for her. How did he die?"

"He was murdered."

Donald sighed. "How do you keep managing to get tied up in these things?"

"I wish I knew, because I'd stop doing whatever I'm doing," Fenella replied tightly.

"I didn't mean to make that sound like an accusation," he said. "I'm worried about you, though. Is Daniel investigating or is it out of his jurisdiction?"

"He's been asked to assist because the inspector in charge hasn't had much experience with murder cases."

"And how is Daniel?"

"As far as I know, he's fine. He brought a friend back from his course with him, so he's rather busy keeping her entertained."

"Her? I see."

"Yes, I suppose you do."

"I'm almost afraid to ask if there's anything else going on there."

"I had dinner at a new restaurant in Ramsey last night," Fenella said. She told Donald the name of the celebrity chef who'd opened the restaurant.

"I've been told the food is incredible, but the man himself is rude," Donald replied.

"He was lovely when I met him. He made us a special ten-course meal and everything was perfect."

"You didn't say who took you to dinner in Ramsey," Donald said casually.

"A man called Todd Hughes. We met at the Tale and Tail. He knows the dead man's father-in-law."

There was a long pause on the other end of the line. Fenella was just about to say something when Donald sighed.

"I didn't realize that Todd was on the island at the moment," he said.

"Yes, well, he is."

"I wonder how long he'll stay this time. I think the longest he's ever stayed was about a month. Then one of his friends will ring with an invitation to some exotic island retreat and he'll be gone for six months or more."

"Really? He told me he was more or less retired."

"Retired from work, maybe, but not from his old lifestyle. He loves to travel and he's never happy in one place for very long. It used to make his wife crazy."

"Well, he's here now, anyway, playing with a local band, The Islanders."

"I doubt he'll still be there in January, when I get back, but if he is, I'd love to see him perform. It's been years since I've had a chance to see him play."

"If they're still playing at the Tale and Tail, you should be able to see him without any problem. There were only four of us there on Sunday night."

"Once the word gets out that Todd is performing, the crowds will pick up considerably," Donald predicted. "Expect a great many women to come specifically to see him, as well. He's never short of female company."

"Thanks for the warning," Fenella said dryly.

Donald chuckled. "I just thought you should know what you're getting yourself into. Todd is a nice man who has led an interesting life. He's also very attractive, and if I stop to think about it, I could get quite jealous of him. That isn't in my nature, though."

"That's good to know."

"And now, sadly, I must go. I like to be at the hospital when the doctor does his rounds, otherwise I only hear things second- or third-hand."

"I hope your daughter continues to improve."

"Thank you. At the moment I'm trying to keep focused on her small improvements and ignore everything else. At some point, before we head back to the island, I'm going to have to discuss some of the harsh realities with her doctors. They believe there are going to be limits to her recovery, but I'm not prepared to hear them yet."

"I am sorry."

"I'm going to try to ring you more often. Talking to you is a small bright spot in my day."

"Even when I tell you about murder and other men?"

Donald laughed. "It's just nice to hear a friendly voice. I don't think I've ever been as lonely as I am right now."

Fenella swallowed a lump in her throat. "I'm sorry."

"I'd better go, otherwise I might just stay here and talk to you all day, and that won't help with Phoebe's recovery."

When she put the phone down, Fenella found that she had tears in her eyes. "He sounded miserable," she told Mona.

"He's worried about his daughter and he's upset that you and Todd are seeing one another. Donald is used to being in control of everything that matters to him, and now he's unable to simply pay for his daughter's recovery or prevent you from seeing Todd. I'm surprised he isn't flying back here to try to convince you to come to New York with him, really. His daughter must be worse that I realized."

"He said the doctors think there will be limits to her recovery."

"How sad," Mona said. "I was very fortunate that I remained healthy right up until the last few weeks before my death. Phoebe is very young. Perhaps the doctors are being unnecessarily pessimistic."

"I hope so."

Fenella had some lunch, after which she wandered into the center of Douglas to do some shopping that she didn't really need to do. She ended up with three books by authors she'd never heard of and a large box of chocolate truffles. Her phone was ringing as she opened the door.

"Hello?"

"You are home," Shelly said. "How was your dinner last night?"

"It was really nice. Todd was great company and the food was amazing."

"Want to tell me all about it over Chinese takeaway?"

"Well, that isn't exactly a chef-prepared ten-course dinner, but I suppose it will do," Fenella laughed. "What time?"

"Tell me what you want and I'll go and collect it and bring it to yours around six," Shelly replied. "After we eat, maybe we could go to the pub and watch the band for a short while."

"That sounds like a plan." Fenella listed a few of her favorites from the local restaurant and then put the phone down.

"I need to vacuum," she told Katie. "There appear to be cat hairs everywhere."

"She does seem to shed a great deal," Mona agreed.

Fenella ran the vacuum and then gave the kitchen a quick clean. While she worked, Mona sat and stared out the window.

"I've been thinking about the case," she said when Fenella finally sat down next to her. "We need to work out what happened to poor Phillip Pierce."

"That's Daniel's job, not ours."

"Yes, yes, of course, but we can talk about it, anyway."

"There's nothing to discuss. We know nothing about the dead man."

"Henry Jones was here, you know."

"Here? In the apartment, you mean?"

"Yes, he came with Todd when they came to play for Max."

"I suppose that's slightly interesting, but I can't see what it has to with the case."

"He brought Karla once. I didn't like her."

"Why not?"

"She was, I don't know, self-absorbed."

"How old was she?"

"It was just a few years ago, so early twenties, I suppose."

"I think everyone is self-absorbed at that age, aren't they?"

"She sang a few songs with the band."

"Did she? She sang a few Hop-tu-Naa songs for us, but no one said anything about her performing with the band."

"Well, she performed with them when they were here."

"That seems interesting, but I'm not sure why."

"Her father seemed to be very protective of her, by the way. And her mother rang her at least twice during the hour or so that they were here."

"Again, that may be interesting, but I can't see that it makes any difference to the murder investigation."

"What if her parents didn't approve of the marriage? Maybe they decided to solve that problem in the easiest possible way."

"Surely divorce is a good deal easier than murder?"

"Maybe, but maybe not. Maybe Phillip blackmailed Karla into marrying him and murder was the only way they could get rid of the man."

"I think your overactive imagination is getting away from you again. We've no reason to think that Karla was anything other than madly in love with her husband."

"But her parents didn't like him."

"I'm not sure that they didn't like him, first of all, but secondly, even if they hated him, it's a huge leap from there to murder."

"Let's talk about the other suspects, then," Mona suggested.

"What other suspects? I don't have the first clue who any of the suspects are."

"I'm sure Karla must be on the top of Daniel's list. The spouse always is, right?"

"I can't imagine that's the case with newlyweds, but for the sake of argument, you can have Karla at the top of your list if you want."

"Good. Her parents must be next, mustn't they? I don't know anything about Phillip's parents."

"Someone told me that they moved across when Phillip was twelve. I would imagine they're in the UK, therefore. I wonder if they'll come over here for the funeral or if they'll have the service over there."

"They should have it here. That way you can attend and see if you can spot the murderer."

"I'm not going to the man's funeral."

"You should. You found the body, after all."

Fenella shook her head. "That isn't how it works. I'd only just met the man. It would look odd if I turned up at his funeral."

"We'll argue about it once we find out where it's being held. In the meantime, we'll assume that Phillip's parents are across and couldn't have killed him. That brings us to Paul."

"Paul? Do you have a motive for Paul?"

"He's still in love with Karla, of course. When he got back to the island and found out that she'd married Phillip, he killed him."

"That would work if there was any evidence that he was still in love with Karla, but there isn't."

"Because he's trying to hide how he feels about her to divert suspicion."

"Maybe. While we're talking about motives, do you have one for Karla?"

"They were married. I'm sure she already had a long list, from the way he hung up wet towels to the way he squeezed the toothpaste, but I suspect if she did kill him it was because she is still in love with Paul."

"They dated briefly, when they were teenagers. No one has said anything to suggest that it was more than a childhood romance."

"So let's talk about the men who work for Manx National Heritage. Do either of them seem likely?"

"I can't imagine any motive for either of them."

"Maybe one of them was secretly in love with Karla."

"I really doubt that. Oliver was a nice man who seemed to love his job. I can't imagine any reason why he would kill anyone, really."

"What about the other man. Josh something, wasn't it?"

"Josh Gentry. What about him? He didn't have any reason to kill Phillip, at least not as far as I know."

"He wasn't happy about the Hop-tu-Naa activities. Maybe he wanted to make sure that they never happen again."

"Surely there are easier ways to sabotage the event besides murdering a man."

"Yes, but maybe it was first thing that came into Josh's head."

"I wonder about Phillip's work," Fenella changed the subject. She couldn't imagine Josh killing anyone, not after the discussion she'd had with the man about vegetarianism.

"He worked for one of the banks, didn't he?"

"Yes, he did. Maybe someone is embezzling or something and Phillip discovered it. There were hundreds of people at Cregneash on Saturday. The killer could have come down, carved a turnip, sang a few songs, and then murdered Phillip and left before the police even arrived."

"I hope Daniel is having better luck solving this case than we are," Mona sighed.

"So do I. Now let's talk about something more pleasant."

"You should ring Todd and thank him for the flowers."

"Oh, I, that is, I didn't even think about that. Surely I can just thank him tonight."

"If you can get to him through the crowds of adoring fans."

Fenella laughed. "There were four people in the whole pub on Sunday. I don't think tonight will be vastly different."

"It would be polite to ring him."

"Yes, okay." Fenella sighed and then picked up the phone. She'd jotted the man's number on the pad next to the receiver. It rang half a dozen times before the machine picked up.

"Oh, yes, hello," she said, feeling completely unprepared. "It's Fenella. I just wanted to thank you for the gorgeous flowers. Shelly and I are planning to come over to hear the band later, anyway, but I thought they deserved a phone call. Okay, well, see you later. Bye." She winced as she put the phone down.

"That was perhaps a bit awkward," Mona said. "Next time we'll practice first."

Fenella flushed. "I'll never be as cool as my Aunt Mona."

"No, dear, but you can at least learn to be more graceful."

A knock on the door brought Fenella to her feet. It was too early for Shelly, which was slightly worrying.

"Daniel? What a surprise," she said a moment later.

"I just have a few more questions for you," he said. "If you have a minute."

"Of course. Come in," she replied. "Shelly will be here soon with Chinese food. Should I call her and tell her to add a few extras to our order?"

"I can't stay," Daniel said quickly. "As I said, I just have a few more questions."

"Come and sit in the living room, then. We can watch the sea as we talk."

"Great." Daniel sat on a couch and stared out the window for several minutes. Mona took the seat next to him and studied him.

"What does he want?" she asked Fenella during the silence.

"How should I know?" Fenella replied.

"How should you know what?" Daniel asked, looking startled.

"Sorry, I was just thinking out loud," Fenella replied, glaring at Mona, who laughed.

"It's a wonderful view. I can't imagine living with it. I'd never shut the curtains."

"Do I have curtains?" Fenella asked. She'd never paid any attention, as she had no interest in shutting off the spectacular view.

"Tell me again about what happened when you walked into the first cottage at Cregneash," Daniel said, taking out his notebook.

Fenella wasn't sure she told the story in exactly the same way again, but she did her best to recount walking in on Karla and Phillip's embrace.

"And then Phillip left and we chatted with Karla for a short while before her parents arrived."

"Repeat that conversation, if you could, please."

Fenella did her best, but she couldn't help but feel as if she was forgetting things. "It's all starting to blur together," she said apologetically when she was done.

"That's fine. I know you're doing your best," he replied, giving her a warm smile that made her heart skip a beat.

"I am," she agreed.

He had her repeat every conversation that she'd had with Karla, Phillip, and Karla's parents again. She tried her hardest to work out exactly what he was looking for, but she didn't feel any the wiser when he was finished.

"Thank you for your time," he said after she'd finished repeating the conversation she'd had with Karla just minutes before she'd found the body. He got to his feet. "I can let myself out."

Fenella followed him to the door. She'd opened her mouth to say something, she wasn't sure what, when someone knocked.

"That worked out just right," Daniel said as Fenella opened the door to Shelly. "Thank you for your time."

He nodded at Shelly and then walked away down the corridor, leaving both women staring after him.

"What was that about?" Shelly asked.

"I wish I knew. He had me repeat all of the conversations that I had with Karla, Phillip, and her parents."

"Why?" Shelly wondered as she and Fenella unpacked the boxes of food.

"I've no idea. He didn't ask any additional questions. He just had me repeat the conversations and then he left."

"How odd. Do you think he suspects one of them of being the killer?"

"I don't know. Maybe? I mean, they had to have known the man better than most, right? And aren't most murder victims killed by the people closest to them?"

"That's what they say," Shelly agreed. "Maybe being single isn't so bad."

Fenella laughed. "You could be right."

They talked about Fenella's dinner the previous evening as they ate.

"It sounds like the perfect evening. Todd sounds too good to be true, really."

"I'm just waiting to find out what's wrong with him," Fenella told her. "There has to be something."

"Donald did warn you that he never wants to stay anywhere for long," Mona pointed out.

Fenella nodded and then remembered that Shelly couldn't hear Mona. "Donald called today. He suggested that Todd will be tired of the island soon and be off on another adventure."

"Maybe Todd will want to take you with him."

"Let's cross that bridge when we come to it," Fenella sighed. "For tonight, let's just go to the pub and have fun."

"I'll go and change," Shelly said. "Now that we know there's going to be a band, I feel as if I should make more of an effort."

"What am I going to wear?" Fenella asked, suddenly nervous. She hadn't known she was going to meet Todd on Sunday when she'd put on that wonderful black dress. How was she going to top that without looking like she was trying too hard?

"Have a look through Mona's wardrobe. If you haven't found anything by the time I get back, I'll help you," Shelly said.

As soon as Shelly was gone, Fenella turned to Mona. "What am I going to wear?"

"Blue," Mona told her. "He's seen you in black and red. It's time for something else altogether. There's a lovely little blue dress on the right side of the wardrobe. It has an asymmetric hem that makes it more interesting than it would be otherwise."

Fenella found the dress in question and slipped it on. "It's lovely," she sighed as she studied herself in the mirror.

"There's a matching hair clip in the bottom drawer. Put your hair up with that and you'll be all set."

It was easier to do what Mona suggested than to try to think of a better idea. The hair clip was beautiful and seemed to hold her hair surprisingly securely. Fenella touched up her makeup and then added a splash of Mona's perfume.

"Will I do?"

"You look very nice. And now I must dash. There's a party at

Peel Castle tonight and I don't want to be late. I don't get many chances to flirt with the Seventh Earl of Derby. I don't want to miss that." Mona faded away before Fenella could question the woman's words.

"She's making it all up," she told Katie as she refilled the animal's food and water bowls. "She's always making up things about the afterlife."

Katie shrugged and then drank some water. Shelly knocked a moment later.

"You look wonderful," she said as Fenella opened the door. "I love that dress."

"Thanks, on behalf of Mona."

Shelly laughed. "What time do they start?" she asked as Fenella locked her door.

"I'm not sure. Todd didn't say. I hope it isn't crowded."

"Crowded? Why would it be crowded? There were only four of us there on Sunday."

"I know, but someone suggested that it might get more crowded once people learned that the band was performing."

It was a cool but clear night as the pair walked the short distance to the Tale and Tail. They were still some distance away when Fenella realized that Mona had been right. There was a long line of people outside the pub, stretching down the sidewalk.

"My goodness, a queue," Shelly said. "There's never been a queue here before."

"Todd Hughes is playing tonight," the man at the end of the line told them. "We flew over from London just to hear him."

Fenella looked at Shelly and then sighed. "Maybe we should just go home," she said.

"But you told Todd you'd be here, didn't you?"

"I doubt he'll notice that I'm missing."

"They should have a special entrance for regulars," Shelly whispered. "I mean, we're here even when no one else is. That should count for something."

"We haven't moved an inch," Fenella said a few minutes later. "The pub is probably full to capacity already."

"It may be, at that," Shelly sighed. "Let's give it a few more minutes before we give up, though."

Fenella nodded, but she was ready to go home. Even if they got inside, it seemed unlikely that they'd get anywhere near the stage where the band was performing. She had Todd's number; she could ring him and explain why she'd missed the show.

A moment later, a familiar face appeared in the doorway. Fenella couldn't remember the man's name, but he was in the band. He walked out the door and walked down the line, eventually stopping in front of Fenella and Shelly. "Todd sent me out to see if you were stuck out here," he said in a low voice. "Come with me."

Shelly and Fenella exchanged glances and then followed the man as he kept walking away from the pub. While they'd been waiting, at least a dozen more people had joined the line behind them, and a small cheer went up from a few of them as Fenella and Shelly left their place in the line.

The man led them to the entrance for the hotel that made up the bulk of the building where the pub was located. They went up the steps, and the doorman held the door open for them.

"Right this way," the man from the band said. He took them down a corridor and through a door marked "Staff Only." From there, they went down a flight of stairs, through a dark basement, and then up another flight of stairs. When they emerged through another door, Fenella looked around. They were in what appeared to be a small storage cupboard.

"This way," the man said. He opened another door, and Fenella blinked in surprise. They were in the very back corner of the Tale and Tail. Fenella had never noticed the small door, and after it swung shut, she realized why. The door had its own bookcase attached, so when the door was shut, it was almost impossible to see. It was only because Fenella knew it was there that she was able to find it again.

"Wow, I didn't know that was there," Shelly said.

"Maybe we should just go right back out again," Fenella whispered. The pub was so full that she could barely see the bar in the middle of the room. There seemed to be thousands of people between her and the stage, and she was already starting to feel claustrophobic.

"I have to get back to the band," the man who'd found them said.

"Good luck," Fenella told him.

He laughed. "I'm just excited that we have a crowd. I thought we were doing well on Saturday at Cregneash, but this is something else. Maybe it will be my big break. I understand a lot of folks from London came over to hear Todd."

"Maybe Paul will get the break he deserves," Shelly suggested.

"I hope so. He needs it more than I do. Music is his whole life. I have a wife and kids and a real job," the man said. "If someone offered me a ton of money to tour with them, I'd go, but it would be a once in a lifetime and we'd put the money away for the kids. But this is all Paul has ever wanted. I hope he gets it."

The man disappeared into the crowd before either of the women could reply. Shelly looked at Fenella and sighed. "Should we try to get a drink or do you want to leave?"

"Let's try to get a drink," Fenella said. "Maybe the bar will clear out a little bit once the band actually starts."

A minute later, as the pair fought their way through the crowd, the band began to play. It seemed as if everyone rushed toward the stage, leaving the bar area nearly empty.

"Phew," their favorite bartender said. "It's crazy in here. The owners have three more staff coming in to help me with the crowds, but I don't know if that will be enough."

"After Sunday, we didn't think we'd have to fight a crowd tonight," Shelly said as the man handed them their usual drinks.

"Word got out that Todd Hughes was performing," the man told her. "I didn't even know who he was on Sunday."

"Neither did we," Fenella muttered.

She and Shelly sat at the bar and listened to the music as they sipped their drinks. Paul seemed to be feeding off the energy of the crowd, sounding even better than he'd sounded on Saturday.

"And now we're going to take a short break," he announced after forty minutes. "We'll see you back here in twenty minutes or so."

"Hold on to your drinks," the bartender said. "It's about to get crazy over here."

10

"Let's go upstairs," Shelly suggested. "We'll still be able to hear the band from up there, and it's bound to be quieter."

Fenella nodded and picked up her drink. She followed Shelly, feeling as if she were fighting against the current, as everyone else in the room seemed to be heading toward the bar.

A quick glance at the stage showed her that the band was completely surrounded by people, including a great many young and attractive women. As she climbed the stairs, Fenella spotted Todd. The women on either side of him weren't exactly young, but they were certainly younger than Fenella. They were both wearing short and tight dresses and, to Fenella's mind at least, too much makeup. One of them leaned toward Todd and then slid her arm around him.

"Come on, move," the man on the stairs behind Fenella barked.

She sighed and then continued on her way to the upper level. It was definitely less crowded up there, but it was still busier than normal. Shelly and Fenella finally found two empty chairs in a dark corner and quickly claimed them.

"We should just go home," Fenella sighed after she'd sipped her drink. "This isn't any fun at all."

"Did you see Todd?"

"He was standing next to the stage with a beautiful woman on each arm."

"Oh, dear. The poor man."

Fenella shook her head. "He didn't look at all unhappy."

Shelly patted her arm. "He's working. I'm sure this sort of thing happens all the time. If you're actually going to get involved with the man, you'll have to get used to it."

"Being single is a lot easier."

"Yes, I suppose it is."

Fenella frowned. "Are you giving up on Gordon?"

"I don't know what I'm doing about Gordon. His being away has given me some time to think, but all I'm doing is getting more confused."

Now Fenella patted Shelly's arm. "See how you feel when he gets back."

Shelly nodded. "Unless I meet someone else between now and then."

"There are plenty of fish in the sea."

"I don't know about that, but I think I'm going to start looking around a little bit. If nothing else, I can always consider it research for my book."

"How is your book coming?"

"Slowly, but I'm getting words on the page, or into the computer, really. I finished chapter four this morning. I need to sit down and work out what's going to happen next before I can continue."

"Good for you."

"I don't know if I'll ever finish it, and even if I do, I may never let anyone read it, but I'm having fun writing it. Okay, I'm having fun some of the time, anyway. It can be incredibly frustrating as well."

"Any time you want to talk about it, you know where to find me," Fenella told her.

"I may have to take you up on that. As I said, I'm trying to work out where the story is going to go next, but I reckon I'll need something around fifteen chapters and I've no idea how to fill them all."

"Boy meets girl. Boy and girl fall in love. Boy and girl have conflict.

Boy and girl get back together and live happily ever after. That isn't anything like fifteen chapters worth of story, is it?"

Shelly laughed. "Not at all. I needed two chapters to introduce the main characters and now I've added in their source of conflict. What can they do for the next hundred pages or so?"

"I don't imagine they can just sit in the pub and chat," Fenella said. "At least not for a hundred pages."

"I should have a scene in a pub," Shelly exclaimed. "I could call it the Bark and Brew and it could be a pub that takes in stray dogs."

"Dogs are a lot more work than cats. Who takes them all for their walks and things?"

"Pub customers could volunteer to walk them. Maybe they even get a free drink for each dog they walk or something."

"It sounds interesting, anyway," Fenella said, "and as it's fictional, you can make sure that it works properly."

"Or maybe it will all go horribly wrong and my heroine will end up with half a dozen dogs staying in her house with her. That might be interesting."

"I'm not sure that interesting is the right word."

"There you are," a man's voice interrupted. "Todd sent me to find you."

Fenella looked up at Paul and smiled. "We wanted to get away from the crowd."

"So does Todd, but he's too polite to push his way up here," Paul replied. "Stan said he brought you in the back way, but he wasn't sure where you'd ended up once the music started."

"We sat at the bar for a while and then came up here," Shelly told the man. "We were just talking about going home, actually. It's too busy to be fun."

"Come down and watch the next set," the man suggested. "You can sit in the reserved seating, right in front of the stage."

"There's reserved seating?" Fenella asked.

"There is now," Paul laughed. "I can't believe the change from Sunday to today. It's a great experience for me, even if it is humbling. I'm the lead singer and the crowd is mostly ignoring me."

"I won't ignore you," a pretty blonde said, slipping her arm around Paul's waist. "I'm Eve and I think you're gorgeous."

"Thanks," Paul replied, blushing as he tried to remove himself from the woman's grasp. "But I need to get back downstairs."

"Maybe we could get together after the show," Eve cooed. She leaned forward and whispered something in Paul's ear. He turned bright red and looked desperately at Fenella.

"You're coming down with me, right?" he asked.

Fenella looked at Shelly, who shrugged. "We may as well, since we're here," Shelly said.

The pair got to their feet and followed Paul toward the elevator. Eve called after them. "I meant what I said. Look for me later."

A large man in a black T-shirt that said "Security" across it was standing at the elevator door. He nodded at Paul and then let the trio into the waiting car. As the doors slid shut, Shelly spoke.

"When did they get security?" she asked.

"The police insisted as soon as the queues started developing just after midday," Paul told her.

"Midday?" Shelly echoed.

"Yeah, Todd is quite famous, really," Paul grinned. "No one has ever queued up to hear me perform."

"Maybe not yet, but maybe some day," Fenella said.

"I hope so, although it's all a bit overwhelming, if I'm honest," the man said. "I love the energy that a big crowd brings, but it's a little scary, too."

The elevator doors slid open and a second security guard nodded at them. "George will walk you through," he told Paul.

A moment later another man in an identical black T-shirt joined them. He was almost as wide as he was tall and he looked mean.

"Ready?" he asked Paul.

Paul nodded and then glanced at Fenella and Shelly. "You go first," he said, gesturing for them to follow George.

"This is crazy," Shelly whispered as George began to push his way through the crowd. He shouted "Security!" at intervals, but most people seemed to be ignoring him. When they finally reached the stage, George stopped.

"Everyone okay?" he asked, looking at Fenella.

"I think so, but that wasn't fun," she replied.

He shrugged. "Everyone just wants to hear Todd Hughes perform. I don't blame them. If I hadn't been hired to help out, I'd be in the crowd myself."

"There are chairs here for you," Paul said, pointing to a small roped-off area to the left of the stage. There were six chairs in the area and they were all empty.

"This makes me uncomfortable," Fenella said as she and Shelly took seats.

"Doesn't it make you feel important?" Shelly asked.

"Not really. And I think half of the people here would happily kill me for this chair."

Shelly looked around at the crowd. "Not half maybe a quarter, though."

Fenella sighed. "We should have stayed home."

"And we're back," Paul said from the stage.

The crowd cheered as the band returned behind him. Todd gave Fenella a huge smile that left her feeling slightly better about being there. An hour later, Todd finished a song with a flourish on the keyboards.

"That was wonderful," Shelly said. "I'm so glad we stayed."

"It was very good," Fenella agreed. "They all have so much talent."

"Maybe the crowd will start to thin out now," Shelly said hopefully. "I could do with another drink, but there's no way we'll be able to get to the bar and back before the next set."

"Ladies, drinks?" one of the men from the band asked. He held up a bottle of wine and then refilled the glasses they'd brought with them from earlier. "Let me know if you need more," he said. "We've half a dozen bottles behind the stage."

"Thank you," Shelly told him.

He nodded and then rejoined some of the other band members who were standing nearby. Paul was talking to a pretty brunette who seemed to be hanging on his every word. Fenella looked around for Todd but couldn't see him. He was probably at the center of the mass of people on the far side of the stage, she decided.

"What a crowd," Henry Jones said as he dropped into the empty seat next to Shelly. "I'd love to think that they all would have turned up if I were the one playing, but I suspect nearly everyone is here for Todd."

"How are you?" Shelly asked.

He shrugged. "I've been better, if I'm honest, but under the circumstances, I suppose I'm doing okay. You were at Cregneash on Saturday, weren't you?"

"Yes, we were both there," Shelly replied.

He nodded. "I knew you looked familiar, but Saturday is something of a blur now. Things had been going so well earlier in the day, too. With Paul back, the band was in fine form, though I say that myself."

"I thought you were wonderful," Shelly said.

"Thank you. How are they doing tonight?"

"The crowd seems to be enjoying themselves," Shelly told him. "I think they're brilliant."

"I wanted to get here earlier, but I couldn't get away. Now I'm in an awkward position, though. I should be ready to rejoin the group by Sunday, but I doubt they'll want me back," he sighed.

"We definitely want you back," Paul said as he joined them. "Todd doesn't want to keep doing this. He's meant to be retired. He'll be thrilled if you come back."

"But you'll lose your crowds," Henry argued.

Paul shrugged. "This was just supposed to be a fun little gig once or twice a week to give us all something to do for a few months until the new year. No one was expecting crowds like this, anyway."

"We'll discuss it tomorrow, at rehearsal," Henry said. "I want to do what's best for the whole band, and especially what's best for you, Paul."

"I appreciate that. I'm sure some of the other guys will want to weigh in tomorrow, too," Paul replied. "Do you need a drink before we start back up?"

"No, I'm fine. There's too much going on at the moment. I'm not drinking."

Paul nodded and then rejoined the other band members at the side of the stage. Fenella still hadn't seen Todd anywhere.

"I hope Karla is okay," Shelly said after a moment.

"She's, well, I think she'll be okay eventually," Henry replied. "I wasn't happy when she and Phillip ran off and got married without telling anyone, but that didn't mean that I didn't like the young man. Anyway, I'm sure that was mostly Karla's doing. She's always been impulsive."

"He seemed quite nice when he was helping us with our turnips," Fenella said.

"Yes, he was very nice. In some ways, that was why I wasn't happy about the marriage. I worried that he was too nice and that Karla would walk all over him. But they were very happy together, really."

"They seemed happy when we met them," Shelly offered.

"I almost wish he wasn't such a nice person. Karla is convinced that she'll never find anyone else as wonderful again."

"She's very young," Shelly said. "She just needs time to recover from her loss."

"It doesn't help that he died in such a horrible way. I'm sixty-two, and this is the first time I've ever known anyone who was murdered. I still can't quite get my head around it, really. It's the sort of thing that happens in books or on television, not to perfectly ordinary people in the real world."

"I'm sure everyone will feel better when the police solve the case," Fenella suggested.

"I don't know. I suppose it's silly, but I keep worrying that whatever they find is going to be even more upsetting to Karla. I mean, the man was murdered. That suggests that he was involved in something criminal, doesn't it? I'm afraid my daughter is going to discover that the man she loved was really a drug dealer or a paid assassin or something."

Fenella nearly laughed out loud. "I don't think either of those things are likely," she said.

"Then who killed him? He was just an ordinary man, living an ordinary life. No one had any reason to kill him," Henry argued.

"The police will work it all out," Shelly said confidently. "Inspector Robinson is excellent at solving murder cases."

"I hope you're right. And I hope I'm wrong about Phillip, but I simply can't imagine why he was killed."

"Maybe it was something to do with his work," Shelly suggested.

"That's an idea. I'll have to talk to Karla about that. She knows more about what he did than I do. I know he worked for a bank, but that's about all I know."

"We're just about ready to start again," Paul announced from the stage. "And we've a special treat for you this set. Henry, will you join us for a few numbers?"

Henry flushed and shook his head. "I'm just here to watch," he said. "Or listen, really."

"Oh, come on, just a few songs," Paul coaxed him. "What do you think?" he asked the crowd.

A moment later the chant of "Henry, Henry" was echoing around the room.

"Do you think they'd stop if they knew that he'd be taking Todd's place in the lineup?" Shelly whispered to Fenella. Fenella nodded.

"Maybe one number, then," Henry said. He got to his feet and the crowd cheered. Paul stepped back to let him up onto the stage, where he crossed to Todd. The two had a whispered conversation, and then Todd took a few steps backwards.

Paul was watching them closely and when Henry nodded, the band began to play. Fenella watched Todd. He stayed on the stage, but didn't actually do anything through the song. At the end of it, as the crowd cheered, Todd slipped off the stage. The stage was brightly lit, which meant most of the crowd probably didn't see Todd as he made his way to the small section of seats where Fenella and Shelly were sitting.

"Can we go now?" he whispered to Fenella as she took the seat next to her.

"They'd riot," she whispered back, leaning close to the man so that he could hear her over the band.

"Maybe they wouldn't notice. Henry is doing a great job."

Fenella nodded, but even to her untrained ear, there was a clear difference in the sounds that were now coming from the stage. Henry was talented, but he lacked the polish that Todd brought to his performance. At least that was how Fenella would have described it if anyone had asked.

Todd took her hand and gave it a squeeze. "I've been trying to get away to talk to you all night, but I keep getting trapped by crowds of people."

"It's fine," she replied.

"But it isn't. This is why my wife rarely came to my shows. I love performing, but with crowds like this it becomes hard work. And this pub isn't really set up for it, not properly. The band needs a place to go to get away from the public between sets and there simply isn't anywhere for us to go."

"I don't think the pub's management was expecting crowds like this," Fenella said.

"No, I'm sure they weren't. It's my fault, of course. I invited a few friends from across because I wanted them to see Paul. As soon as word got out, things went crazy."

"Henry said he might be ready to come back by Sunday."

"I hope he is. I'm ready to go back to being retired right now," Todd said emphatically.

As the band finished another song, the crowd applauded, but Fenella could hear a real difference from earlier. "I think the audience has noticed that you're gone," she said.

"Time for me to slip back up on stage and lend a hand, then," he sighed. "Please stay after we finish. Five minutes with you at the end will make it all worthwhile."

Fenella hesitated. She was ready to go home.

"Or go," Todd said quickly. "I won't blame you one bit if you leave. I probably would, if I were in your shoes."

"I just don't know what Shelly wants to do," Fenella replied as the band started another song. "If she wants to go, I'll go with her."

"Spend the day with me tomorrow, then," he said. "I'll ring you in the morning to arrange it all."

"Okay," Fenella replied, surprising herself.

He leaned over and gave her a quick kiss. "I still want you to stay," he told her. "But I truly do understand."

As the crowd clapped a few times at the end of the song, Todd dashed away. He was back on stage, standing behind Henry, a moment later. After a few songs where both Henry and Todd played, Henry waved to the crowd and rejoined Fenella and Shelly.

"You're very good," Shelly said quickly.

Henry laughed. "Thank you, but I know my limits. Todd is a much better musician. Playing with him just then was probably the high point of my musical career."

Now that Todd was back, the entire room felt different. Fenella found that she didn't want to leave nearly as much as she listened to Paul and the band. When they finally stopped, she looked at Henry. "Will they play another set?" she asked.

He glanced at the clock and then looked around the room. "I expect so. It's not that late and it's still pretty busy. I hope, for the sake of the people who were still queuing when I arrived, that enough people have left to allow them to let everyone else in."

"Do you want to stay or go?" Fenella asked Shelly.

"One more set? Let's stay," Shelly said. "I'm really enjoying myself."

A couple of the men from the band came over and sat with them during the break. Henry reintroduced them to the women and they all chatted easily amongst themselves. After a while, it became obvious to Fenella that both men were flirting with Shelly. As they were both around her age and seemed quite nice, she settled back to watch what would happen next.

"We're all going back to Stan's after the show," one of the men, called Mark, said. "You ladies should come with us. His wife is going to have food and drinks ready for us."

"I think I need to go home and get some sleep," Shelly replied. "I'm not used to late nights like this."

"You were here on Sunday, too," Tim, the other man, interjected. "When we didn't have a crowd."

Shelly nodded. "We saw you at Cregneash on Saturday as well."

"Oliver introduced you to us, didn't he?" Mark asked. "Things were a bit crazy down there, but I definitely remember you."

Shelly blushed. "It was busy, with all the families and small children."

"And then the murder," Tim added. "That was horrible. Sorry, Henry, I'm sure you don't want to talk about it."

Henry shrugged. "I'm sure everyone on the island is talking about it, aren't they? Karla is afraid to leave the house. She's sure everyone will point and stare."

"Once the police work out what happened, the talk will all die down," Tim said. "I reckon he had some trouble across and came to the island to get away from it. Whatever the problem was, though, it clearly followed him here."

"Trouble across?" Henry echoed. "Yes, that seems a good possibility. I don't know much about his life across."

"Ready?" Paul asked from a few feet away.

Mark and Tim got to their feet. "You're staying for the next set, aren't you?" Tim asked Shelly.

"I suppose so," she replied, looking at Fenella.

"Excellent," Mark said. "We can talk when we're done for the night."

As the two men walked away, Henry chuckled. "Those two always did go for the same women," he told Shelly. "Don't let them fight over you, though. Pick one and let them both know. Tim's first wife had an affair with Mark and the band nearly broke up over it."

Shelly shook her head, blushing fiercely as she did so. "I don't think..." she began.

"Tim would be a better bet, really. Mark is still married, although they've been separated for a few months now. But Tim is single and it would be good for him to find a nice woman to spend some time with. I suggest you focus on him, really," Henry said.

Shelly looked at Fenella. "Which one was Tim?" she hissed softly.

Fenella laughed. "The better-looking one," she replied.

The last set seemed to go by very quickly. Fenella sipped wine from the bottle that Tim and Mark had brought with them when they'd come over. She and Shelly clapped as loudly as everyone else when the band finally finished their last song.

"Paul's very good, but Todd was carrying the whole band for the last three songs," Henry said. "Paul needs to work on his stamina. He's too young to get tired out that easily."

"I thought it was all wonderful," Shelly said.

"I'm sure most of the audience did as well," Henry replied.

The band members began to pack up their instruments. Todd looked over at Fenella and then shook his head.

"He's going to have to sneak out another way," Henry said. "Otherwise the crowd will never leave. Everyone wants to talk to him."

Fenella watched as two of the security men walked Todd toward the hidden door. They disappeared through it as a few people shouted Todd's name.

"I'm going to go and pack up Todd's things," Henry said.

Fenella and Shelly stood up. "Now what?" Shelly asked.

"I've no idea. Should we leave?"

Shelly glanced at the stage as Mark jumped off of it. "You aren't thinking about sneaking away, are you?" he asked, winking at Shelly.

"We were just discussing it," she replied.

"You really should come to the party at Stan's house," he said.

"I'm exhausted," Shelly told him. "I'm not used to late nights."

He laughed. "I'm not either, really, but we don't do this very often. I'm just reliving my wild youth. Not that it was that wild, if I'm honest."

Fenella watched as the security team began to clear the room. After a few minutes, she could actually see the bar in the middle of the space. It didn't seem that long before the only people left were the bar staff, the security men, and the band, aside from Shelly and Fenella.

"I'm glad that's over," Todd said as he reappeared next to Fenella. "It was fun, but I'm too old for this."

"We won't have the same problem on Sunday," Henry said. "We'll be lucky to have half a dozen people in our audience."

"We'll come," Shelly said, glancing at Fenella, who nodded.

"And I'll come," Todd said with a grin. "Just to watch, though." He put his arm around Fenella. "Maybe we can sit together," he suggested.

"Maybe," she replied.

He frowned. "You're angry with me," he said, dropping his arm.

"No, I'm not," she countered. "I'm just tired. We enjoyed the show, but now I need some sleep. Katie will have me up at seven tomorrow no matter what time I get to bed."

"Tell her that I said you must be allowed to sleep until eight," Todd replied. "She liked me. She'll listen."

Fenella laughed in spite of her tiredness. "I hope you're right."

"I'm always right. But now I believe we have a party to go to, don't we?" he asked Mark.

"Stan's wife is doing food," he replied.

Todd grinned. "I'm far too wound up to go home and go to bed. I'd love it if you'd join me," he told Fenella, "but I will understand if you won't."

"I'm sorry, but I'm too tired," she replied. "Maybe another time."

"Henry, you'll come, won't you?" Todd asked.

Henry shook his head. "I need to get home. I hadn't planned on staying this long. Harriet is worn out from looking after Karla. I need to get back and help her."

"We'll see you at rehearsals tomorrow, though, right?" Mark asked.

"Yes, I'll be there tomorrow, but not Thursday. Actually, we're having a memorial service on Thursday afternoon at two o'clock," Henry said. "I'm sure Karla would be grateful if you could all come along and pay your respects to Phillip."

A murmur went through the band. "Sure," someone said. "Yeah, I'll be there," someone else added.

"You ladies are welcome as well," Henry said to Fenella and Shelly. "I'd much rather have a large turnout so that Karla has lots of different people to speak to during the afternoon. Phillip's parents will be there as well. I'm sure they'd appreciate hearing what you thought of their son."

Fenella nodded while she desperately tried to think of a reason why she couldn't go to the service. The last thing she wanted to do was speak to Phillip's parents.

"Let me walk you home, at least," Todd said in her ear as Henry turned to go.

"You have to get to your party," Fenella reminded him.

"The guys are still packing up," he said. "Anyway, they'll start without me. I don't mind being a few minutes late."

Shelly and Tim were chatting together as Fenella finished her last sip of wine. She put her glass down and smiled at Todd. "Let's go, then," she said. "Shelly? Are you ready?"

"Yes, of course," Shelly said.

"I'll walk you home," Tim offered.

"Oh, that's okay, I mean, we're fine," Shelly stammered.

"But I'll feel better knowing you got home safely," he countered. He offered her his arm and after a moment she took it.

Todd winked at Fenella. "They're cute together," he whispered.

"You'll have to tell me all about him," she replied. "Shelly is very important to me."

"We're all getting too old to play the games that were common when we were younger," Todd said as they walked out of the building.

"Todd, Todd," a woman's voice shouted. The woman who rushed toward them looked to be around fifty. "I love you so much," she said. "Come home with me."

Todd sighed. "I'm sorry, but I'm seeing someone."

The woman gave Fenella a dismissive look. "You can do better," she snapped.

"I don't happen to agree," Todd said lightly. He put his arm around Fenella and began to lead her away.

"Todd," another voice called. This one was male.

He sighed. "This is going to be a long walk, isn't it?" he muttered to Fenella.

"Todd, I'm such a huge fan of your work. I have a demo I want you to hear. It's my own song. I have it on my phone. Listen," the young man said in a rush.

Todd held up a hand. "I'm sorry, but now isn't the time. I'm too tired to give it proper attention. Ring my office and make an appointment to come and see me. Tell Helen, that's my receptionist, that I said it was okay."

"Really? Seriously? Thank you so much."

The man was still babbling as Todd and Fenella took a few more steps. When someone else called Todd's name, he stopped. "Hey, Tim, take Fenella with you," he said.

Tim and Shelly were only a few steps away. They stopped and turned to see what was going on behind them.

"I need to get back inside," Todd said to Fenella as another middle-aged woman advanced toward them. "By tomorrow no one will remember who I am, but for tonight I need to hide."

"I understand," Fenella replied.

As the woman began to tell Todd how much she loved him, Todd pulled Fenella into a kiss. For a moment Fenella let herself get lost in the experience, but that wasn't easy under the circumstances. When Todd lifted his head, he sighed. "Some day we'll laugh about this," he whispered as the woman began shouting his name again.

"I hope so," Fenella replied.

She turned and caught up to Tim and Shelly as Todd rushed back into the pub. Tim walked them to Shelly's door and then gave Shelly a polite kiss on the cheek. "Maybe we could have dinner one of these nights," he suggested.

Shelly gave him her phone number while Fenella hunted around in her handbag for her keycard. She purposely didn't find it until Tim was walking back toward the elevators.

"Thanks," Shelly said before she let herself into her apartment.

"I'll talk to you tomorrow," Fenella told her friend. Feeling as if she wanted to either laugh, cry, or scream, Fenella gave Katie a midnight snack and then crawled into bed. "Oh, and Todd says you mustn't wake me before eight," she told the animal just before she fell asleep.

11

When Katie began tapping Fenella's nose the next morning, she groaned. "It can't be morning. I just shut my eyes."

"Merrrow," Katie said before she jumped down and ran into the kitchen. Fenella could hear her complaining loudly in front of her empty food bowl a moment later.

Sighing, she sat up in bed and looked at the clock. It was eight, which either meant that Katie had understood and listened to Todd or that the kitten had simply overslept. Knowing she'd had an extra hour of sleep made Fenella feel slightly better, anyway. She gave Katie her breakfast and set the coffee maker going before she took a shower.

"What should I wear?" she asked her reflection.

"Where are you going?" Mona asked, making Fenella jump.

"Can't you make some noise as you come in or something?" Fenella demanded.

"I'll try to remember to do just that," Mona promised. "Tell me about last night. How was the pub?"

"Crowded. Very, very crowded. Apparently a bunch of people from London heard that Todd was playing in a band here and they all turned up to listen and then throw themselves at him."

"Oh, dear. That doesn't sound at all fun."

"Parts of it were fun, actually. The band was excellent, at least when Todd was playing. He stepped out and let Henry do a few songs, and the difference was considerable."

"I'm sure the audience didn't appreciate that."

"They behaved, anyway. But it was a long and late night and I wasn't really comfortable surrounded by all those people."

"I hope Todd was attentive in spite of the crowds."

"I'm sure he did his best. It was difficult. He tried to walk me home, but three different people stopped him within a few feet of the pub's entrance. He finally gave up and went back inside. They had security inside."

"Security at the Tale and Tail? That must have been something to see. I hope the books all made it safely through the night."

"From what I could see, no one was interested in the books," Fenella assured her.

"What are you doing today, then, that has you wondering what to wear? You're usually happy with jeans and a sweatshirt."

Fenella flushed. "I like to be comfortable when I'm just staying home and relaxing."

"Which is all you normally do, so today must be something special. Let me guess. You're seeing Todd."

"He said something about our spending the day together, maybe."

"Doing what?"

"He didn't say."

"That's a problem. For now, perhaps a nice pair of trousers and a light jumper would be best. You can always change if necessary."

"A jumper?"

"Yes, what you'd call a sweater," Mona sighed. "You really must make an effort to learn to speak English."

Fenella didn't bother to argue. Instead, she opened Mona's wardrobe and flipped through it. "How about this one?" she asked, holding up a light grey sweater.

"It's nice, but I think the green one on the end will highlight your eyes. There are some dark grey trousers in the third drawer that should work well with the green jumper."

Fenella had been living with Mona for long enough to know better than to argue with her when it came to clothes. She dug out the trousers and pulled them on. "They fit perfectly," she said.

"Of course they do."

Fenella was going to ask her aunt why, but decided against it. Mona wouldn't have explained anyway, and maybe she was better off not knowing. The sweater did exactly what Mona had suggested. It made Fenella's eyes looked brighter and larger.

She made herself some breakfast and then paced around the kitchen for several minutes. "What time do you think he'll call?" she asked Mona after a while.

"What time did you get home?"

"It was late, but he was going to one of the band member's houses for a party after. I'm sure he didn't get home until very late indeed."

"So he probably won't be up for hours yet. You may as well stop pacing and read a book or something." She faded away as Fenella headed for a bookcase.

Fenella grabbed the first book she touched on the nearest bookshelf and curled up with it on a couch. She'd read the first three pages before the phone rang.

"Hello?"

"Fenella? It's Daniel. How are you?"

"Daniel? Oh, hi," she said, feeling flustered.

"You sound surprised."

"I was expecting someone else," she said, immediately regretting the words.

"I'm sorry to disappoint you."

"No, not at all," Fenella said too quickly. "It's fine. I'm fine. How are you?"

"I'm okay, thanks. I was just wondering if you've seen any of the people involved in the Phillip Pierce case since Saturday," he replied. "You often seem to find yourself in the middle of everything, so I thought it was worth asking."

"The Islanders, the band that played at Cregneash on Saturday, have been playing at the Tale and Tail," Fenella replied.

"Have they really? No one mentioned that to me. I heard there was something going on there last night, but I thought someone said that a famous musician from across was performing."

"That's Todd Hughes. He was a session musician for a whole bunch of famous bands. He's been filling in for Henry Jones since Saturday."

"Should I ask how you know all of this?"

"Shelly and I met everyone in the band at Cregneash," Fenella explained. "I told you in my statement that Oliver introduced us to all of the guys. Shelly and I were at the pub on Sunday night when they came in and did a few sets."

"Sunday night, not last night?"

"We were there last night, too, but we saw them on Sunday first," Fenella explained.

"Tell me exactly what happened on Sunday, please," Daniel said, sounding annoyed.

Fenella did her best to remember everything she could about the evening. She told him about talking with Paul and about how she and Shelly were just about the only people there. She tried to avoid saying much about Todd, but she had to mention meeting him.

"I saw him perform once," Daniel said. He named a band that Fenella remembered as being huge in the eighties. "I didn't realize he was on the island."

"He is, and he's mostly retired, but he agreed to help out because he wants to help Paul."

"Really? I'm sure his connections will be useful for Paul."

Fenella told Daniel everything that Todd had said about working with Paul.

"It sounds as if you and Todd have become quite good friends in the last few days," Daniel said when she was done.

"We had dinner together on Monday night," Fenella said, feeling as if she might as well just tell the man everything. "He took me to that new place in Ramsey, the one with the celebrity chef. The chef and Todd know each other."

"How nice," Daniel said. "Did you go and see him perform last night, then?"

"Yes, Shelly and I went, but it was really crowded. Paul arranged for us to have seats near the stage so that we could enjoy the show, though."

"Paul arranged them or Todd did?"

"I'm not sure. Paul was the one who found me and Shelly where we were hiding on the upper level of the pub, though."

"So you saw the whole band again last night. Did you talk to anyone about the murder?"

"Henry Jones was there, too. He said a few things."

"Tell me everything," Daniel sighed.

Fenella did her best to repeat the various conversations that had taken place during the evening that related to Phillip's murder. When she was finished, Daniel asked her a few questions.

"When do you plan to see Todd again, then?" he asked eventually.

"I don't know. We don't have any firm plans, although Henry invited Shelly and me to Phillip's memorial service tomorrow. I imagine Todd is planning to attend."

"I'm also planning to attend. You can introduce me to Todd." Daniel put the phone down before Fenella could reply.

"I wasn't going to go," she protested as she hung up the receiver.

When the phone rang again a short while later, Fenella thought about letting the answering machine pick up. She really didn't want to talk to Daniel again.

"Hello?"

"Good morning," Todd said brightly. "I've just woken up and I feel energized by the thought of seeing you. Let's spend the day together. Where would you like to go? Paris is fun, but flights might be a problem on such short notice. I suppose London would be easier. What about Dublin? It's lovely this time of year."

"How about Castletown?" Fenella suggested. "Or Peel?"

Todd laughed. "I suppose we could do Castletown or Peel. Have you been to either of the castles?"

"I've been to both. They're both wonderful."

"I've never been all that interested in history. Which castle is better?"

"You've never been to either?"

"No, I haven't."

Fenella sighed. "They are both worth a visit, and you should also visit all of the island's museums and other historical sites, too. The island has an incredibly rich history."

"So which castle do you want to visit today?"

"Some parts of Castle Rushen are still in use today, which is amazing as it's medieval. Peel Castle is mostly ruins, but some sections of it are even older than Castle Rushen. Which appeals to you more?"

"As it may well rain, I think maybe Castle Rushen is a wiser choice. I hope it has a roof over it?"

"It does, and most of Peel Castle does not, so you're probably right."

"I'll come and collect you in about an hour. I haven't had a shower yet. As soon as I woke up, I wanted to hear your voice."

Fenella blushed. "I'll be ready to go," she promised.

A loud coughing noise made Fenella jump. "Are you okay?" she asked Mona as the woman came into view.

"I'm fine. You did ask me to make noise as I arrived, remember?"

"Yes, but that wasn't what I was expecting."

"What would you prefer? I can see about getting angels to sing, or maybe a small angel with a harp could play a few notes. Would that be better?"

Fenella rolled her eyes at her aunt. She was tempted to tell Mona that she wanted the harp, just to see what Mona would do, but knowing Mona, she'd find a way to make it happen, just to annoy Fenella.

"Anyway, It's nice to hear the phone ringing once in a while," Mona said as Fenella put the receiver down. "Who rang the first time? I was busy and missed the conversation."

"It was Daniel," Fenella replied.

"He's heard about you and Todd, then. Interesting."

"I don't think that's the case. He said he'd called because he thought I might have seen some of the people involved in the murder in the last few days. He said I have a knack for running into people, or something like that."

"He's right. You do seem to find yourself in the middle of these things quite regularly."

"I don't do it on purpose."

"Of course not."

Fenella frowned. "I truly don't."

"And now you're going to spend the day with Todd. That will be nice."

"It should be. Anyway, he's not involved in the case. He wasn't even on the island when Phillip was killed."

"How do you know that?"

"He told me that he was in London that day."

"Did you ask him for an alibi?"

"No, not at all. It just came up in conversation."

"Interesting. I wonder if Daniel has asked the man for an alibi."

"I can't see why Daniel would have spoken to him at all. Todd wasn't at Cregneash when Phillip died and I don't think he really knew Phillip, either. He and Henry are friends, of course, but that only ties him to the case in a minor way."

"Maybe," Mona said, "but you need to get ready, don't you?"

"We're going to Castle Rushen. I suppose what I'm wearing will do."

Mona gave her a critical look. "It will do, but you could wear a dress or a skirt. Castle Rushen is indoors, after all."

"I could, but this is more comfortable."

"Comfort isn't the most important concern."

"I'm not sure I agree with that."

Mona sighed. "And yet we share at least some common DNA. How odd."

Todd arrived almost exactly an hour later. "Good morning," he greeted Fenella. "And hello, Katie."

The kitten wandered over and let the man give her a few quick pats before she dashed away. "Shelly will be over to give you your lunch," Fenella reminded the animal. "She may even bring Smokey over for some play time."

"Shelly has a cat, too? I assume Smokey is a cat?" Todd asked.

"Yes, Smokey is a cat. She and Katie are good friends."

"Are you ready to go, then?"

Fenella nodded. She picked up her handbag and followed the man out of the apartment. After locking the door, they headed for the elevators.

"I've driven past Castle Rushen once or twice, but I've never really paid any attention to it," Todd said after they were in his car, heading south.

"How can you not pay attention to a massive medieval stone castle?" Fenella demanded.

Todd laughed. "As I said, I've never been that interested in history."

"I'll try to remember that as we go along, but you'll have to remember that history is my passion."

"Really? All those dates and battles and wars? I could never remember everything in the right order. Don't ask me what order the kings and queens came in, either. I can never remember, although I'm pretty sure Henry VIII came after seven other Henrys."

Fenella laughed. "History doesn't have to be about dates, battles, and wars, or even kings and queens. I'm fascinated by the people, the ones who are barely mentioned in the history books but who actually lived and breathed on this planet all those years ago. I walk around Castle Rushen and I wonder what it would have been like to be a servant there when the seventh Earl of Derby was in residence or a prison guard during the years when the castle was a prison. Dates aren't what matters when you study history. It's the people who matter."

"When you put it that way, it does sound a bit more interesting, anyway. When was the seventh Earl of Derby here? Did he live at Castle Rushen? Pretend I know nothing about the island's history and tell me everything."

Fenella laughed. "I'm going to guess that you truly don't know anything about the island's history," she said.

"I didn't grow up here, remember. When I did live here, I wasn't here very much, really. My wife wasn't interested in history, either, or we might have toured the castle during one of my visits."

"The seventh Earl of Derby did live at Castle Rushen. He was, I believe, the only Earl of Derby to ever actually live on the island, even though they'd been the island's rulers for many years. At one time they held the title of "King of Mann," but it was deemed safer to switch to "Lord of Mann" so as not to antagonize the King of England."

"That makes sense. What sort of time period are we talking about?"

"The first Earl of Derby's second wife was the mother of Henry VII," Fenella told him. "By the time we get to the seventh earl, we're right in the middle of the English Civil War."

"Which side was the earl on?"

"The Royalists, of course. As Cromwell's army advanced across England, Derby and his family escaped to the island. He put together an army of sorts and headed back to England, where he was captured and executed."

"You know a lot about the island's history, but you said you didn't grow up on the island, or am I remembering that incorrectly?"

"Not at all. I was born on the island, but my family moved to the US when I was a child. I've only been back here since March. While I did my degrees in history, I never paid much attention to the island until I got back. I've bought just about every book I could find on the island's history now, though, and I'm doing my best to learn all that I can about the island."

"It does sound interesting. I'm almost looking forward to seeing the castle now."

Fenella frowned. "We can do something else, if you aren't really interested in the castle."

"Not now we can't. I'm expecting you to make history interesting for me for the first time."

"That sounds like quite the challenge."

"I'm sure you're up to it."

Fenella nodded. The island's history was so rich and fascinating that she was certain she could find some element within it that would interest the man. "You know about the island's music, anyway. A lot of the songs that the band perform are Manx," she said.

"I just read the music and try to follow along, though. I don't know anything about the origins of the songs we play."

"I'm afraid I don't, either. I'm sure Henry probably does, though."

"If he doesn't, Harriet will. She's the one who's obsessed with the island's past. That much I know about her for sure."

"She did say that she'd been volunteering with Manx National Heritage for a long time."

The drive, in Todd's American sports car, didn't take long. Once they reached Castletown, Fenella gave the man directions to the parking area for the castle.

"What's the little white building?" Todd asked as they began to walk toward the castle.

"The Old Grammar School," Fenella replied. "It's the oldest roofed structure on the island. It was originally built as a church, but was later used as a school."

"Can we go inside?"

"I think it's closed to the public, at least at the moment."

A small sign on the building's front door confirmed Fenella's words.

"That's disappointing," Todd said. "I want to soak up as much history as I can now."

"There's plenty at the castle," Fenella assured him.

An hour later, he pulled her onto a convenient bench. "This is exhausting," he said. "I haven't had this much information crammed into my head since school, and that was a fair few years ago."

"We can stop reading all of the signs and just walk through the rest of the building, if you want."

"No, I truly want to take the time to read the signs and learn about the castle. It is really interesting, if a bit overwhelming. It's very well presented, and I sort of feel as if we're getting a window into the past. I can't imagine being a prisoner in one of these rooms, though. It's a horrible thought."

"They're cold and damp and dark," Fenella shivered. "I think I'd be quite claustrophobic if I had to spend any time in one."

The large rooms where the Derbys had entertained were warmer and more comfortable, at least. The tour ended at the old kitchens.

"I can't imagine trying to cook under those conditions," Fenella said.

"I can't cook, so I'd have to agree."

"You can't cook?"

Todd flushed. "I was married very young and my wife was a good cook. When I was on the road, food was always provided from somewhere. Now that I'm on my own, I simply go out or get takeaways. Cooking seems like too much bother."

"Cooking can be great fun," Fenella said, "and there's something very satisfying about sitting down to a delicious meal that you prepared yourself."

"I'll have to take your word for that."

Fenella thought of a dozen other things she wanted to say, but she bit her tongue. The man was over sixty. If he didn't want to learn to cook, it wasn't really any of her business. "How about the gift shop?" she suggested as they walked down the stairs to the courtyard.

"I do enjoy a bit of shopping," Todd replied.

The gift shop was all but empty as the pair walked in. A middle-aged woman was behind the counter. "If you need anything, let me know," she called before she went back to reading her book.

"I should buy a book on the island's history," Todd said. "I'm quite embarrassed by how little I know, really."

"They have some very good ones," Fenella replied. The pair walked over to the selection of books. As Fenella pointed out a few of her favorites, the door to the shop swung open.

"Harriet, my dear, are you okay?" the woman behind the counter asked. She rushed toward the woman who'd just entered and pulled her into an awkward embrace. "I can't imagine how you must be feeling, you poor, poor dear," she gushed.

"I'm fine," Harriet Jones replied firmly. "It's all very sad, especially for poor Karla, but stiff upper lip and all that, after all."

"Yes, but such a horrid tragedy," the other woman said. "And murder," she added in a loud whisper.

Harriet glanced around. When her eyes met Fenella's, she sighed. "I wasn't expecting to see you here," she said in a tone that almost sounded like an accusation of some wrongdoing.

"She's with me," Todd interjected, sliding an arm around Fenella.

"Todd, I didn't see you there," Harriet said. "It's good to see you. Henry was very grateful that you allowed him to play for a short while last night. It was good for him to get away for a few hours."

"It's good to see you, too," Todd replied. "We're all hoping Henry will be back for good now, but I can keep filling in if he isn't up to it. We know you've all had a huge shock."

Harriet glanced at the woman who'd been behind the counter and then walked quickly to where Fenella and Todd were standing. "Yes, it was a huge shock," she agreed in a very low voice. "Especially for Karla, of course."

"I hope she's okay," Todd said.

"She has good hours and bad hours," Harriet replied. "Today she was feeling strong enough to agree to my coming here for my regular shift. I've been neglecting my volunteer work quite dreadfully since Saturday, you understand."

"I'm sure Manx National Heritage was able to manage without you for a few days," Todd said. "Karla had to be your first priority."

"Yes, well, they've been very accommodating, but I know that they rely on their volunteers. I hated to let them down, even for Karla."

Todd nodded. "But she's feeling better today?"

"She says she is, anyway. Tomorrow is the memorial service. I'm sure that will be an ordeal. Phillip's parents arrive later today. No one is looking forward to that, either."

"I'm sure they're devastated," Todd said.

"Yes, of course they are, but they were quite rude to Karla when she rang to tell them about Phillip's death. They almost seemed to be blaming her for some reason or other."

"I'm sure it was just the shock of it all," Todd suggested.

"I suppose so. The situation wasn't helped by the fact that they hadn't actually told his parents that they'd married. Phillip wanted to tell them in person. They were going to go across to see them sometime in November."

"How awkward," Todd murmured.

"Karla had to give me the phone halfway through the conversation. Phillip's mother was hysterical and saying all manner of horrible things."

"I'm sure you can understand that it was shock and grief talking," Fenella said.

"Yes, I suppose so, but Karla took it all very badly. She's threatening to stay home tomorrow so that she doesn't have to see Mr. and Mrs. Pierce."

"She should do whatever feels right to her," Fenella suggested.

Harriet shook her head. "She needs to be at the memorial service. What will people think if she isn't there? Phillip was her husband, after all."

"At least they told you and Henry about the marriage," Todd said.

"Yes, although I would have preferred to hear about it before it happened, rather than after. She's my only child. I would have liked to have had a chance to attend her wedding."

"She's young. Perhaps she'll marry again one day," Todd replied.

Harriet shrugged. "Right now she's insisting that she'll never look at another man again, that her heart will always and forever belong to Phillip. I'm pretty sure that sentiment won't last, though."

"As I said, she's very young," Todd said. "The manner of the man's death makes it all worse somehow."

Harriet shivered. "I can't even begin to imagine how Phillip managed to get himself murdered. He was a very ordinary man in every possible way. Surely it takes something extraordinary to drive someone to murder?"

"I don't know about that," Fenella said. "Sometimes murders are committed over incredibly mundane things."

"I told Henry that perhaps it was a disgruntled parent who didn't like his or her child's turnip," Harriet told her. "It sounds awful, but that seems as likely as any other possibility. People that I know simply aren't murdered, you see."

"This is the first time in my life that I've ever known anyone who was murdered," Todd said, "and I'm sure it's odd for Fenella as well."

Fenella gave him a weak smile. At some point she'd have to tell him about everything that had happened on the island since she'd arrived, but this didn't seem the time.

"Someone suggested that it might have had something to do with the man's work," Todd continued.

"His work? He worked in a bank, processing loan and credit card requests and other boring things like that. I can't imagine anyone killing over that, can you?"

"Perhaps someone he turned down got unreasonably angry," Todd suggested.

Harriet shrugged. "He didn't turn people down in person. The bank managers did that job. He simply evaluated their files, or some such thing, from the main corporate offices. I doubt anyone who applied even knew that Phillip existed."

"Who do you think killed him?" Fenella asked. She knew the question was bordering on rude, but she couldn't stop herself from blurting it out anyway.

"I keep thinking it must have been something completely random," Harriet said after a minute. "Maybe someone stumbled into the barn, found that the turnips had run out, and lost their temper. That seems as likely as anything, at least to me."

"I hope the police find the killer quickly," Todd said. "I'm sure everyone will feel better knowing that he or she is behind bars."

"It must have been a man," Harriet said stoutly. "Phillip was strong enough to overpower a woman."

"There are some very strong women out there," Todd countered. "Anyway, I've not heard exactly how he was killed. Perhaps he was simply hit over the head with something. That could have been done by a woman, surely."

Harriet shook her head. "It was a man. I'm sure of it. Someone who was unhappy with the festivities at Cregneash, or maybe someone from Phillip's office who didn't like him. Karla and I are going to take a long holiday once the memorial service is over. We both feel as if we need to get away. I love the island, but it's difficult knowing that someone was murdered here."

"Are you sure the police will let you go?" Fenella asked.

"What do you mean?" Harriet demanded. "They can't stop us."

"I believe they can, during a murder investigation," Fenella told her. "You'll need to ask Inspector Robinson about that."

"I've no intention of talking to the police about anything," Harriet replied. "Karla and I have answered all of their questions at least a dozen times. If we want to go on holiday, that's our business."

Fenella thought about arguing, but she didn't want to upset the woman any further. What she would do, though, was mention the woman's plans to Daniel. It was possible that both Harriet and Karla had been eliminated from his list of suspects. If that was the case, they would probably be free to take their vacation.

"Did you actually tour the castle or simply come in to do some shopping?" Harriet changed the subject.

"We toured the castle," Todd replied. "Fenella was a wonderful tour guide. She knows a lot about the island and its history."

"Do you?" Harriet raised an eyebrow.

"Only what I've read in a few books. I've been meaning to talk to Marjorie Stevens, though. I'd really like to do some research on some aspect of the island's history."

"Are you qualified to do that?" was Harriet's next question.

Fenella flushed. She was tempted not to reply, as her qualifications weren't any of the other woman's business. "I wasn't aware that I would need special qualifications in order to do research," she said, "but I do have bachelor's, master's, and doctoral degrees in history."

"What were you looking for in here, then?" Harriet asked Todd.

Fenella swallowed several rude remarks as Harriet talked with Todd about the various books on display. Several minutes later she and Todd were on their way out of the shop. Todd was carrying a large bag full of books.

"You will be at the service tomorrow, won't you?" Harriet had asked as she'd rung up the man's purchases.

"Yes, and I'll be bringing Fenella with me," he'd replied.

"Really?" Harriet had given Fenella a dismissive glance and then gone back to ignoring her.

I wasn't going to go, Fenella thought, but now I think I will.

12

"She didn't mean to be rude," Todd said as he and Fenella crossed the parking lot back to his car. "She's very aware that she finished school with just a few qualifications. University wasn't even a consideration for her. I'm sure all of your degrees intimidated her."

"She was the one who asked me if I was qualified to do research," Fenella reminded the man.

"Yes, I know. Please make allowances for her. She's under a great deal of stress right now."

"I'd just as soon avoid her from now on," Fenella muttered.

"Does that mean you won't come to the memorial service with me tomorrow? I was really hoping you'd come."

"I'll come, and I'll even be polite to Harriet Jones if I have to be, but you'll owe me a huge favor."

"That's a deal," Todd laughed. "For now, how about some lunch?"

There was a small Italian restaurant nearby. Fenella had eaten there before, so she knew the food was excellent. The dining room was about half full when they arrived, but it filled quickly while they were eating.

"Tell me more about you," Todd invited after they'd ordered.

"I told you everything before, I'm sure."

"Of course you haven't. What was your childhood like in the US?"

"I suppose it was fairly typical, or at least I didn't know any better if it wasn't. I have four older brothers, but most of them were already out of the house before I really became aware of them."

"They're a lot older, then?"

"John, the oldest, was seventeen when I was born. The others followed at two-year intervals, or nearly. James was almost twelve when I came along."

"What a lovely surprise for your parents."

Fenella laughed. "I'm not sure that's exactly how they felt about it at the time, but that is how they always described it to me when I was younger. They'd been planning to move to America, you see, and I rather upset their plans."

"But it all worked out in the end."

"Yes, it did, just a few years later than originally expected. My father was American. He'd met my mother during the war."

"That sounds romantic."

"I'm sure it sounds much more romantic than it was, but they were married for a great many years, and as far as I know they were very happy together."

"I often wonder if my wife and I would still be together if she hadn't passed away," Todd said. "As I said, I was faithful and I loved her, but the traveling took its toll on our relationship. I do still miss her, though, even after all these years."

"I'm sorry," Fenella said softly.

"What about you? Are there any men in your past that you haven't recovered from losing?"

Fenella thought about the question for a minute. "Not really. I fell madly in love once, with a man who cheated on me and broke my heart. By the time I'd recovered from that, I was already involved with another man, but he and I were barely more than friends, in spite of spending ten years together."

"I hope he felt the same way, the man you were with for ten years, I mean."

"He's still calling me, asking me to come back to him," Fenella admitted. "That's mostly because I took care of him, not because he loved me, though."

"Are you sure?"

Before Fenella could reply, the waiter delivered their food. That gave her a moment to give the matter proper thought. "I don't think Jack and I were ever truly in love. We loved each other and we cared about each other, but it was never a great romance. I certainly never felt the same way about him as I did about the man who broke my heart. It was different for Jack, though. He'd dated a few different women over the years, but he'd never had a serious relationship. I don't think he was all that interested in women."

"Do you think he's gay?"

"No, I don't think he's all that interested in other people," Fenella tried to explain. "He's a genius, truly he is, but at military history and nothing else. When we started dating, he hadn't balanced his checkbook in twelve years. His mother did all of his cooking, cleaning, and laundry for him and I'm sure she was the one reminding him to pay all of his bills on time. I was so upset about everything that happened when my previous relationship ended that I enjoyed feeling needed, at least for the first year or two."

"And then it started to feel like hard work."

"Yes, exactly that. I've no one to blame but myself, really, because I took over all the jobs that Jack's mother had been doing and I never complained, but as the years went past, I started to want to find a partner, rather than having what felt like an overgrown child."

"But Jack was perfectly happy with you running his life for him, I'll bet."

"Yes, he was. I don't know if I would have ever found the strength to leave him if I hadn't inherited Mona's fortune."

"So now you're just hoping that Jack finds someone else so you can stop feeling guilty," Todd suggested.

"That's about right. I keep telling myself that I shouldn't feel guilty. The man is nearly sixty years old, for heaven's sake. But I do sometimes feel as if I abandoned him."

Todd patted her hand. "Your happiness is important, though. You can't get back together with the man just to assuage your guilt."

"Oh, I have no intention of getting back together with the man," Fenella laughed. "I'm just glad there's an entire ocean between us and that Jack doesn't have a passport."

Todd laughed. The waiter cleared their empty plates and handed them dessert menus. After they'd ordered, Fenella spoke.

"He's a fan of yours, by the way."

"Jack is? Should I be flattered?"

"He's jealous that I've been able to meet you and he hasn't."

"Something else about which you mustn't feel guilty," Todd said.

After dessert they headed back toward Todd's car. "But what's going on at the Old Grammar School?" Todd asked as they went.

The door to the building was open and Fenella could see someone moving around inside it. "I've no idea, but maybe we can have a sneaky look inside while we're finding out," she replied.

They crossed to the door and Fenella peered inside. A man was straightening rows of chairs. When he turned around, she recognized him.

"Oliver," she said. "What a lovely surprise."

Oliver Wentworth smiled at her. "Ms. Woods, what brings you to Castletown?"

"I brought a friend to tour Castle Rushen," she explained. "We were both disappointed to see the Old Grammar School was shut. Are you planning on opening it to the public soon?"

"We're doing a good deal of work in here at the moment, so we're only open for prearranged tours and school groups, but as you're here, you may as well have a quick look around," the man said. "Come in and shut the door behind you, otherwise we'll have a crowd and I'll get into trouble."

Fenella and Todd stepped into the small building and Todd shut the door.

"It's very small in here," Todd said, glancing around the space.

"It was built as a church, but it was later used as a school," Oliver told them.

"How many students did they cram in here?" Todd wondered.

"You'd be surprised," Oliver said. "We can get far more children in here than you'd expect when they come on school trips. Kids are little."

Fenella laughed. "I taught at a university. Those kids were huge."

The pair took a quick tour of the space while Oliver gave them a brief history of the site. When they were done, Fenella was quick to thank him.

"This was fascinating, thank you," she said.

"You're more than welcome. I have a group of thirty kids coming tomorrow morning to see the place. They'll be far less enthusiastic," Oliver laughed. "But are you all recovered from everything that happened on Saturday?"

Fenella shrugged. She wasn't sure if the man knew that she was the one who'd discovered the body or not. If he didn't know, she wasn't about to tell him. "It was pretty horrible," she said.

"Yes, it was. Josh is arguing strongly for canceling the Hop-tu-Naa festivities, at least at Cregneash, for next year. We've had to cancel everything else that was planned for this year already, of course."

"Josh didn't seem too pleased with all the visitors," Fenella said.

"No, he doesn't like tourists coming to his home and trampling all over everything," Oliver replied. "That's more or less a direct quote, although I shouldn't really be talking about the man, should I?"

"You sound a bit frustrated," Fenella suggested.

Oliver sighed. "Cregneash is a wonderful place, but Josh is crazy if he thinks that it can support itself without the funding from ticket sales. He wants to run a model farm using all of the old techniques, but he doesn't appreciate that those aren't particularly cost-effective. If it were up to me, we'd be having a lot more events at Cregneash and if it were up to Josh, it would be closed to the public entirely. Sometimes the pair of us find it easier to locate middle ground between our views than other times."

"I'm sorry you've had to cancel the rest of this year's activities," Fenella said.

"So am I. I hate disappointing the people who were planning to attend even more than I hate the lost revenue."

"What do you think happened to Phillip?" Fenella had ask.

Oliver shrugged. "I barely knew the man. I have to assume that he had enemies. Don't we all?"

"I hope I don't," Fenella told him. "At least not enemies who would murder me."

"You're right, of course," Oliver replied. "I suppose I haven't really been giving the matter much thought. I've been busy trying to reschedule the Hop-tu-Naa activities at other sites and to get us some publicity so that people don't drive all the way to Cregneash to find it closed. I really just pushed the murder right out of my head."

"You must know his wife fairly well. I understand she volunteers with Manx National Heritage regularly," Fenella said.

"Karla? I don't know her well, but I know her mother. Harriet is one of our most dedicated volunteers. It's unfortunate that she grew up in a time when women didn't work after their marriage. She should have had a career, really. Marriage and motherhood weren't enough for her. I shouldn't complain, of course; she's become invaluable to MNH."

"We saw her at Castle Rushen this morning," Todd said.

"She shouldn't be working already." Oliver shook his head. "Not after her huge shock on Saturday."

"Perhaps she'd rather be at work than sitting around with too much time on her hands," Fenella suggested.

"I suspect she needed a break from Karla," Oliver said in a low voice. "That girl can be very demanding."

"She's very young," Todd interjected.

"Yes, and rather spoiled as well," Oliver said. "Which is a mean thing to say about someone who was just widowed under the worst possible circumstances, I know."

"Are you planning to attend the memorial service tomorrow?" Fenella asked.

Oliver shook his head. "I've offered to work, as many of the our staff do want to attend. Someone has to keep the sites running, but Harriet has a great many friends at Manx National Heritage. They all want to pay their respects, for Harriet's sake."

"And Karla's, surely," Fenella suggested.

"Maybe. No one knows Karla as well as Harriet, though. She's considerably younger than most of the other volunteers. I suspect most of the people at the service tomorrow will be Harriet's friends or Henry's."

"The Islanders will be there," Todd said.

"Surely Karla has friends her own age?" Fenella made the statement a question.

Oliver looked at her and then shrugged. "She must, I suppose, but I've never met any of them. The only person her age that I remember seeing her with regularly, was Paul Baldwin. They were a couple for a while when she was younger, but that was years ago, of course."

"Were you surprised when she married Phillip?" Fenella asked.

"Surprised? Now that you mention it, I suppose I was. I only met him on Saturday when they turned up together. She volunteered him to help with the turnips. I don't think he was best pleased, really. I think he thought that they would be spending the day together, but he didn't complain, at least not to me."

"I understand he grew up in the island but moved when he was in his teens," Fenella said.

"Yes, that's what he told me. He had vague recollections of carving turnips when he was a child, but he said he'd only done it once or twice. He was a quick study, though. I only had to show him the basics and he caught on quickly."

"The perfect volunteer," Todd said.

"Yes, exactly that. I said something to him about being glad that he'd married into the family, as Harriet was one of our best volunteers and I was sure she'd rope him into helping with lots more things in the future. He just laughed and said something about him not knowing what he'd been getting into when he'd married Karla."

"Can you remember his exact words?" Fenella asked.

"It was something along the lines of 'and there's something else I didn't see coming when I married Karla,' or words to that effect. Why does it matter?"

Fenella shook her head. "I'm just curious, that's all. I thought the pair seemed very happy together, but that suggests that maybe it wasn't going as wonderfully as it appeared."

"I'm not sure that it matters," Oliver said.

"Except the police are still looking for a motive for the man's murder," Fenella reminded him.

"Even if the marriage wasn't all sunshine and roses, you can't be suggesting that Karla killed him," Oliver replied. "That simply isn't possible. They'd only been married a week and when I saw them together they seemed incredibly happy."

"I thought they seemed happy, too," Fenella agreed, "but someone did murder the man."

"Yes, but as I said before, he must have had enemies. Enemies that have nothing to do with Karla or Manx National Heritage. He'd only just moved here from across. He must have had some trouble over there and brought it here when he came over," Oliver said.

"I'm sure the police will work it all out," Todd interjected. "And now we should let you get back to work. We've taken up a lot of your time."

"I was done here anyway," Oliver replied. "I'm floating between sites today, trying to tie up a lot of loose ends and handle little issues. My next stop is Castle Rushen, actually. We need to start working on Christmas at the Castle in the next few weeks."

"What's Christmas at the Castle?" Fenella asked.

"It's a big charity fundraiser at Castle Rushen," Oliver explained. "Different charities from around the island each decorate a room inside the castle. It started out with only a few charities and a few rooms, but it's grown to the point now where just about the entire castle gets decorated."

"It sounds wonderful," Fenella exclaimed.

"There's a big charity auction at the end, where all the decorations get auctioned off, along with a great many other things that are donated to the event. All of the money raised is split between the various charities and Manx National Heritage," Oliver added. "All of the ticket money from the weekends when the event is open is also shared between the charities."

"When does it start? I don't want to miss it," Fenella said, pulling out her phone.

"It will run on weekends starting around the middle of December,"

Oliver replied. "It will be heavily advertised, as well, so you've no worries about missing it."

"Excellent," she said, making a note in her calendar. She loved Christmas anyway, and she couldn't wait to see Castle Rushen decorated for the holidays.

"You should go to the auction evening," Oliver told her. "There's food and wine and The Islanders will be playing. That's one of the reasons why Paul came back, I'm told. He loves Christmas at the Castle and didn't want to miss it."

Fenella nodded. "I'm not sure I'd want to buy an entire room full of Christmas decorations, though," she said. "Although I've not really thought about how I'll decorate for Christmas this year yet."

"Mona had some beautiful decorations," Todd told her. "I played for her and Max a few days before Christmas one year and the flat looked fabulous. There must be boxes of decorations somewhere, I'm sure."

"I can't imagine where, but maybe I've overlooked a few things," Fenella said, trying to think where large boxes of Christmas decorations could be hiding in her apartment.

"Most of the people who buy the room decorations from Christmas at the Castle are doing so for their businesses," Oliver explained. "We have several businesses, including a church or two, that buy rooms every year. They throw everything into storage and then decorate with it all the following year, then they donate the lot to charity shops who sell the individual components to the general public."

"I'm going to have to have a look around and see what I actually have at home," Fenella said. "I may need a room full of decorations for this year."

"We can't really help you, then," Oliver laughed. "The charity auction is usually on Christmas Eve and the decorations don't come down until the new year."

"Then I may have a large shopping trip in my future," Fenella said. "I love shopping for Christmas, though, so I don't mind a bit."

Oliver walked them to the door of the building and then followed them outside, locking the door behind him. "I'm off to the castle," he said. "It was nice seeing you again."

"Likewise," Fenella replied. "I'll probably see you at Christmas at the Castle."

"I hope you do."

Todd took Fenella's hand as they walked back toward his car. "I don't know if I'll be here for Christmas or not," he said. "I often spend Christmas in the Bahamas with some friends."

He named a few famous people, leaving Fenella shaking her head. "I don't think the island can compete with that sort of star power," she laughed. "Christmas at the Castle sounds wonderful, but on a rather different level."

"You're more than welcome to join me in the Bahamas," he said lightly. "I promise you'd have fun." He opened her car door for her and she slid inside. As he walked around the car, she tried to think of the best way to frame her reply.

"I'm flattered by the offer, but I think I'm more suited to Christmas on the Isle of Man than the Bahamas," she said once he'd started the car. "I can't even imagine what that would be like, really."

"Imagine white sand beaches, a staff of hundreds for a few dozen guests, unlimited gourmet food, the best wines and champagnes, that sort of thing."

"It sounds amazing, but it doesn't sound like Christmas," Fenella sighed. "I'm afraid I'm going to miss the snow that we always had in Buffalo, but at least here it should be cold. Warm weather and sunshine simply don't go with Christmas."

Todd laughed. "We could go skiing somewhere if you'd like." He named another famous person. "He owns a ski resort in Switzerland. One whole wing is reserved for him and his family and friends every Christmas. There would be skiing and ice skating with food and wine and everything else lovely."

"I really want to spend this Christmas on the island," Fenella said after a moment. "It's my first Christmas since I moved here, after all. Maybe another year I'll feel like traveling, but not this year."

"Are you sure it isn't just me you want to avoid?" Todd asked in a teasing tone.

Fenella laughed. "I'm enjoying getting to know you, but I'm not sure I'm ready to run away with you for Christmas," she said. "Even if I were madly in love with you, I truly do want to be spend this Christmas on the island, though."

"You aren't madly in love with me yet?" Todd demanded. "I must be getting old. Women used to fall madly in love with me the moment I met them."

"It's not you, it's me," Fenella countered. "I'm too old to fall in love quickly. It takes me ages to make any decisions these days, usually because I forget what I was trying to decide on."

Todd laughed again. "You're considerably younger than me, anyway. But it's only October. It's far too early to be worried about Christmas, anyway."

As they drove back into Douglas they chatted about Castle Rushen and everything they'd seen that day.

"It was a real treat, getting to see the Old Grammar School," Fenella said, "but I think my favorite part of the day was the dessert at lunch."

Todd laughed. "I was hoping you were going to say my company, but I suppose I can't compete with chocolate gateau."

"Your company has been excellent," Fenella told him. "I just hope I didn't bore you with too much history."

"Not at all. It was fascinating and it makes me feel as if I should have paid attention more in school. I thought history was dull and boring, but you really brought it to life."

"I'd give the credit to the castle. There's something about walking around a building that old that makes the stuff in the history books feel a lot more relevant."

Todd parked in front of Fenella's apartment building. "What about dinner?" he asked. "We can go anywhere you'd like. The restaurant in Ramsey is open again tonight, if you wanted to go there again."

"I ate far too much at lunch to want another ten-course dinner. Maybe we could go somewhere local. Although I don't know where you live, so maybe Douglas isn't local for you."

"I do live in Douglas," he replied. "Not far from here, actually. If you'd like, we can have dinner at my home. I'm sure I can find a caterer that can accommodate us on short notice."

"That sounds like far too much trouble. There are several dozen restaurants within walking distance of here. I'll be happy with any of them."

"We had Italian for lunch. How about Chinese for dinner?"

"Sure, there are three places nearby. Do you have a preference?"

Todd named the restaurant at the opposite end of the promenade. "It's a bit of a walk, but I think it has the best food."

"I like it there, too, although the desserts are better at the one near the sea terminal. Since we had dessert with lunch, it's probably best that I won't want it with dinner, though."

Todd chuckled. "It may just be a two pudding day," he told her. "Do you find it difficult to adjust to British English?"

"It's just different. I find pudding very strange to say because it's a specific thing in the US and I've never actually seen what I would call pudding on a UK pudding menu."

"It's like custard, right? But most often chocolate?"

"I suppose that's the nearest equivalent. Can you get chocolate custard?"

"I'm sure someone has tried it at some point, but I don't think I'd like it."

"Custard has eggs in it, though, and American pudding doesn't."

"Are you hungry now? Should we go straight to dinner?"

Fenella looked at her watch. "Although all this talk about pudding and dessert has made me a little hungry, I think it's too early for dinner. Anyway, I need to get Katie her evening meal, and I'd like to change my clothes, as well."

"Shall I come back for you in an hour, then?"

"If you like. You're welcome to come up and visit with Katie if you don't need to go home yourself, though."

"I will, if you don't mind, then. I'd rather spend the hour with you than home alone."

"Maybe you need a pet," Fenella suggested after they'd climbed out of the car.

"I'm not home enough. I had a dog for a few months when I was in

LA, but I was always coming and going and it wasn't fair to him. He was a lovely animal and I still miss him when I think about it, but I ended up giving him to one of the roadies to give to his daughter. She was about nine at the time and she gave the dog a wonderful home, at least."

"I never really thought about having a pet, but Katie adopted me," Fenella explained. "She just walked into my apartment one day and hasn't left."

"Most people would have taken her to a shelter," Todd suggested.

Fenella opened her apartment door. Katie rushed up to greet them. As Fenella picked her up and gave her a quick cuddle, she looked over at Todd. "How could I possibly have taken her to a shelter?" she asked.

Todd smiled. "I'm not sure I could have done it, either, really. She's a very sweet creature. My wife had a cat, actually two of them, one after the other. They were very much her pets, though, not mine. They usually ignored me completely when I was around."

"Well, Katie seems to like you," Fenella said as Katie wound herself around Todd's legs.

"She's just happy I've brought you back to get her dinner."

"Shelly left you a note on the counter," Mona said as she appeared in the living room. "She brought Smokey and the cats had a good play together."

Fenella found the note, trying to act as if she were surprised, since Todd wouldn't have heard Mona. "Smokey and I had a lovely long visit with Katie. She had her lunch and three treats from the treat packet. I filled up her water bowl before I left," Fenella read from the paper.

"Mmmeerrooww," Katie said from the kitchen. She was sitting in front of her empty water bowl, frowning.

"Shelly filled it up before she left," Fenella reminded her. "That was only a few hours ago." She put fresh water into the bowl and then added Katie's dinner to her food bowl. "It's a little early, but I'm going out," she said to her pet. "You could leave it for a short while, if you don't want to be hungry later."

Katie stared at her for a minute and then began to eat. Fenella sighed. "I tried to tell her," she said to Todd.

He laughed. "Are you ready to go out, then?"

"I was going to change into something a bit nicer," she said hesitantly.

"You look lovely," he assured her. "More than good enough for where we're going."

"You should change," Mona said. "I don't know where you're going, but Todd can afford to take you somewhere special where what you're wearing won't be at all appropriate."

There was no way for Fenella to reply to her aunt, so she ignored her. "Do you want to sit and chat for a while before we go?" she asked Todd.

"We could. Or I could walk around your flat and admire your furniture. I love antiques."

"If you know anything about them, I'd love to learn more," Fenella said. "I love everything here, but I don't know anything about any of it."

"I can tell you about every piece," Mona said. "I bought them all, after all."

Todd walked around, admiring nearly everything, while Mona made faces at him behind his back. Fenella had to struggle not to laugh at the woman's antics. When she couldn't take it any longer, she interrupted Todd.

"I'm getting hungry," she said. "Let's go and get some dinner, shall we?"

"Sure, that sounds good," he agreed easily. "Are we still going for Chinese, or would you prefer something else?"

"Chinese is fine. Just let me freshen up and we can go. Give me five minutes."

Fenella shut her bedroom door and then crossed to the large mirror in the corner. She was touching up her makeup when Mona joined her.

"Chinese? Really? The man can do better than that."

"I'm fine with Chinese. I don't have to be taken out for expensive meals all the time," Fenella hissed. "We went out for lunch, too, you know."

Mona sighed. "I don't think Todd properly appreciates you. He should still be trying to impress you with his wealth and sophistication."

"He spent the entire day listening to me talk about history, a subject that he told me he finds boring. I'm already impressed."

Mona chuckled. "Again, I find it difficult to believe that we're related. History? All day?"

"We went to Castle Rushen. What else should we have talked about?"

"You could have talked about the ghost," Mona suggested. "Everyone loves a good ghost story."

"It's the seventh Earl's wife who haunts Castle Rushen, right? We did talk about her, not as a ghost, but about her time on the island."

"Yawn. Surely it's more interesting that she's still haunting the castle, waiting for her husband to return from the war?"

"That's actually really sad," Fenella sighed.

"It's also not strictly true. Oh, it sounds quite dramatic and Charlotte loves for people to believe it, but she's really just hanging around because she likes being at Castle Rushen. She enjoys popping in to surprise women and predict their future for them."

"She does?"

"Oh, yes. If you come to the castle with a man and you see Charlotte, you will know whether the man you are with is the right man for you or not. If she's smiling, you are with your soul mate, but if she's crying, he's not for you."

"How does she know?"

Mona shrugged. "I suppose she simply guesses."

Fenella frowned. "I hope the young women on the island aren't seriously taking advice on their love lives from a ghost."

"Why ever not?" Mona demanded. "You are."

13

It was a lovely crisp autumn evening and Fenella enjoyed the walk from her apartment to the Chinese restaurant. It was fairly quiet there, with only a few other couples scattered around the dining room. Todd asked for a quiet table in the corner, a request they were easily able to accommodate.

The food was excellent, as always. "I'm stuffed," Fenella said after her last bite. "It's a good thing I don't really like their desserts, or puddings, I should say."

"Everything was excellent," Todd agreed, "and now we get to walk home along the promenade, which is one of the best things about living on the Isle of Man."

"The scenery here is amazing," Fenella agreed as they began their stroll toward home. "I can't understand why the island isn't more popular."

"I believe the weather has something to do with it," Todd said as he glanced upwards.

"It does look as if it might rain," Fenella admitted, "but it nearly always looks as if it might rain. It probably only rains about half the time."

Todd laughed. "The Bahamas are hot and sunny all year round."

"That must get incredibly boring."

"Maybe, but it makes a perfect holiday location."

"If you like hot and sunny, sure. I'm not really one for spending my time on the beach, though. I burn easily and I get bored, too. What else is there to do?"

"I mostly go for the company and the food," Todd told her. "I'm not a fan of lying on the beach, either."

They walked in companionable silence for a few minutes before Todd reached over and took her hand. "I hope you don't mind?" he asked.

"No, not at all," Fenella replied. "Although it does sort of make me feel like a teenager again."

"There's nothing wrong with that, surely?"

Fenella laughed. "I suppose not."

"As we're behaving like children, let's stop for ice cream," Todd suggested a moment later.

The small shop across the road looked as if it was getting ready to close for the night. Todd dragged Fenella inside. "We aren't too late for ice cream, are we?" he asked the bored-looking teenaged girl behind the counter.

She looked up from her magazine and shrugged. "The manager will be here in a few minutes to shut the shop. You'll have to be quick."

Todd opened the freezer case and pulled out a frozen treat. "Which one for you?" he asked Fenella.

She studied the selection for a moment and then picked the one that looked the best. Todd paid and they were back out the door before the manager arrived. Fenella unwrapped her treat and took a bite.

"This is really good, and I'm not even hungry," she said after a moment.

"As we're walking while we're eating, the calories don't count anyway," Todd told her. "I think we might have to keep walking past your building if we want to finish our ice cream before we go inside, though."

"I don't mind walking a bit further."

"I'm not looking forward to tomorrow," Todd said a short while later.

"The memorial service? It's going to be very sad, I imagine."

"I'm not looking forward to seeing Karla. I've known her since she was a child. I feel dreadfully sorry for her."

"I'm sure there will be lots of people there to support her. Henry and Harriet will be with her as well."

"I worry about Phillip's parents, too. I'm sure they're incredibly upset. I've no idea what to say to them."

"Just tell them the truth. Tell them that you didn't really know Phillip, but he seemed like a lovely young man who was very happy with the island and his wife."

"I'm not sure that's entirely true," Todd frowned. "I mean, he did seem like a nice man, but I don't know that he was very happy on the island. He said something to me about being sent over to deal with a few issues, which made me think that he wasn't planning on staying forever."

"I didn't know that. I wonder if Karla did."

"I'm sure she must have. That has to be the sort thing they discussed before they got married, surely," Todd said.

"You'd think so, but they did marry on impulse, remember."

"I hope you aren't going to suggest that Karla killed the man when he told her that he wasn't planning on staying on the island forever," Todd said.

"No, not at all," Fenella said quickly, even though she wondered if the idea had merit. "At least you can tell his parents that you thought he and Karla were happy together, can't you?"

"Yes, of course. That I can say. They seemed very much in love and very happy."

"So tell Mr. and Mrs. Pierce that and then move on. They'll have a great many people with whom to speak, I'm sure."

"I hope so. I'm sort of hoping that there will be so many people there that I can skip speaking with them, if I'm honest."

Fenella smiled. "I know what you mean. Do you have any idea how many people are expected?"

"Henry said it could be quite crowded, but he really wasn't certain.

The band will be there, of course, and many of Harriet's friends from Manx National Heritage. Henry said that the bank will be sending some representatives, but he wasn't sure how many. Then there will be Karla's friends and coworkers."

"Do you think she has many friends?" Fenella asked, thinking about what Oliver had said about the woman.

"I don't know. Henry never said anything to suggest that she had trouble making friends or anything like that, but he may well have not confided in me. We're friends, but only because of the band. I'm afraid I'm not very good at getting close to people because I'm always traveling."

Fenella felt as if there was a warning in the man's words. They walked to the sea terminal and then turned around.

"Woof," Winston said as he bounced toward Fenella.

"Winston, how are you?" Fenella asked. The big dog let her pet him and then demanded the same from Todd as Fenella fussed over Fiona.

"It's good to see you," Harvey Garus said, "and Todd. I didn't know you knew Fenella," he added as they all fell into step together.

"We met at the Tale and Tail on Sunday last week," Todd explained. "I was filling in for Henry and she was one of the four people in the audience."

"So a little bit different from Tuesday night," Harvey laughed. "I thought I would have a little listen Tuesday but I couldn't get anywhere near the place."

"You should have rung me," Todd told him. "I could have made arrangements for you to come in through the back. I did that for Fenella."

"It was fine. I didn't really want to leave Winston and Fiona home alone, anyway," Harvey shrugged. "I was just going to show my support, but I reckoned you had plenty of support in a crowd that big."

"It was a great crowd," Todd told him. "They were very enthusiastic."

"And loud," Fenella muttered under her breath.

"What happened on Saturday was a bad thing," Harvey said. "How's Henry holding up?"

"He was at the show on Tuesday," Todd replied. "He even played a few numbers. He's upset, obviously, but he's getting through it. I think he's more worried about Karla than anything else."

"Anyone have any idea who killed the man or why?" Harvey asked. "I don't believe I'd ever met the murdered man. He and Karla can't have been together for very long."

"They'd only been married for a week," Fenella told him, "but they knew each other as children until Phillip and his family moved away when he was twelve."

"Really? I wonder if young Karla fell for him all those years ago, then. It seems like something she'd do, really. She's always seemed lost in her own little fairy tale worlds."

"Maybe that's why she seemed to fall for him so quickly," Todd said. "Maybe she'd never really stopped caring about him from the time she was twelve."

"But she had other boyfriends," Fenella pointed out.

"She did, aye. She was with Paul Baldwin for a long time," Todd said.

"Well, I hope the police find the killer quickly. I'm sure Karla will sleep better at night knowing that he or she is behind bars," Harvey said. "Are you going to the service tomorrow?"

"Yes, Fenella and I will be there," Todd told him.

Harvey glanced at Fenella and then smiled at Todd. "I'll see you there, then. I didn't know the dead man, but I feel as if I should attend out of respect for Henry."

"I think nearly everyone there will be there for Henry or Harriet," Todd said. "I don't think anyone on the island knew Phillip well, aside from Karla, of course."

Fenella gave the dogs a bit of extra attention before Harvey continued on to the apartment building next door to hers. In her building, she and Todd took the elevator to the sixth floor, and he walked her to her door.

"I've a few things I need to do tomorrow morning," he told her in an apologetic tone, "but we can have lunch before the service if you'd like."

"Sure, that sounds great," Fenella said.

With their plans made, Todd gave her a gentle kiss and then

watched as she let herself into her apartment. She dropped her handbag onto the nearest table and then sank into a chair without turning on any lights.

"What's wrong?" Mona asked a moment later.

"Everything I keep hearing keeps pointing to Karla as the killer," Fenella said, "and I can't quite get my head around that."

"Tell me what was said tonight, then," Mona suggested.

Fenella repeated the various conversations that she'd had with Todd and then the chat with Harvey. "I don't know why, but every time someone talks about Karla, he or she says something that makes me think she killed her husband," she concluded, "but that simply doesn't seem possible. They'd only just been married a week."

"You keep saying that every time you talk about them, but I can't see what that has to do with anything," Mona said. "If they'd been married for a year, would that make it seem more likely? What about six months? At what point do you draw the line and say that after that many days or weeks or months it becomes more likely that she killed him?"

"I don't know, but one week seems an incredibly short space of time to go from being so in love that you want to marry someone to wanting that person dead."

"Maybe she wasn't so in love, then," Mona suggested.

Fenella frowned. "She acted as if she were madly in love with him when I saw them together."

"Maybe she's simply a very good actress."

Fenella nodded slowly. "Maybe I need to get some sleep. I think tomorrow is going to be a long day."

"While you're sleeping, I'll try to come up with a plan," Mona said. "There must be a way to trick her into confessing tomorrow. We just have to come up with the exact right question for you to ask her."

"I don't want to ask her anything. I'm going to the service because Todd asked me to come with him. I'm not going to confront a grieving widow just because I can't shake the feeling that she may have killed her husband."

"I'm not suggesting you confront her. You just have to say something that lets her know that you're suspicious and then step back and watch what she does."

"Yeah, because that worked so well when we tried it once before," Fenella snapped. "Except it didn't work well at all. It ended up with me running down the beach being chased by a killer with a knife. That's not an experience I'd like to repeat."

"You'll be at a memorial service surrounded by people. She isn't going to try anything there."

"Maybe not, but what's to stop her coming here after the service and killing me?" Fenella demanded. "I'm sure Todd or Harvey would happily give her my address if she asked for it."

Mona frowned. "As I said, you go and get some sleep. I'll come up with the plan while you're sleeping."

"I don't need a plan," Fenella replied as she headed for the bedroom. "I'm not even going to speak to the woman if I can help it."

After the conversation with Mona, Fenella wasn't surprised that she found it difficult to sleep that night. After tossing and turning for several hours, she finally fell into a restless sleep.

"Yes, I did kill him," Karla said to her. "He didn't want to stay here, you know. He tricked me. He got me to marry him and then, after it was too late, he told me that he wasn't planning on staying on the island. He wanted to go back across once he'd finished his projects here."

"You could have divorced him," Fenella suggested.

"That would have taken ages and been hard work," Karla replied. "This was much easier, and this way I get all sorts of sympathy and extra time off work, too."

"I'm going to have to tell the police," Fenella told her. "You can't be allowed to get away with it."

"Oh, I'm going to get away with it," Karla laughed. "The police will never believe you. I'm a grieving widow. Look, I'm wearing a black dress and everything."

Fenella looked at the woman's long black dress. As she stared at it, it began to grow and then swirl up around both her and Karla. The long skirt began to wrap itself around Fenella, growing tighter and tighter as Karla laughed and clapped. Fenella tried to fight her way out of the yards and yards of fabric, gasping for air as it tightened its grip. She tried to scream, but she couldn't seem to catch her breath.

"Meerroow?" a voice said in her ear. "Meeerroooooooooowwwww."

Fenella opened her eyes. Katie was standing on her chest, looking at her with concern. Somehow Fenella had managed to wrap herself in her bedding with her arms held down at her sides and her legs hopelessly tangled in sheets and the duvet.

"What a mess," Fenella said as she climbed out of bed. It took her several minutes to make the bed again. When she was done, she looked at the clock. There were still six hours to go before Katie would want her breakfast, but going back to bed didn't hold much appeal for Fenella. The last thing she wanted was to find herself back in the middle of that nightmare.

She padded into the kitchen in her slippers and got herself a drink of water. Mona was sitting on one of the couches staring out the window. "I wasn't sure if I should try to wake you or not," she said as Fenella sat down next to her.

"Next time, wake me," Fenella replied.

"I can try, but I don't know if you can hear me when you're asleep."

Fenella shrugged. "It's worth trying the next time I'm having a nightmare. That one was pretty awful."

"Was it about Karla?"

"Yes, she confessed to killing Phillip because he wanted to move back across, and then her dress wrapped itself around me and tried to squeeze me to death."

Mona shivered. "Maybe it's good that ghosts don't sleep," she said softly.

"I'm awfully tired," Fenella said a short while later.

"Go back to bed. I promise you the nightmare won't come back."

Fenella thought about questioning Mona, but she decided that she'd rather just believe her and go to bed. She was asleep as soon as her head hit the pillow and she slept soundly until eight the next morning.

"You didn't wake me," she said to Katie as she slid out of bed.

"Meereew," Katie replied from her spot in the center of the bed.

"I know I kept you up last night, too, but you usually still wake me," Fenella replied. She got Katie's breakfast and started a pot of coffee before she took a shower. Breakfast was toast with jam and a bar of chocolate.

"It's an indulgence, but I'm still feeling stressed from last night," she told Katie as the kitten watched her eating the sweet treat.

"You'll be sorry you had that now when you want it later," Mona predicted as she walked into the kitchen.

Fenella flushed and shoved the last bite into her mouth. "I'm already sorry I ate it now," she sighed, "but it did taste good."

"We need to find you something appropriate to wear," Mona said. "Something black or dark grey, I think."

"I suppose so," Fenella replied. The pair went into the bedroom and went through the wardrobe. Mona had an extensive collection of black dresses, so it didn't take them long to find one that Fenella liked.

"That will do," Mona agreed as Fenella twirled in front of the mirror. "Now we can talk about my plan."

"I don't want to hear your plan," Fenella replied as she changed back into her jeans and sweatshirt. She'd change again just before Todd was due.

"Just hear me out before you decide," Mona told her. "I don't ask you for much, really, do I?"

And you've given me a wonderful new life, Fenella added silently. Feeling as if Mona was trying to guilt her into listening, she sighed. "Go ahead, then."

"I think you should start by talking to Phillip's parents. They would know whether Phillip was planning to return to the UK or not," Mona said. "Then once you know that, you can confront Karla with your knowledge."

"I'm not going to confront anyone about anything."

"But you can ask her about it, surely? Just casually, in conversation."

"He may not have even been planning to leave."

"Exactly, and maybe Karla wanted to leave and was disappointed that he wanted to stay. You need to find out what Phillip wanted to do and then find out how Karla felt about it."

"Or I could go and sit quietly with Todd and then leave without speaking to anyone."

"How are you going to solve the murder that way?"

"It's Daniel's job to solve the murder, not mine."

"Well, he doesn't seem to be doing a very good job of it. Perhaps he's too busy with Tiffany to give it his full attention."

"Perhaps he's already made an arrest and we simply haven't heard about it yet. Or maybe he's about to arrest someone, but he's still gathering evidence."

"Or maybe he's lost and hasn't a clue, and he needs your help."

"The last memorial service that I attended ended in an arrest and a lot of upset. I'm hoping this one will be far more civilized."

"The last one only ended in an arrest because your brother confronted the killer," Mona reminded her. "Otherwise the police would probably still be trying to solve that case as well."

Fenella shook her head. "I'm going today for Todd's benefit and not for any other reason. I will be polite and speak to people, but I'm not going to ask anyone any rude questions."

"I wasn't going to suggest you ask any rude questions," Mona countered. "There's nothing rude about asking the man's parents about his future plans."

"Except the man is dead and doesn't have a future. I'd rather not remind them of that."

Mona sighed. "I'm sure he's very happy in the afterlife, if that makes you feel any better. Maybe he's even haunting Cregneash, although if I were him I'd haunt Karla, wherever she is. Of course, he may simply have chosen to move on and leave this life behind. Most young people do. They've far less to stay behind for, of course."

A dozen questions sprang to Fenella's lips. "If I were him, I think I'd stay here until the police found my killer. Of course, I'd try to communicate with someone to let them know who'd killed me."

"It isn't that easy," Mona sighed. "There are some elements of it that I don't even understand, so I can't explain them to you, anyway."

"This would be easier if you could go and talk to him and ask him what happened."

Mona nodded. "It would be, wouldn't it? Unfortunately, I haven't any real connection with Cregneash, so I've no way to get there. And there's no reason to believe that Phillip is haunting Cregneash anyway. He could be anywhere, but he's probably long gone."

"What if I drove your car to Cregneash?" Fenella asked. Mona had surprised her once by appearing in the passenger seat of the sporty little car.

"That might work if you're prepared to drive it right into the barn where the body was found. I'm assuming that's the most likely place for Phillip to be, although even if he is there, it's possible I wouldn't be able to see him or speak to him."

Fenella sighed. "We'll just have to leave everything to Daniel, then."

"Where has that man been? Whenever you've been caught up in a murder investigation in the past, he's visited or rung daily. He always said he liked to talk things through with you."

"I suppose he's talking things through with Tiffany now. As she's a trained investigator, that's probably smart."

"There's nothing smart about that woman," Mona said darkly. "You should be trying to get between them."

"Get between them? How am I supposed to do that?"

"He'll be at the memorial service, won't he? Perhaps when he sees you with Todd he'll realize what he's missing."

"Perhaps, or maybe he'll feel justified in finding another woman when it becomes clear that I'm not sitting at home pining for him."

Mona shrugged. "If he gives up on you that easily, he wasn't right for you anyway. I have confidence that it's all going to work out in the end, though."

"I don't. Not even a little bit," Fenella sighed. She glanced at the clock and then gave Katie an early lunch. With that chore out of the way, she changed back into the outfit that she and Mona had chosen earlier. Moving everything she needed into a black handbag filled the last few minutes before Todd was due.

"You look lovely," he told her when she opened the door.

"You look very handsome," she replied, taking in the dark grey suit with the lighter grey shirt under it. The grey of his tie fell somewhere between the two shades, with a dark grey pinstripe running through it.

"Thank you. I only have a few suits because I rarely need them in my professional life. I do have one that's bright red. I used to wear it at

Christmas, but I think I may be too old for it now. Anyway, it didn't seem appropriate for today."

"No, probably not."

"Ready for some lunch?" he asked as he offered his arm.

"Yes, please," Fenella replied. She and Todd walked a few steps down the corridor, but Fenella stopped when she heard a door open behind them.

"Shelly? Hello," she said brightly.

"Hello," her friend replied. "I'm glad I bumped into you, actually. I've been thinking about the memorial service today for Phillip Pierce. Are you planning to attend?"

"I'm going to go with Todd," Fenella replied, nodding at her companion.

"I'm of two minds about going," Shelly sighed. "I didn't know the man, but I liked him when we met and I feel as if I should be there to pay my respects somehow. When John died, the entire service was overwhelming, but I remember so many little bits of conversations from the day. Some of my favorite memories are from people who didn't know him well but had kind things to say about him anyway."

"You're more than welcome to come with us," Todd offered. "We're just going to get some lunch first. You're welcome to join us for that as well, if you'd like."

"I don't want to be in the way," Shelly replied hesitantly.

"We're just going to the pub next door for lunch," Todd laughed. "I think Fenella will probably appreciate your company at the memorial service, too. I'll probably end up talking with Henry and the rest of the band and poor Fenella will end up on her own."

"In that case, I'll come," Shelly said. "I need to change, though, so maybe I'll skip lunch."

"We can go and get a table," Fenella suggested. "Knowing you, you'll want the cottage pie and a cup of tea, right?"

Shelly laughed. "I am rather predictable, aren't I? Yes, please, unless they have steak and kidney pie on special today. They don't do it very often, so it's a real treat when they have it."

Shelly went back into her apartment while Todd and Fenella continued to the elevators.

"I hope you didn't mind my inviting her along," Todd said as they rode the car to the lobby.

"Of course I don't mind. Shelly is my closest friend on the island."

"I thought it would be helpful if she was at the service, just in case I do get dragged away by the rest of the band."

"You're right about that. I don't want to be sitting all alone there. I don't think I'll know very many people."

The pub was quiet and the only thing on special was beef stew. Fenella ordered cottage pie for both Shelly and herself, and after a moment, Todd made it three. Shelly arrived, dressed in black, just before the food did.

"I don't know if I've ever seen you in plain black," Fenella said.

"I don't usually wear it, but it seemed best for today's service. I probably won't know anyone there so I really don't want to stand out," Shelly explained.

The trio talked about nothing much as they enjoyed their meal. Todd insisted on paying for everything, including a very generous tip. After they finished, they headed to his car.

"Can you actually fit a person in the back of your car?" Fenella asked as they walked out of the restaurant.

"I brought a different car today," he replied. "There's plenty of room for passengers in this one."

The gorgeous car was luxurious and comfortable and Fenella had to swallow a sigh as she sank into the thickly padded leather passenger seat. In theory she could afford to buy herself something like this, but she was far too practical to indulge herself in such luxury. There seemed little point in having a car this nice when the farthest she was going to drive was no more than half an hour away.

"Here we are, then," Todd said a short while later as he pulled into the parking lot of a large church. "We're a few minutes early, I think."

"Let's wait here until we see someone we know go in," Shelly suggested. "Then again, I don't think I'm going to know anyone, anyway."

"You know the others in Henry's band," Fenella said, "and you've met Karla and her parents."

"Beyond them, it's really just Phillip's coworkers who will be here, and I'm not sure how many of them could get the afternoon off. Except for Phillip's parents, of course. That might be them now." Todd nodded at a car that was parked nearby.

Fenella watched as an older couple climbed out of the car. It had a sticker on the rear bumper from one of the island's car rental companies. The man, who had been driving, came around to help the woman out of the passenger seat. They were both dressed in black and they both looked almost unbearably sad. He was bald and wore thick glasses. His companion stood up and then turned to get a cane from the car. She had a cloud of white hair on the top of her head. Her face was free of makeup and she'd clearly already been crying.

"They look so sad," Shelly said.

"Sometimes I'm very grateful that I never had children," Todd remarked.

Fenella swallowed a lump in her throat. She'd lost her only child in the very early stages of her single pregnancy. That loss had left her unable to conceive again. The pain of the experience had never fully left her, even though she'd learned to live with it over the years.

"There's Henry and Harriet," Shelly said. "Is that Karla with them?"

The couple were making their way through the parking lot, escorting someone wearing a thick black veil.

"It must be, mustn't it?" Todd asked. "The veil is a bit dramatic, I think."

Fenella watched as the trio walked past the other couple who were still slowly making their way toward the church. Henry said something to them, but he didn't stop. Harriet was staring straight ahead and didn't even glance at the pair. It was impossible to tell what Karla did behind her veil.

"We should probably go in," Todd said a moment later after they'd seen a few of the band members arrive.

As they began to get out of the car, another car pulled into the lot. Fenella stiffened as she recognized Daniel's car. He parked nearby.

"What's she doing here?" Shelly hissed in Fenella's ear as Tiffany climbed out of the passenger seat of Daniel's car.

14

"Good afternoon," Daniel said, nodding toward Fenella and her friends.

"Hello," she replied. She introduced Daniel and Tiffany to Todd.

"I didn't realize that the police really come to murder victims' memorial services," Todd said. "I thought that was just something they do on television for dramatic effect."

Daniel shrugged. "I prefer to be there whenever large groups of witnesses to a homicide are gathering."

"Witnesses?" Todd echoed. "I'm sure you mean suspects."

Daniel didn't reply; instead, he glanced at his watch. "We should get inside. We don't want to be late."

Fenella stood still and let Daniel and Tiffany walk in front of them. Shelly made faces at Tiffany behind the other woman's back, making Fenella chuckle softly. Todd gave her a curious look, but there was no way that Fenella could explain why she disliked Tiffany so much.

The inside of the church felt dark and somber. Daniel and Tiffany took seats near the back, but Todd headed down the aisle toward the other band members who were near the front.

"Maybe Shelly and I should sit back here," Fenella whispered, stopping near the middle of the church.

Todd frowned. "You're more than welcome to sit with the band."

"Yes, but I think we'd both feel more comfortable back here. You go and sit with your friends. We'll catch back up with you after the service."

Todd hesitated and then nodded. As he continued on his way, Fenella and Shelly slid into seats.

"Thank you for that," Shelly whispered. "I'm not up to dealing with Mark and Tim right now."

"I'm a terrible friend," Fenella gasped. "I forgot all about them. What's been going on?"

"Nothing, really, although they've both been ringing. I've been putting them off because I'm not sure what's going on with Gordon, but I'm tempted to let Tim buy me dinner or maybe lunch."

"You should. Maybe if you started seeing someone else, Gordon would make a decision."

"Maybe, or maybe I'll just hide back here and avoid them both."

Fenella didn't get a chance to say anything further as the church suddenly went quiet when the vicar entered.

"We're here today to pay our last respects..." he began. Fenella was only half listening as he talked. It was obvious from his remarks that he didn't know Phillip, and after a few very vague comments, she began to wonder if he'd ever even met the man. Once he'd moved on to the standard service, the vicar seemed less uncertain. Fenella found herself watching Henry and Harriet as the service continued.

The veiled figure that could only be Karla was sitting between them. Henry and Harriet exchanged glances several times, but Karla didn't seem to move at all as the vicar spoke. In contrast, the couple who Fenella assumed were Phillip's parents sat with their arms around one another. The woman sobbed, although she was clearly trying to do so as quietly as she could. The man had tears streaming down his face which he wiped away periodically.

"And now I'd like to invite Mr. and Mrs. Pierce to come up and share a few thoughts about their son," the vicar said.

Fenella only just stopped herself from leaning forward to make certain she could hear.

"Phillip was a good son," his father said. He cleared his throat several times. "We were happy that he'd come back to the island that had been his childhood home. He still had friends here, Paul and Karla among others."

The man nodded at Paul, who was sitting next to Henry. Paul seemed to be staring straight ahead.

"He had a good career and we have to believe that he'd found happiness with his wife, Karla, although we didn't get the opportunity to get to know her the way we might have liked." The man stopped and looked over at his wife.

She sighed and then took his place in front of the microphone. "I don't understand," she said in a low voice. "I'll never understand why someone killed him. It was a senseless and pointless thing to do. Phillip never hurt anyone. All he wanted was a nice quiet life." She shook her head and then turned and walked back to her seat with her husband on her heels.

The vicar returned to the lectern and invited Henry and Harriet to speak.

"We were only just getting to know Phillip, but we were enjoying the experience very much," Henry said. "Karla isn't feeling well enough to speak today, so I'll just thank you all for coming on her behalf. There will be a reception in the church hall following the service. Everyone is welcome to attend."

Harriet patted his arm and then the pair returned to their seats. While they'd been speaking, Karla had slid over to sit next to Paul. When her parents returned, they sat next to each other on the other side of Karla.

"That was odd," Shelly whispered. "Her moving over to sit with Paul."

"Maybe she felt she needed someone next to her while her parents were speaking," Fenella suggested.

Shelly shrugged. "Maybe she should have said a few words herself," she whispered back. "I managed to thank everyone myself at my husband's funeral, even though I've no idea now what I actually said."

Fenella watched as Paul whispered something to Karla. The girl seemed to nod behind her veil.

At the vicar's invitation several other people got up and said a few words about Phillip. There was a single representative from the bank there. He praised Phillip's work ethic and personality. A couple members of the band spoke, but only in general terms. Fenella knew that they were doing so out of respect for Henry. It was clear that they didn't really know Phillip.

It felt much the same when a few of Harriet's friends from Manx National Heritage took their turns to speak. They said nice things about the dead man, but Fenella couldn't help but feel as if they hadn't really known him.

"And now, as Mr. Jones already said, there's a reception in the church hall," the vicar finally concluded the service. "Please join the family for tea and biscuits."

"I could do with a cup of tea," Shelly said as she got to her feet. "That was terribly sad."

"It was," Fenella agreed.

She and Shelly joined the line of people who were making their way through the church and into the connected church hall. As they walked into the large room, Fenella noted that Henry, Harriet, and Karla were standing on one side of the room while Phillip's parents were on the other.

"I don't think they like one another," Shelly whispered.

"No, and no one is speaking to Mr. and Mrs. Pierce."

"We should go and say something, shouldn't we?" Shelly asked.

Fenella was sure Shelly didn't want to speak to the grieving parents any more than she did, but she felt the same sense of obligation that Shelly did. They simply couldn't ignore them, even if it seemed as if everyone else was doing just that.

"Good afternoon," Fenella said when they reached the couple. "I'm Fenella Woods. I only met your son on Saturday, but he was incredibly kind in helping me carve a turnip very badly."

Mr. Pierce chuckled, but it was clearly forced. "Thank you, my dear," he said. "I'm Oscar and this is Audrey. Phillip was our only child and we're both really struggling right now. Mr. and Mrs. Jones have been very kind, but they don't truly seem to understand."

"I can't imagine what you're going through," Shelly said after she'd introduced herself. "I was never blessed with children myself."

"It is a great blessing," Audrey said, "and one that I'm grateful for, even with the way that things turned out. We had our son for twenty-six years, eighteen weeks, and three days, and they were the happiest years of my life."

Oscar put his arm around his wife. "They were the best years," he sighed. "Phillip truly was a good man, and we aren't just saying that because we've lost him. He worked hard and was building up a very successful career. In spite of how busy he was, he always remembered to ring home on a Sunday afternoon to check on us. He worried about us because we're getting older, when we should have been the ones worrying about him."

"I didn't want him coming back to the island," Audrey said in a low voice. "It's a lovely island, but it's so far away. I preferred when he was only an hour away and could visit us on Sundays."

"I suppose, now that he was married, he was planning to stay on the island," Fenella said after an awkward pause. As soon as the words were out of her mouth, she frowned. While she wasn't, strictly speaking, questioning the couple, the remark still felt nosy.

"He wasn't, though," Oscar replied. "This was just a temporary assignment. He was going to be here through the new year, but then he wasn't sure what was coming next. There was some talk about sending him to Scotland for a short while or maybe even abroad."

"My goodness," Shelly exclaimed. "You would have missed him."

"Yes, but, well..." Audrey began and then trailed off as a tear slid down her cheek.

"I'm sorry," Shelly said quickly. "I wasn't thinking."

"You're fine," Oscar assured her. "There's no right or wrong thing to say under these circumstances. We appreciate you taking the time to speak with us, regardless. No one seems to want to even do that."

"I suspect everyone else is too busy getting biscuits and tea to talk to anyone at the moment," Fenella said after a quick look around. There were long lines at the refreshment tables and only a few people speaking to Henry and Harriet. Karla was standing on her own a few feet away from them, seemingly staring at a blank wall.

"Would you like a cup of tea?" Shelly asked the couple. "I'm happy to get something for you."

"No, thank you," Oscar said. "I suppose we'll wander over there in a few minutes, more for something to do than anything else."

"I'm not hungry," Audrey said softly.

"I know, dear, but you haven't eaten in days. Phillip wouldn't want you to make yourself unwell," her husband replied.

"Mr. and Mrs. Pierce? I'm Daniel Robinson from the Douglas Constabulary. I'm sorry for your loss," Daniel interrupted.

"I didn't realize the police were here," Oscar said, "and you've brought your daughter along?"

Daniel flushed as Fenella and Shelly exchanged glances and struggled not to laugh. "This is Tiffany Perkins. She's a police inspector from another jurisdiction. She simply happens to be visiting the island right now."

"Ah, nice to meet you," Oscar said.

"I think we should get some tea," Shelly whispered to Fenella. As Daniel spoke to the bereaved parents, they slipped away.

"He doesn't look that much older than Tiffany," Fenella said after she and Shelly had filled up cups and plates.

"Clearly he does to Oscar," Shelly replied. "It would have been inappropriate to have laughed out loud, but I was tempted."

They sipped their tea and nibbled their way through a few biscuits as they watched people come and go. A number of people spoke to Henry and Harriet, and a few tried to speak to Karla, but she didn't seem to answer anyone. The members of the band all went up together to talk to Henry, but only Paul stopped to say something to Karla.

"She's talking to him, anyway," Shelly remarked.

To Fenella it seemed as if the pair were having an animated conversation. Paul didn't look very happy with whatever Karla was saying to him, though.

"Maybe we should wander over and offer our condolences," Fenella suggested.

"Yes, let's," Shelly agreed.

"It was kind of you to come," Henry said. "I'm afraid it's all a bit of a blur, though. Tomorrow, I probably won't remember that you were here."

"Make sure you sign the book of condolences," Harriet told them. "Karla will want to keep that forever to remember Phillip by."

"Perhaps you can get it copied for Phillip's parents," Shelly suggested. "I'm sure they'd like a copy."

Henry and Harriet exchanged glances. "Yes, that's an idea," Harriet said softly.

"How is Karla doing?" Fenella asked. She glanced over at the woman, who was still talking with Paul.

"She's doing better, but she's insisting on staying close to Paul, as he reminds her of Phillip, being that they all grew up together," Henry said.

"It's good for her find comfort wherever she can," Harriet added.

"Yes, of course," Henry said, "but I do wish she'd speak to a few other people as well. So many people have been kind enough to come to support her."

"I can try to talk to her again," Harriet said in a reluctant tone.

"No, leave her," Henry replied. "I don't want to cause a scene, not here today."

"I'd like to tell her how sorry I am," Fenella said. "I hope that's okay."

"You can tell her, but please don't be offended if she doesn't reply," Henry answered.

Fenella nodded, and then she and Shelly took a few steps closer to Karla. Paul looked over at them and smiled.

"Karla, here's Fenella and Shelly. You remember them from Saturday."

"No," the girl replied in a flat voice.

"They came to the Hop-tu-Naa celebrations. I met them when they came to try out the dancing," Paul told her.

"Whatever," the girl said.

"We're very sorry for your loss," Fenella said. "You and Phillip seemed very happy together when we met you."

A long silence followed Fenella's words. Finally Shelly broke it.

"We enjoyed doing our turnip carving with Phillip. He was very patient with us."

Karla didn't reply. Fenella exchanged glances with Paul, who shrugged. "It's all been very difficult for everyone, Phillip's untimely death," he said.

"Yes, I'm sure it has," Fenella murmured.

"Mrs. Pierce, I'm not sure if you remember me, but we spoke shortly after your husband's death," Daniel said from behind Fenella. "I'm with the Douglas Constabulary and I wanted to extend my deepest sympathies on your loss."

"It was kind of you to come," Paul said.

"Did you come expecting to get a confession?" Karla asked.

Daniel shook his head. "Not at all. I came to pay my respects and to observe everyone. It's all part of building a picture of the victim and of his family and friends."

Karla nodded slightly.

"And I'm Tiffany Perkins," the girl interjected. "I'm a police inspector, but not here on the island. I'm visiting Daniel at the moment."

"Where do you work?" Paul asked.

"I'm between postings at the moment," Tiffany replied.

"Have you ever thought about doing private security?" Paul wondered. "I have a friend who runs a private security firm in London. They're always looking for attractive young women with police training to join their crew. They seem to get lots of applications from men, but very few from women."

"It's not something I've ever given any thought," Tiffany told him, "but I'm intrigued. If you have your friend's contact details, maybe I'll give him a ring."

"I may have his card," Paul said. He pulled out his wallet and looked through it. "I don't have it with me, but I have it all in my phone. If you give me your number, I'll text you his details."

"Paul, I don't feel well," Karla said in a voice that was shaking. "I need to sit down."

Paul took the woman's arm and led her to a cluster of chairs in one corner of the room. It looked as if they'd been moved there to get them out of the way, rather than for people to use, but Paul guided Karla into a chair and then sat down next to her.

"I'll just go over and get those details," Tiffany said to Daniel.

"Why not leave it for today," he replied. "He has enough to worry about right now."

"It won't take a minute," Tiffany insisted. She walked across to the couple and said something to Paul. He nodded. Fenella thought that Karla must have said something because a moment later Tiffany came back, frowning.

"There's something not right about her," she said angrily to Daniel.

"Karla? What do you mean?" he asked.

"She doesn't seem to want Paul talking to me," Tiffany replied. "It was weird."

Daniel's phone buzzed before he could reply. He pulled it out and frowned at the screen. "I need to take this," he said before walking away.

"So, why haven't you found Phillip's killer yet?" Henry asked Tiffany a moment later.

Tiffany looked like a deer caught in headlights for a minute and then she shook her head. "I don't work for the island's police," she said. "Finding Mr. Pierce's killer is Daniel's job."

"Surely, if you're here, you can help," Henry insisted. "What's taking so long?"

"Homicide investigations are complicated," Tiffany replied. "Daniel's approach is very different to mine, as well."

"What would you do differently?" Henry wanted to know.

"When I investigate a murder, I always start by thoroughly investigating the person who found the body," Tiffany replied. She glanced at Fenella. "Oftentimes, the person who finds the body only does so because he or she knew it was there in the first place."

"I'm not sure I know who found Phillip's body," Henry said. "We were all dancing and singing and then the police arrived. No one ever said who found the body."

"I did," Fenella said reluctantly. "I was trying to avoid the dancing so I thought I'd see if Phillip needed any help clearing up from the turnip carving."

"Except Karla and I had already helped him with all of the tidying up," Henry said.

"I didn't know that at the time," Fenella countered. "Anyway, I just wanted a place to hide for a short while."

"What were you hiding from, exactly?" Tiffany demanded.

"I just said, I didn't want to get caught up in the dancing," Fenella replied. "I was tired and I really just wanted to sit down and rest."

"You do seem to find a great many bodies, though, don't you?" Tiffany challenged her. "And whenever you find a body, you seem to spend a great deal of time with Daniel."

"As Daniel has been off the island for several weeks, I haven't spent much time with him at all lately," Fenella replied.

"And you sound incredibly bitter about that," Tiffany said mockingly. "Daniel seems to be convinced of your innocence. He reckons that you wouldn't have murdered a man you didn't even know. I can't help but wonder if you weren't trying to find your way back into Daniel's arms by creating a new case for him to work on with you, though. He's told me all about how you've helped solve so many other cases for him. Not just when you've found the body, either, but you've even helped with cold cases, haven't you?"

Fenella flushed. "I don't think any of this matters right now," she said tightly.

"It matters if you were missing Daniel so you killed Phillip so you'd have an excuse to see him," Tiffany suggested.

"Except Phillip was killed in Cregneash, which is outside of Daniel's jurisdiction," Shelly pointed out.

Tiffany shrugged. "With the training that Daniel had just completed, it was obvious that he'd be called in to help with the case. Fenella had to know that."

"I didn't know any such thing," Fenella told her, "and I didn't have anything to do with Phillip's death."

"You found Phillip's body?" Karla asked from behind them.

Fenella swung around and looked at the girl. "Yes, I did," she replied softly.

"How did he look?" she asked.

Fenella closed her eyes and then quickly opened them as an

unwanted image of the dead man flooded her memory. "I didn't do much more than glance at him," she replied. "It was obvious that he was dead. All I wanted to do was get away from him and call the police."

Karla nodded behind her veil. "Do you really think she killed him?" she asked Tiffany.

Tiffany shrugged. "I'm just saying that if it were my case, I'd be taking a good long look at her, that's all. Anyone who finds as many dead bodies at Fenella Woods has to be trouble."

"I don't think that's at all fair," Daniel said in a level tone from behind Tiffany. "Fenella has had a run of very bad luck, but that's hardly her fault."

"You'd think, with all of her money, that she'd be able to afford to stay out of trouble," Tiffany said.

"What is that supposed to mean?" Shelly demanded.

Tiffany smiled smugly. "As I understand it, Fenella is worth millions. She doesn't have to worry about little things like police investigations. She can simply fly away to somewhere exotic while the police clear up whatever problem she's stumbled across this time."

"Except she's never done anything like that," Daniel said.

"But she could," Tiffany replied. "It must be wonderful to not have to work for a living, all because her aunt was a whore."

Fenella took a step closer to the woman. "Mona was many things, but she was never a whore," she said tightly. "I don't know why you don't like me and I really don't care. Just do us both a favor and stay well away from me and my friends."

"You should stay away from police investigations, then," Tiffany said mockingly.

"As you don't actually work for the police, I think perhaps you should stay away from them as well," Fenella replied. "Why are you here today, anyway? Memorial services aren't really for nosy spectators."

"Why are you here?" Tiffany challenged.

"She's here because I asked her to come with me," Todd spoke up from the edge of the crowd that had developed around them. "I've known Henry for more years than you've been alive, which I think explains why I'm here."

Tiffany shrugged. "Daniel invited me to come with him," she said.

"Actually, you invited yourself along," Daniel countered. "I only agreed because you promised to be quiet and simply observe. If I'd known you were going to start throwing wild accusations around, I wouldn't have agreed to your coming."

"You're too close to the situation," Tiffany said. "You can't see things clearly like I can. Your good friend, Ms. Woods, keeps stumbling over dead bodies. There must be a reason why."

"I think that's enough," Daniel said.

"Why does she keep finding dead bodies?" Karla asked. "Did she kill Phillip?"

Fenella flushed. She looked around and realized that every person in the room was listening intently to the conversation. "Of course I didn't kill anyone," she said in the lightest tone she could manage. "It's a crazy idea."

"Someone killed him," Karla said, her voice quavering behind her veil. "And no one had any reason to kill him."

Fenella briefly considered asking the woman about Phillip's plans to leave the island, but it would probably look as if she were trying to shift the blame from herself to the grieving widow. Whatever she thought of Karla, this wasn't the time or place to start asking her questions.

"I've given several statements to the police about everything that happened on Saturday," she said. "If they want to arrest me, they know where to find me." She turned on her heel and began to walk toward the door.

"I don't think you killed him," Audrey Pierce called after her.

"Me, either," her husband added.

"Thank you," Fenella said, feeling sad that they'd had to listen to everything that Tiffany had said. Tiffany's wild remarks wouldn't have helped them feel any better about what had happened to their son.

"I know you didn't kill anyone," Todd said as he caught up to her. He took her hand and walked with her to the door. Shelly caught up to them a moment later.

"Of course you didn't kill anyone," she said loudly. "Tiffany is just jealous of you and your friendship with Daniel. Maybe she killed Phillip just so that she could blame his death on you. That makes as much sense as her explanation."

"Daniel, you aren't going to let her get away with saying that, are you?" Tiffany demanded.

Fenella didn't wait to hear Daniel's reply. She walked out of the church hall with Todd and Shelly. They made it back to Todd's car before anyone spoke.

"That was horrible," Shelly said.

"It was pretty grim," Todd agreed. "What is wrong with that young woman?"

"She wants Daniel and she's afraid that he's in love with Fenella," Shelly said.

"Should I be worried about Daniel, then?" Todd asked Fenella.

She climbed into the car and sat back in the seat with her eyes closed. Once the others were inside and Todd had started the car, she spoke.

"I doubt very much that Daniel will ever speak to me again after that," she said, trying not to cry. "He and I were friends before he went away on a course. He brought that girl back with him and we really haven't spoken since."

"Friends? Or something more?" Todd asked.

"We were moving toward something more, but then he had to go away," Fenella explained.

Todd nodded. "I won't ask any more questions, not for now. You've had a very upsetting afternoon. I'd rather not make it any worse."

"Thank you," Fenella said softly.

He drove her and Shelly back to their building. "I was going to offer to buy you dinner, but I suspect you might prefer a quiet night in tonight," he said to Fenella at her door.

"Yes, I think I would. I'm exhausted."

"I'll ring you," he promised.

Fenella nodded and then let herself into her apartment. The tears were already falling as she pushed the door shut behind her.

"What happened?" Mona demanded.

"Tiffany Perkins happened," Fenella replied. "If she ever turns up dead somewhere, I hope I have an alibi."

"Tell me everything," Mona insisted.

Fenella really didn't want to talk about it, but she knew that Mona wouldn't stop nagging until she'd heard the whole story. She tried to soften Tiffany's words when she got to the part about Mona, but Mona wasn't having it.

"What word did she really use?" she asked when Fenella stumbled over a suitable synonym.

"She called you a whore," Fenella said after a moment.

Mona chuckled. "I've been called worse. She's wrong, of course, but I don't care what she thinks and neither should you."

"I'm more concerned with what Daniel thinks," Fenella said sadly.

"Daniel doesn't care about my past," Mona told her. "I suspect he may be worried about the money, though. No doubt Tiffany has convinced him that you couldn't possibly be interested in a man with an ordinary job and a standard income."

"I didn't know about the money until recently."

"Yes, I know, and that was better for you and Daniel. Tiffany is a much bigger problem than the money, though. You only need to talk to Daniel and explain that the money doesn't matter, but you can't do that until you get rid of Tiffany."

"I hope you aren't suggesting that I kill Tiffany," Fenella said. "In spite of my propensity for finding dead bodies, I couldn't kill anyone, not even her."

"I wasn't suggesting that at all," Mona said. "What you need to do is solve Daniel's case for him and show that woman that you're not only prettier and richer than her, but you're also smarter."

"Sure, that'll be easy. We can do that. I'm sure you have lots of ideas," Fenella said sarcastically.

"I do, actually. What did Karla say to you when you ran into her just before the dancing started?"

"I don't know. Something about wondering where her husband was, why?"

"Try to remember her exact words," Mona said. "There's something there but I want you to remember it for yourself."

"She said she hoped he wasn't going to miss the dancing because he was busy cleaning up the barn. She said something about helping him do that after the day was over," Fenella recalled after a minute's thought.

"And what did Henry say today?" Mona asked.

"He said that he and Karla had already helped with the tidying up," Fenella remembered.

"Exactly. Someone is lying. Daniel simply needs to work out whether it's Karla or Henry."

"It must be Karla," Fenella said, "but I still can't quite believe that she killed her husband."

"Because they were newlyweds," Mona yawned. "Perhaps Daniel should check to see if Karla had any life insurance on her new husband."

Fenella shook her head. "That's too terrible to think about."

"But it provides a motive. Otherwise we're back to wondering whether she wanted to stay on the island or not. You never did ask her, did you?"

"No, it wasn't the time or place."

"I won't argue, but you might suggest that line of questioning to Daniel."

"Except I'm not going to suggest anything to Daniel," Fenella said. "I'm not going to call the man."

"If you don't ring him, Karla might get away with murder." Mona said.

"Daniel will work it out for himself," Fenella said without any conviction.

"Ring him," Mona said.

"And if Tiffany answers?"

"Tell her exactly what you think of her before you ask for Daniel."

15

"I can't do it," Fenella said after she'd started dialing Daniel's number three times. "I'm going to have Shelly ring him."

"Just make sure he knows that you were the one who noticed Karla's lie," Mona insisted.

Shelly came over when Fenella rang. Fenella did the same thing that Mona had done, having Shelly recall the two different conversations. When Shelly realized the discrepancy, she got very excited.

"Karla killed her husband," she said. "Let's go and confront her."

"No!" Fenella exclaimed. "We need to tell Daniel and let him handle it."

"And you want me to ring Daniel so you don't have to talk to him," Shelly guessed.

"Yes, that's it exactly," Fenella admitted.

Shelly looked as if she wanted to argue, but after a moment she dialed Daniel's home number.

"Ah, yes, is Daniel home, please?" she said a moment later. She made a face at Fenella as she did so.

"I'd rather not say who's calling," she said next. "It isn't any of your business." A moment later she sighed and put the phone down. "Tiffany didn't like my answer."

"Try his mobile number," Mona urged.

"Maybe he isn't home," Fenella said. "Try calling the station. At least you can leave a message there and he might actually get it."

When Shelly put the phone down a minute later she frowned at Fenella. "Do you have a mobile number for him?" she asked.

"I do, but I'm not sure I should be letting anyone else use it," she said.

"We've solved his murder for him. He should be grateful," Shelly replied.

"Yes, I suppose so, but, well, it's awkward. He gave me the number back when we were friends. I haven't used it for a long time."

"What if we rang Mark Hammersmith?" Shelly asked.

"I'm not sure about that," Fenella replied, "but maybe we could call Inspector Nichols. It's his case, after all. I don't want to get Daniel into any trouble, but you did try to reach him first."

"That's a great idea," Mona said. "Then Inspector Nichols can solve the case, and Daniel will be left looking foolish. Just make sure that he lets Daniel know the source of the critical information."

"Do you have his number? He isn't going to be at the station at this hour, is he?" Shelly asked.

"Let's try there first," Fenella suggested. "Maybe he's working late."

Shelly called the non-emergency number for the police station in the south of the island. Inspector Nichols was working and happy to take her call.

It only took Shelly a few minutes to tell the man why she'd rung. "I tried to ring Daniel Robinson with this, but I couldn't reach him," she added when she was done.

"I'll ring Daniel," he told her. "As we're both working the case together, I'll take him along when I go to question Karla and her father about the inconsistencies in their statements."

Shelly put the phone down. "I think we need a trip to the pub," she said after she'd hugged Fenella.

"I think I need to call out for pizza and have an early night," Fenella told her. "I'm completely exhausted."

Shelly looked as if she wanted to argue, but after a moment she nodded. "Can I join you for pizza, then?" she asked. "I'm too wound up to sit home alone tonight."

"Of course you can. Bring Smokey over so the cats can play while we talk," she suggested.

It was nearly a week later when the news broke. The newspaper headline caught Fenella's eye as she did her shopping.

"Pierce Widow Charged in Husband's Murder," it read. Fenella grabbed the paper and read the article while standing in the middle of the aisle.

As soon as she'd finished reading, she rang Shelly. "Have you seen today's paper?" she demanded.

"Not yet. I'll get one later. Why? What's in it?"

"Karla's been arrested," Fenella told her.

"Really? Tell me everything."

"There isn't much more in the article, really. It just says that Karla has been arrested and charged with killing Phillip. I'll bring you a copy of the paper when I come home, but I've told you most of it already."

When Fenella got home, she had a message on her answering machine from Todd.

"Want to come and see the band tonight?" he'd asked. "We'll be at the Tale and Tail. I'll be filling in for Henry. He's, well, not in a fit state to do much of anything at the moment. Paul isn't much better, if I'm honest. I'm on my way to the pub now for an emergency practice. If you come before six, you shouldn't have any problem getting in, but if you do, come in the back way."

Fenella and Shelly talked over the story in the paper and then agreed to go to the pub. "Maybe we'll find out more from the band," Shelly said.

"Have you heard much from Mark or Tim?" Fenella asked.

Shelly flushed. "I've been avoiding them both, which makes me less excited about tonight, but I don't know how to politely discourage Mark without putting Tim off as well."

"I'll help you tonight," Fenella promised.

They were at the pub shortly after five. The band was busy setting up. Todd rushed over as they walked in.

"I've been meaning to ring you every day, but things have been a bit crazy," he told her. "I had to fly over to play at a birthday party, and then when I got back things with Karla blew up and I've been trying to help with that ever since."

"What happened?" Fenella asked.

Todd shrugged. "The police found inconsistencies in her statement and pulled her in for more questioning. Apparently she kept contradicting herself until she'd talked herself into a corner. I gather she ended up confessing because she couldn't keep her story straight any longer."

"How are Henry and Harriet doing, then?" Shelly asked.

"They're both upset, of course, but I think they had their suspicions. Henry told me that he knew that Karla and Phillip had been fighting a lot," Todd explained.

"You said Paul was upset. Why?" Fenella wanted to know.

Todd glanced over at the stage where a miserable-looking Paul was talking with some of the others.

"According to Henry, Karla killed Phillip because she wanted to get back together with Paul. Apparently she only married him to make Paul jealous, or that's what she's saying now. She claims she never stopped loving Paul, but he was too focused on his music to notice her, so while he was gone, she decided to show him what he was missing."

"Poor Phillip," Shellly sighed.

"I hope that her original plan was to simply divorce the man once Paul returned, but for some reason she decided to make it easier on herself and just get rid of him immediately," Todd told them. "Paul's badly shaken because her plan was actually working. He was spending a lot of time with her, helping her recover from her grief, and he told me that he was starting to fall for her again. If the police hadn't worked out what really happened, her plan may well have worked."

"What a mess," Fenella sighed.

"Yes, exactly that," Todd agreed, "but the whole awful incident has brought about one good thing, I suppose. Mark and his wife are back together, at least for the moment."

Shelly smiled. "That is good news," she said.

The band was good, even though Paul wasn't at his best. Todd played well to the large but not capacity crowd. When the night was over, Shelly and Tim went to have a drink together while Todd walked Fenella home.

"I'm going to New York for a few days," he told her. "I'm going to a wedding." He named a Broadway producer that Fenella knew had produced some of New York's biggest hits in the past few years. "I'll ring you when I get back." He gave Fenella a passionate kiss and then left her at her door.

A few days later Fenella received an unexpected text.

"Tiffany has gone back to the UK where she belongs. I hope I'll see you around. Daniel."

After many hours of debate with Mona, Fenella chose not to reply.

ACKNOWLEDGMENTS

I couldn't do these books without a great deal of help.

Thanks to my editor, Denise, who still hasn't managed to teach me anything, but doesn't complain about correcting the same mistakes over and over again.

Thanks to Linda at Tell-Tale Book Covers, who manages to find time to do the wonderful covers for this series in between a million other demands on her time.

Thanks to my beta reading team, who make several small improvements in every title before it goes live.

And thanks to my readers, who keep me writing!

INVITATIONS AND INVESTIGATIONS

AN ISLE OF MAN GHOSTLY COZY

Release date: November 16, 2018

Fenella Woods is pleased when police inspector Daniel Robinson asks for her help with another cold case. It isn't the first time he's asked her to share her thoughts on an old case, but things have been difficult between the pair since Daniel returned from a lengthy course in the UK.

Ronald Sherman disappeared nearly seven years ago. It seems everyone who knew the man has a different idea as to why. Fenella and her friend, Shelly Quirk, find themselves talking to a number of different people about the missing man.

As if helping Daniel isn't enough to keep Fenella busy, she's planning a banquet for her first Thanksgiving on the island. Sending invitations and sharing recipes with the chef at the restaurant she's chosen seems to take up a lot of her time.

Can Fenella and Shelly work out what actually happened to Ronald? Is Daniel hoping to rekindle his romance with Fenella over witness statements? Will Fenella's Thanksgiving feast be a success or is it a disaster waiting to happen?"

BY THE SAME AUTHOR

The Isle of Man Cozy Mystery Series
Aunt Bessie Assumes
Aunt Bessie Believes
Aunt Bessie Considers
Aunt Bessie Decides
Aunt Bessie Enjoys
Aunt Bessie Finds
Aunt Bessie Goes
Aunt Bessie's Holiday
Aunt Bessie Invites
Aunt Bessie Joins
Aunt Bessie Knows
Aunt Bessie Likes
Aunt Bessie Meets
Aunt Bessie Needs
Aunt Bessie Observes
Aunt Bessie Provides
Aunt Bessie Questions
Aunt Bessie Remembers
Aunt Bessie Solves

BY THE SAME AUTHOR

The Isle of Man Ghostly Cozy Mysteries
Arrivals and Arrests
Boats and Bad Guys
Cars and Cold Cases
Dogs and Danger
Encounters and Enemies
Friends and Frauds
Guests and Guilt
Hop-tu-Naa and Homicide
Invitations and Investigations

The Markham Sisters Cozy Mystery Novellas
The Appleton Case
The Bennett Case
The Chalmers Case
The Donaldson Case
The Ellsworth Case
The Fenton Case
The Green Case
The Hampton Case
The Irwin Case
The Jackson Case
The Kingston Case
The Lawley Case
The Moody Case
The Norman Case
The Osborne Case

The Isle of Man Romance Series

BY THE SAME AUTHOR

Island Escape
Island Inheritance
Island Heritage
Island Christmas

ABOUT THE AUTHOR

Diana grew up in Northwestern Pennsylvania and moved to Washington, DC after college. There she met a wonderful Englishman who was visiting the city. After a whirlwind romance, they got married and Diana moved to the Chesterfield area of Derbyshire to begin a new life with her husband. A short time later, they relocated to the Isle of Man.

After over ten years on the island, it was time for a change. With their two children in tow, Diana and her husband moved to suburbs of Buffalo, New York. Diana now spends her days writing about the island she loves.

She also writes mystery/thrillers set in the not-too-distant future as Diana X. Dunn and middle grade and Young Adult books as D.X. Dunn.

Diana is always happy to hear from readers. You can write to her at:

Diana Xarissa Dunn
PO Box 72
Clarence, NY 14031.

Find Diana at: DianaXarissa.com
E-mail: Diana@dianaxarissa.com

Printed in Great Britain
by Amazon